THE UNDERCOVER DUKE

THE 1797 CLUB BOOK 6

JESS MICHAELS

THE UNDERCOVER DUKE

The 1797 Club Book 6
www.1797Club.com

Copyright © Jesse Petersen, 2018

ISBN-13: 978-1985119932

ISBN-10: 1985119935

For more information, contact Jess Michaels

www.AuthorJessMichaels.com

For Jenn LeBlanc, Kate Smith, Grace Callaway, Sara Ramsay and all the wonderful writers who have helped me figure out what to do and reminded me I love to do it.

And for Michael. Twenty-one years and you still listen to me as I pontificate about Star Wars, soap operas and the best kinds of cheese. You are a saint.

PROLOGUE

February 1811

It was wrong. It was all wrong. Lucas Vincent, Duke of Willowby, felt that wrongness like an icepick in his gut as he crept around the perimeter of the country estate. He paid attention to the feeling, for he had long ago learned to trust his instincts. They were what kept a spy alive.

Of course, that didn't mean he didn't still do his job. Today he moved forward despite that feeling. Perhaps *because* of it. After all, he'd also long ago determined that it was his destiny to die in the field, for his country, with honor.

If today was that day, then so be it. There was little to live for beyond that sense of honor. He had no relationship with his family and he had cut away his friends—his dear friends who had once been like brothers—over the years since he had discovered the truth of himself.

"Willowby!"

The harsh whisper of his name drew him from maudlin thoughts and he turned, weapon drawn, to find George Oakford's wise, lined face peeking out from behind a shrubbery. Oakford was a friend and a talented surgeon who used his extensive gifts to save the lives of those who served the crown.

He was also not supposed to be here.

Lucas eased over to him. "What are you doing here?" he whispered.

Oakford looked toward the house with a scowl. "I heard rumors that you were coming here to suss out a traitor," he said, rage potent in his low tone. "And since we've lost three good men under terrible and suspicious circumstances in the last six months, men I've watched die because I did not have the talent to save them, I knew I had to come and support you. Orders be damned."

Lucas reached out and gripped the older man's arm. There were very few people in this world he trusted more than George Oakford, and relief washed over him in a wave. "I admit, I'm pleased to find you here. I have a sense of dread and I wouldn't mind the support of your presence."

Oakford's eyebrows lifted in surprise. "It's just you?"

Lucas nodded. "Yes. I was meant to only observe, Stalwood's orders. He has an abundance of caution, as you know."

Oakford's lips pursed. "He always has. Sometimes I think to his detriment."

Lucas couldn't disagree, even though he respected the spymaster, as he knew Oakford did, too. He continued, "When I saw the men unloading weapons round the back, when I saw them bringing carriages full of lightskirts as entertainment for their evening, it was evident something very big is happening here tonight. If I can stop it before it does, it could save the lives of thousands of men on the battlefield. And perhaps keep even one more spy from dying for this operation at the hands of a craven coward."

Oakford held his gaze for a long moment. "You've always been the best of your kind, Willowby. Whoever is running this operation should fear the consequences you are about to rain down on them. I'm certain they deserve it."

"*We're* raining those consequences down, Oakford," Lucas said.

"But I need to get a look at who our traitor is. There's been activity in that chamber up there, but I haven't been able to get a clear view of whoever is inside."

He pulled out his spyglass and handed it over. Oakford looked up at the window Lucas had indicated and lowered the glass. His finely wrinkled face was pinched in an expression of disgust. "I see what you mean," he said. "What's your plan?"

"There's a trellis along the north wall," Lucas explained. "It leads to a thin ledge on that second floor, which I can use to creep around the window of the chamber next to the one our traitor is occupying. If I can manage to get inside, I might even be able to incapacitate him without causing a stir. We could be in and out without a fight."

Oakford lifted his eyebrows. "I'm impressed with you, Willowby. But then, I always am."

Lucas fought the urge to puff up his chest at the compliment. Oakford didn't give them often. "Congratulate me *if* I can carry out the plan. There are guards circling the property, but they're like clockwork. In less than one minute they'll go by again, and assuming we're not caught—"

"You intend to climb the wall and have our man dead to rights," Oakford finished.

"Shhh," Lucas said, ducking a bit lower behind the bush and tugging Oakford with him. They stayed perfectly still as two men, the guards Lucas had been tracking, walked by between the line of bushes where they hid and the house. They were talking and Lucas strained to hear them as they strolled off to the next area of their inspection.

"Where...went...Cal—"

"Could you understand them?" he whispered, hoping that Oakford's position closer to the men might add to whatever Lucas had heard.

Oakford shook his head. "Not really. A few words here and there."

Lucas pressed his lips together. "They started saying a name, I think. Started with 'Cal.' If they were referring to our traitor, there are quite a few options within the department."

Oakford nodded. "But they could have just as easily been referring to someone quite outside your case."

"I suppose we'll find out soon enough. Stay here, watch for trouble and be ready to ride to the village to bring the magistrate if things go very wrong."

He slipped from the bushes without waiting for the answer and made his way to the trellis, where he began to climb. He'd always been good at physical things, even as a child. Now that aptitude paid off.

He was almost to the top, his fingers reaching out to the ledge when he heard the crack of a pistol being fired below. He didn't have time to pivot, to look, when the gun fired again and he felt a searing pain in his leg.

His fingers slipped and he toppled backward. He was falling, falling, and then the ground was there, hard and unforgiving beneath his back. His head bounced off something and the world began to swim, his ears ringing as he struggled to sit up despite the pain that seared through his entire body.

"Oakford," he grunted, rolling slightly.

The surgeon was on the ground behind him, splayed out and still. Dead, Lucas realized through his fog. The first shot. It had struck Oakford. He rolled to his front and was unable to keep from crying out in pain as he belly-crawled toward his friend. A man he'd known since his first days in the War Department. A man who'd saved his life more than once.

He wasn't more than a foot from Oakford when there was a third shot that rang out from behind him. He felt the bullet slice through him and collapsed against the ground. The world was spinning, becoming black. There were voices around him now. He recognized they were the voices of the men who had attacked them. Killed him. He could handle that.

But that they'd killed Oakford made his last moments pure agony.

"Why—" one voice said, slow and like it was coming through a deep ocean.

"You—no—bastard," the other voice replied, just as unrecognizable. Lucas lifted his head in one last attempt to see what supposed friend had betrayed them all, but the world spun as he did so and then went entirely dark. The last things he experienced were loud pops and then nothing.

CHAPTER 1

Fall 1811

Diana Oakford stood at the low table in her kitchen, binding bundles of plants with twine. She hummed as she did so, keeping a rhythm that made the work go by steadily. She liked the practice, actually. It cleared her mind, doing this repetitive thing.

It kept her from thinking too much about painful subjects that were best left unpondered. Subjects that would likely drop her to her knees if she allowed them to haunt her. She pushed even the hint of them aside now as she worked and refocused herself on the task at hand.

She became so lost in the act that she jumped when there was a light knock at the door she'd left open behind her.

She pivoted and gasped as she found that her visitor was none other than the Earl of Stalwood. Her hands shook as she set her herbs down and stared at him. How well she knew him and how little at the same time. The man had been an old friend of her father and had come in and out of their home for as long as she could remember. But he was also the spymaster for the War Department, as secretive as he could be kind. A man who had taken her father away on more than one occasion until one horrible day when she'd been told he would never return again.

She hadn't seen Stalwood since the private memorial service for her father in London more than six months before. Seeing him now brought back a rush of painful emotions that she fought to rein in before she spoke.

"My lord," she managed to squeak out as she moved toward him. "I-I did not expect you."

He inclined his head. "Perhaps I should have sent word of my impending arrival," he said. "To be honest, I feared you would not receive me if you knew my intentions. I feared a great many other things, as well."

She wrinkled her brow at his cryptic remark and then motioned him into her kitchen. "I would not turn a friend of my father away. Please, do come in. I'm afraid I can only offer you a seat at my kitchen table, for I do not have the fires lit in the parlor."

"That will be more than enough," he reassured her as he entered the room and took a seat at the table where she'd been working. She hustled to move the bound piles of herbs aside and he smiled up at her. "You are like him."

She hesitated as she turned away. "Mmmm. Not exactly like," she said. "May I get you some tea?"

"Yes," he said, and was silent for a few moments as she stirred the fire and swung the heavy pot of water over the flame. She felt his eyes on her, though. Felt him watching her. Her stomach coiled in anticipation of whatever he would say next. "I need your help, Diana."

She froze in her place, staring into the dancing flames for a long moment before she faced him at last. His expression was impassive and unreadable. So like her father. Spies were like that. She had always hated not knowing what was in Papa's heart. Not being able to see if he shared her pain when there was loss or damage in their lives.

It had always made her feel so very alone.

"My help," she repeated softly, unable to keep the tremble from her voice.

He nodded slowly. "Yes. We have an injured spy. Badly hurt in the field some time ago. We've been fighting as hard as we can, but he has not healed as fully as we'd like. We need a better healer."

"You have not yet found a replacement for my father as surgeon?" she asked, folding her arms though that wasn't any kind of barrier to what this man's words inspired in her.

Stalwood's expression flickered, and for half a second she saw all his grief. "No," he said, emotions gone again. "There will never be any replacing him, I fear. The men who trained under him are good, of course, but they are only shadows of him. I cannot reach out to anyone outside our circles for fear they would be put in danger by our secrets. Or would not understand the delicacies of working with spies."

She lifted her chin. "And you think I do?"

"I know you do."

She flinched and turned back to the fire. She wrapped a cloth around the heavy kettle and poured it out into the more delicate teapot slowly.

"He needs hiding, too," Stalwood continued, his words in a rush like he was trying to keep her from fully digesting them.

Of course she did. They were shocking words and Diana almost laughed at the ridiculousness of this conversation. "*Hiding*," she repeated, letting the word roll from her tongue. "So he is in danger. He *is* danger."

Stalwood bobbed his head once. "Yes." His voice was soft but firm.

"And you've come to me, despite all that. Despite what that kind of danger has cost me." He flinched and so did she. This man didn't know the half of it. "Why?"

Stalwood took a long breath as she poured his tea at last. Only when she'd set the pot down did he say, "Because this man was injured the same day your father died. They were together."

Diana's ears began to ring and she sat down hard in the chair across from Stalwood. She gripped her hands into fists against the tabletop and stared at him. She knew so little of her father's death. Only that he'd died in the field. Only that she would never see him again or hear his heavy footsteps on the stair.

She longed to know more. She feared it too. "My father was with someone else?"

Stalwood shifted. "Yes," he said softly.

"I have never asked you for details," she said, dropping her chin so she would not have to look at him. "But I want them. You are asking me to endanger myself, I want to know how."

"I can give you some information," he said after a long and heavy pause. "Your father went against orders to help this man. He was... he was investigating a traitor from within. It went very wrong. My spy was badly hurt and many servants and your father were killed."

Her stomach turned. Her father had made a life out of saving the lives of those in service to their king. And now to hear that one of them had betrayed her father? Killed him?

She wanted to scream. She wanted to break everything around her. She wanted to find the man who had killed her father and she wanted to destroy him as he had destroyed her.

Instead, she glared at Stalwood. "How do you know the man who was injured was not the betrayer, himself?"

"He isn't." Stalwood shook his head. "We've extensively researched. And I know him. He is not the one."

"Who is he?" she asked.

Stalwood cleared his throat. "When I say his name, it is with the express understanding that this will never leave this home. Never leave your lips."

"Am I being indoctrinated as one of your spies, my lord?" she asked.

He shrugged. "In a way, yes. Am I clear on the subject?"

She nodded. "Yes."

"It is the Duke of Willowby."

Her lips parted. "A duke. Do you mean the Undercover Duke?"

Stalwood drew back in surprise. "You know of him?"

"My father spoke of him by that nickname sometimes," she said. "Never by his formal title or his given name. I knew nothing more than that. And that Papa cared for the man."

Stalwood was quiet, and she knew he was letting her ponder the information before he said, "Does that mean you will help Willowby?"

She straightened and glared at him. "As I said before, this business of yours, of his, it has taken more than enough from me. More than you can imagine."

"I know that, Diana," Stalwood said. "And I hope you know that I would not ask this of you unless we had a dire need."

Diana pushed to her feet and walked away from him, breathing in the fragrant scent of herbs that always filled her kitchen. He was manipulating her, of course. As much as she liked Stalwood, it was in his nature as a spy to do so. To get what he wanted.

Worse, it was working, no matter how she recognized the truth of it. She thought of her father, dead now for half a year. She knew what he'd say if he were here. She could almost hear him, whispering to her in that voice she hadn't heard in months.

He would talk to her about honor and courage. About duty. Always duty, above all else.

She bent her head. "Very well," she said on a sigh. "Bring him here, then."

Stalwood rose behind her and she faced him. He looked different now. Like he was past the gentleness required to get her agreement. Now she was one of his soldiers and he was in charge.

"London would be better," he said. "We're still investigating, and I can place guards to ensure your safety with more ease there."

She pressed her lips together in irritation. She didn't want to be in London. Not this time of year. But there seemed to be no choice.

"Fine," she said. "But at my father's home there. My herb garden is a necessity I cannot deny myself."

He seemed to consider the request and then nodded. "Very well. No one will suspect he is there, for certain. That could work out very well. How long will it take you to get there?"

She looked around, already making mental lists of what she would need to do and gather. "A week at most," she said. "I could be there Thursday next."

"Excellent. I will be certain you have what you need there. Will you have servants to contend with? We'll need an explanation for Willowby's arrival."

She shook her head. "I do not keep a servant. I can manage myself well enough."

Stalwood's brow wrinkled as if he did not understand. Of course he would not. Men like him had a dozen servants. This duke would probably expect white-gloved treatment too.

She sighed at the thought.

"I will make sure you have a driver. Safe and vetted by my department. He will take you to London and be at your disposal there. If you want no one else, I will not interfere. The fewer people involved in this situation, the better."

She nodded. "I agree."

"Then I shall leave you to your readying. With my thanks," he said, moving toward the door where he had entered less than half an hour before.

"Stalwood," she said before he could leave her.

He turned. "Yes?"

"You will find whoever is responsible for my father's death."

His expression softened a bit. "I will do everything in my power, my dear. *Everything* in my power."

"Good day," she whispered past a suddenly thick throat. He tipped his hat to her and then he was gone, leaving her alone to think of what she had agreed to.

And ponder what a terrible mistake it would likely turn out to be.

. . .

L ucas shifted as the carriage turned and he was rocked against the wall. Every muscle in his body protested with screaming pain and he gripped his fists against the leather carriage seat to keep from crying out.

How he hated being injured. Being weak. How he hated that it all felt so commonplace to him now. Pain was just part of life.

The carriage came to a stop and he looked out the window as the servants began to move to help him. It was a small cottage that they'd come to. One that looked like every other cottage in The Hale, a part of London he'd never been to before. He knew all the worst parts through his job, and the best thanks to his upbringing.

He hated them both equally. But this place was suspended somewhere in between. Not too high and mighty, but neat and tidy, well maintained. Anonymous.

The door opened and the men Stalwood had tasked with helping him appeared. Their faces were grim as one said, "Ready, Your Grace?"

Lucas winced at both the recognition of the pain about to come and the title that was used to address him. "Yes," he ground out, his voice rough as he reached out to steady himself on waiting arms. He staggered forward, trying in vain to keep his grunts of agony in as he was helped down.

The men looked away as they guided him up the stairs to the cottage door. They were spies, like he was, sent to do this menial task because they were the only ones to be trusted with the secret of his location. He knew what they saw when they looked at him: their future. And it wasn't one they wanted, so they distanced themselves.

The door to the cottage was already open and the men helped him in. They didn't hesitate as they all but carried him up another short flight of stairs and down a hall to an open door. Lucas had to believe this had all been prearranged. He did not yet even know who it was who would be taking care of him during his time here. Stalwood had said a healer, but nothing more.

A healer. Internally, he scoffed. He'd been poked and prodded and tortured by many a man who called himself that. The amount of healing that had followed was laughable. He was broken, perhaps irretrievably, and that sent a wash of rage and pain through him more powerful than any caused by the physical.

"Let me go," he snapped, staggering from the arms of those helping him and all but collapsing against the edge of the bed.

The men seemed unmoved by his ill humor. All but one left him there. The last was named Simmons. Lucas glared at him. He'd trained this particular pup years ago, and now the boy stared at him like he was a dotard, lost to his youth and usefulness.

"Is there anything I can do?" Simmons asked, all that pity heavy in his mournful tone.

"No," Lucas said through clenched teeth as he turned his face. "Just get out."

"Well, that is a pretty way to talk to someone who is helping you!"

Lucas turned at the sharp, feminine voice that had said those harsh words. There, standing in the doorway, staring at him like he was a monster, was a woman. Not just a woman, a goddess, it would seem. She had dark hair with deep red highlights, a finely shaped face and full lips. Her eyes were the most spectacular green he had ever seen. Like jade stolen from faraway lands that he could only dream of now.

At this moment, those green eyes were narrowed and filled with anger as she folded her arms and shook her head. Her censure made him feel a strange sense of...shame. An odd sensation he rarely experienced. He'd cut that away a long time ago.

"Mr. Simmons, is it not?" she asked, turning to the other man in the room.

"Yes, miss," Simmons said, and his gaze flitted over their companion. Lucas recognized the interest that lit in his eyes. The same he felt in his own belly.

Only the younger man likely had a better chance than he did in his current state.

"Thank you for your help. I believe I can handle the situation from here. Please send word to Lord Stalwood that we are settled."

Simmons glanced at Lucas and then back to the woman. "Of course, miss. I will be one of the guards rotating here. If you have any trouble, if you *need* anything, put a candle in the front window and I will come at once."

The young woman nodded, and seemed oblivious to Simmons' regard as she motioned him toward the hallway. "I appreciate that kindness. Good day."

Simmons shrugged ever so slightly and left. Once he was gone, the young woman turned toward Lucas, those sharp eyes still filled with slight disgust and judgment.

"Hello," she said, stepping into the room. "I trust the room will be comfortable, even if it does not meet your standards."

Lucas leaned on the bed with his undamaged arm, mostly because he was not entirely certain he could stay upright on his own. "I have no standards, I'm afraid. Ask anyone in my acquaintance."

Her lips pursed in what seemed like annoyance at his quip and she moved toward him. "Let me help you."

He recoiled as she reached out. "I can get myself into the bed."

Her brow wrinkled, and when her gaze swept over him, he felt her judgment even more powerfully. She glanced at his face and shrugged. "So you say. Then I shall let you get settled on your own if that is your choice at present. I will return in an hour to bring you some food."

She said nothing else, nor did she wait for his answer to her statement. She merely turned on her heel and marched from the room, tugging the door behind herself as she left.

When she was gone, Lucas collapsed against the mattress, too exhausted and pained to even try to remove his boots. He had no idea who the lady was, nor her role in the next few weeks of his life.

Perhaps she was the healer's wife or daughter. Perhaps she was a servant. He supposed he would find out soon enough.

Whatever the answer, her presence, as lovely as it was, did not change the facts of his life. He did not want to be here, and he was going to do everything in his power to get away from this place as soon as possible.

CHAPTER 2

Diana cursed herself as she walked up the stairs toward her father's old chamber, the room where the Duke of Willowby now waited, and she hoped in a better mood. Not that it had been his mood she'd been pondering since she left him a few hours before.

No, she hadn't been thinking of *that* at all. She'd been thinking of how different the man had been from the image she'd created in her head. Thanks to her father, spies had come in and out of her life for decades. She had no romantic notions about them, no sweeping ideas about them all being young or handsome. Most she'd known had been thinkers, not fighters. Men who were good at puzzles and could talk about pedantic questions for hours, even days.

So when her father had talked about the Undercover Duke, when he'd described the titled spy, she'd had a picture of a pampered, middle-aged popinjay. Someone...soft.

But this man was anything but soft. He was hard. His face was hard, his jaw was hard, his eyes were hard. He had a scraggly beard and long hair that curled wildly around his face. He was obnoxious too. She would grant him some allowances for the pain he was obviously in, but he had no call to speak so unkindly to those who helped him.

And yet, despite all that, he was handsome. Yes, *handsome*. She'd been trying to avoid that observation, pretend it away, but there was no way to do so. The Duke of Willowby was undeniably handsome and unmistakably young.

And she was going to be spending copious amounts of time alone with him. Any ladies' handbook would speak to the wildly inappropriate nature of that fact.

"Thankfully, I'm not a lady," she muttered as she shifted the items in her arms, drew a steadying breath and opened the door to the chamber once more.

She gasped as she did so. The duke had found a place on the bed, sort of cockeyed across the mattress so that his still-booted feet hung off the edge. What he *had* managed to remove was his shirt, and as she entered the room, he made a pained sound and stood, giving her a good look at a masculine and well-formed chest.

One with a very ugly scar across the left shoulder. It was red and ragged, not completely healed. In fact, it looked as though it had been opened and reopened over the months. She could only imagine the horrible pain that this man had endured.

"This is most inappropriate, Miss—Miss...*Miss*," the duke said with a shake of his head. "I must insist you fetch one of the men at once."

She managed to lift her gaze from the handsome chest and the ugly scar, and met his gaze. "The men?" she said with a laugh as she set her tray with her supplies and a plate of food on the table by the door. "Aside from the guard outside, who I have no intention of calling, there are no men here, Your Grace."

A look of pain washed over his face. "Don't call me that."

She tilted her head. "Not Your Grace?"

His lips pressed together hard and he shook his head slowly. "I prefer not."

She considered that a moment and then took a step toward him. "Very well. What would you like me to call you, then?"

"Lucas is fine," he ground out, and she could see he was trying to control the same snappish tone he'd used earlier on the men helping him.

Lucas. She thought of the name, rolled it around in her head. Calling a duke by his Christian name was almost as inappropriate as hanging about alone with him in her cottage. Especially considering the wide variance in their positions.

"Are you certain I could not call you Willowby?" she pressed.

That pained look crossed his face again. "That is the same as calling me Your Grace."

She did not respond, but stepped forward again and reached out with the intention of beginning her examination of the wound on his shoulder. She knew he had another on his leg, but for now she would focus on the easiest one to deal with.

But before she could touch him, he backed away. She tilted her head as irritation flowed through her. "Your Grace—"

"Lucas," he snapped, and there was the harsh tone.

She pursed her lips as she fought her own sharp tongue. "Fine, *Lucas*. You knew you were coming to a healer, I assume you understand that I must touch you."

His eyes went wide. "*You* are the healer?"

She blinked at the utter confusion and disbelief in his tone. "Yes," she said slowly. "Did Stalwood not tell you?"

"Bloody Stalwood," Lucas muttered. "No, he only told me I was being moved for my safety and so that I could be attended to by a healer. He never said it was a woman."

She spun around, holding her arms out. "And yet here I am. And this is what I was asked to do by Stalwood. What I must do to honor my father and his memory."

Once again Lucas looked anything but certain. He leaned closer, exploring her face before he said, "Who is your father?"

She swallowed. It seemed Stalwood had left her to a great deal of explanation. "He didn't tell you that either? I—my father was... George Oakford, Your Grace. My name is Diana."

All the blood promptly exited the face of the handsome man before her, and he reached out to steady himself on the nearest pillar on the four-poster bed. He stared at her, his eyes wilder now.

"George Oakford," he repeated after what felt like an eternity. "George Oakford, the surgeon for the crown?" His voice shook. She heard all the emotion in it, the emotion that matched her own. Grief and loss, anger and guilt.

Slowly, she nodded. "Yes. That's the very one."

His hands gripped into fists, and for a moment she thought his knees might go out from under him. Then he stepped around her and headed for the door.

She pivoted and reached out, catching his good arm. "What are you doing? Where are you going?"

"I-I must leave," he said, his tone distant, almost like he was telling himself rather than her. "I can't stay here."

"Why?" she said, holding tight even when he moved his arm to try to extract himself from her grip.

He stopped fighting and instead looked down at her. His dark brown eyes met hers with an intensity that pinned her in her place. Made her stop breathing.

"Your father is dead because of me, Miss Oakford. He's dead because of *me*."

E motions Lucas had fought hard to gain control over all his life were now washing over him like a violent storm. He had made his confession, thinking this woman would recoil or cry or call him names. Instead, she was just *staring* at him. The silence that stretched between them was worse than any condemnation he had expected.

As was the look on her lovely face that was so pained and

confused. Now that he knew who she was, he did see her father in her. In her eyes, mostly. Her eyes were like Oakford's.

"Stalwood told me that you were injured the day my father died," she said at last. Her tone was very calm. "But he did not say that his death was your fault. I want an explanation."

Lucas nodded. "You deserve that," he admitted as he pushed away from her and limped across the room to a chair before the fire. With an apologetic look for the rudeness of his action, he sank into the cushions and drew a deep breath to gain some control over the pain.

She was silent as she moved to take the opposite chair from his own. Those jade eyes flitted over him, observing like the best of spies. He found himself wondering at the outcome of her assessment.

"Tell me," she repeated. An order, not a request.

His mouth felt dry as kindling and his tongue felt thick. Somehow he managed to speak. "I was pursuing a traitor to the Crown. One within our own ranks."

"Stalwood suggested as much," Diana said. "And that things went wrong."

"I was told not to pursue, but to observe," Lucas said, bending his head as memories washed over him like a tsunami. "I didn't listen. I should have listened. I should have requested more help. Your father wasn't even supposed to be there. But you know him."

A ghost of a smile crossed her face. "Yes, I do know him," she said. "He was not one to follow orders."

"No, but this time we should have." Lucas scrubbed a hand over his face. "I thought something massive was about to happen. Something dangerous. I decided to go in instead of simply observe. Your father was covering me. But we were both shot, I in the leg while I was climbing up a building. I fell and was even more injured. When I turned, your father had already been hit. I was trying to help him when I was shot a second time."

Her face was still impassive, but he saw the glitter of tears brighten her eyes as she dipped her head and stared into her clenched hands in her lap. "It does not sound as though what happened was your fault," she said at last.

That little absolution hit Lucas in the gut for a moment, but he shook away the forgiveness he did not deserve. "I was the one who should have decided to act more prudently. I should not have asked your father to help me violate my orders. But for me he would still be with you. He died trying to protect *me*."

She was silent again, and he allowed the silence, despite how much he wished to recoil from it. At last she said, "That seems like all the more reason for me to wish to help you, Your Grace."

He wrinkled his brow. "You cannot mean that."

She stood and looked down at him. "I certainly do. I have an obligation not to let my father's sacrifice be for nothing. As do you. You will not leave, Your Grace. You will stay and you will allow me to help you. For my father."

"Miss—"

She turned away. "Rest again. I have left food by the door. Tomorrow will be a better time to discuss our next course of action. Good night."

She didn't wait for his response this time any more than she had the last time she walked away. And he did not offer any, but just watched her depart and leave him alone with his guilt and his rage and his pain.

CHAPTER 3

Diana had not lived in her bedroom in London for almost exactly a year. Even when she'd come for her father's service, she had stayed at an inn, her room paid for by Stalwood. The last time she'd been here, her heart had been broken and she'd never wanted to return to this place and all its horrible memories. Now she sat on her bed, and that same heart was broken all over again, not just by memories, but by the details the Duke of Willowby had just shared about her father's death.

"It's too much," she whispered out loud into the silent darkness that offered no comfort or solace. "It's just too much to bear."

Grief overcame her then, and she sank against her pillows, her sobs racking her body as she relived every broken moment of the last few years of her life. All the pain, all the loss, all the shattered dreams washed over her in an unrelenting wave.

She rocked against the pillows as the grief went on and on, and then she was being lifted, turned into a broad chest as warm, strong arms came around her. She leaned into that chest, letting the strength of those arms comfort her before reality came back. She lifted her face toward the very handsome one of Lucas.

"You shouldn't—" she began, though it was a weak refusal. In truth, it had been a very long time since someone had offered her physical comfort. Right now she wanted nothing more than to curl into him.

He shook his head. "Shh now," he soothed, that rough, hard voice now gentle and even kind. He guided a hand up to the back of her head and tugged her back to his chest. His fingers smoothed through her hair. "Shhhh."

She went limp, all her last resistance erased with the safety she felt in this man's arms. Perhaps it was an illusion, actually, she could almost guarantee that it was. But in this moment, she could not pull away.

So she sobbed against him, pouring out everything she was normally too strong to share. And he said nothing. No empty platitudes, no request that she tell him what was in her heart. No demand that she erase her feelings to make him more comfortable.

He just held her until the tears had stopped and she could finally breathe again.

She shifted slightly and lifted her gaze again. He was looking down at her. They were sitting on the bed together. He had no shirt. She had changed into her night-rail long ago.

In that moment, she realized how very intimate their position was. Especially when she could feel his clean, warm breath stirring her lips. When his dark eyes bore down into hers and held her captive.

His fingers tightened against her back, the rough pads stroking over her bare skin with exquisite intimacy. He was going to kiss her. She knew it as well as she knew her own name.

More than that, she wanted him to do it. In this moment when she was so raw and emotional, when she felt her loneliness with a sharpness that stabbed through her heart, the kiss felt like exactly what she needed more than anything.

But just as his lips dropped, reason screamed in her head for her to pull away. To remember the last time she had trusted a spy with her body. With her heart.

She jumped up and he let her go without comment. Her cheeks flamed and she turned her face so she wouldn't have to look at him as she said, "You ought not to be up, Your Grace."

"Lucas," he corrected once more.

She looked at him. In the half-dark his expression was impossible to decipher. He was a blank page, with no feeling about her weeping, about their near kiss, about anything at all. God, how that reminded her of her father and how he could put a wall down that separated them.

"Lucas," she surrendered, for it seemed pointless to continue belaboring the fact. "You need to rest."

He arched a brow. "Do you think me so ungentlemanly that I could hear a lady weeping in an adjoining room, weeping over something *I* did, something *I* said, and not come to ensure she was well?"

She ducked her head once more. She had not the talent he did to shutter her heart. There were times she wished she did. Tonight, for instance.

"I am well," she whispered. "And I'm here to help *you*, so I assure you that I will not trouble you with my emotions again."

He shrugged his good shoulder. "It was not any trouble tonight."

"Either way, we should get you back to bed," she insisted, and took a step toward him before she stopped. If she was going to help him, she was going to have to touch him. Touch that hard chest, be close to him like she had been when he almost kissed her. An entirely inappropriate thought to be having about someone she was meant to assist.

"I can manage," he said, but as he turned to go, he buckled slightly and she rushed forward to steady him.

"I should have investigated your wounds more closely this afternoon," she admonished herself as she slung his arm around her shoulders and began to help him back to his chamber. "Tomorrow I will be more thorough."

He laughed deep in his throat, and she jerked her gaze to the side to look at him. There was something almost feral about this man. Wild and dangerous, but infinitely alluring. And it was something she could not feel. Would not feel. Not ever again.

L ucas jerked awake, gasping in a huge gulp of air. Pain ripped through his shoulder and his leg. Always pain, his constant companion.

Where was he? He looked around the small chamber, flooded with light from outside and settled back against the pillows with a sigh. Oh yes, he remembered now. He was in George Oakford's London cottage.

Diana Oakford's cottage, he supposed. She must have inherited all her father had when he died. Including his duties. Something Lucas would have to discuss with Stalwood when the earl came to see how things were going. Diana did not deserve to be thrown into such a dangerous world. She ought to have been dancing and court-ing, not sobbing in her chamber over a man she was being forced to help.

Of course that had led to him touching her. Lucas shuddered at the memory. He hadn't come in to hold her, just to ensure her safety. But he couldn't help himself. And once he had...oh, he'd wanted to do far more than just hold her.

The door to the chamber opened slowly and he sat up straighter and gathered the covers around his naked body as Diana entered. She jolted as she found him watching her.

"Good morning," she said as she set her tray down on the table. He could see it contained food, and his stomach growled. "I didn't think you were awake. When I passed by earlier, you were still asleep."

He set his jaw. The idea of her checking in on him in his sleep felt very intimate. It also showed him how soft he'd become in the months since he was injured. He'd always been a light sleeper and would wake at the tiniest sound, ready to fight. He hated this new reality.

"I am awake, though, as you can see," he said.

"Let me look at your wounds, at last," she said, moving toward him.

He shifted. At present, he had a hell of a cockstand and he didn't want her seeing that. "No," he said.

She stopped and stared at him. "No?" she repeated. "What do you mean, no?"

"Just what I said." He folded his arms across his chest. "I don't need you poking around at me like half a dozen surgeons have done before. None of them could help me. I must simply learn to live as I am now."

Her brow wrinkled. "That is ridiculous. I'm certain I could make your life more comfortable, if you will only let me."

He rolled his eyes. "Said like a true physician. And then you'll slather donkey shit on me and leave me to sit in my own stink for a week."

She drew back. "That I would not do, I assure you. What you describe is practically medieval, Lucas."

He smiled a little at her surrender at calling him by his given name. At least *that* battle had been won. On to the next he went. "When can I leave?"

She blinked at him, like she didn't understand the question. "Leave? You're hurt."

He shrugged his uninjured shoulder. "And I have no doubt that I will find a way to compensate for those injuries. So what is the point of staying here?"

"And what would you do if I gave you the clearance to go?" she asked, and now her own arms folded. Of course, that only drew his attention to her breasts, but he tried to maintain focus. This was a negotiation, after all—he could not let himself be distracted.

"*You* give me clearance." He chuckled. "I do not think you have the rank to hand out such a thing."

Her bright green eyes snapped and narrowed. "Stalwood asked me to help you. Until I say you are ready to go, I assume he will not give you whatever it is you want."

He frowned. She might be right about that. So it was time to try a different tactic. "And what if I said that I wanted to pursue whoever killed your father?" he asked, hating how pain flared across her face before she reined in the reaction. Hating he'd caused her such pain. "I am far more qualified than anyone else on that case."

"No," she repeated, softly but firmly.

His eyes went wide at the dismissive finality of that rejection. "Am I wrong to assume you want whoever did this to be brought to justice?"

"Indeed, I do," she said, her voice getting louder. "But not if it comes at the cost of your life. Which is probably what would happen based on the fact that you can hardly walk from one chamber to the next without assistance."

He sat up straighter and was rewarded by blinding pain that ripped through his damaged body. Pain that proved her point and made him even angrier. So he directed it at her because there was nowhere else to put it. Not unless he wanted to face truths that would change his world forever. "You have no idea what I'm capable of, my dear," he growled. "And if you cared about your father, you would let me do my duty."

She flinched at those words, cruelly said and immediately regretted. He waited for her to cry again or to demand that he leave, as he deserved. But instead of doing those things, she merely speared him with a long stare. "You may be accustomed to everyone doing what you say when you say it, *Your Grace*, but I will not. My duty is to Stalwood, to my father's memory and to my oaths as a healer. Your wants and needs and tantrums do not come into the equation."

He pushed to his feet out of the bed. As the covers fell around him, he remembered he was naked beneath. And yet Diana didn't shy away at that fact. To the contrary, he watched, fascinated, as her gaze flitted up and down, settling for far too long at his cock. The one that slowly eased to attention once again under her gaze.

Desire pulsed between them, just as it had the night before. It was sudden and powerful, and in that moment Lucas wondered if he might be able to use it against her to get what he wanted. To get out into the field again before he ran mad with waiting and being useless.

She swallowed hard, and to his shock she stepped closer to him. She focused on his face as she said, "Do you want to get well? To go back into the field?"

He nodded slowly. "More than anything."

She gritted her jaw before she said, "Then let me help you. Give me a month."

He caught his breath. A month? That was impossible. He'd already been useless for over half a year. Another month was a waste of time, especially since he had enormous doubt that the end of it would be any different than the start. He would still be in pain. He would still be useless. His destiny would remain the same.

"To do what?"

She sighed. "To try to undo what surgeons far less skilled than my father have done to you. I won't lie to you, Lucas—it will hurt like hell. You will curse my name a hundred times. But let me."

Her voice was so calm and comforting and confident. She truly believed she could help him. And in that moment, he found a wild faith in the same. One he tamped down immediately for it was ridiculous.

"And if I refuse?" he asked.

She threw up her hands. "Then you fail my father. You fail yourself."

She pivoted and left the room. He stared as she did so, taken aback not only by her parting barb and how much it stung, but by her. She was beautiful, of course. No man wouldn't look at her and want. Need. But beneath that exterior was a strength of iron. A determination so powerful that it made him believe what he hadn't believed in a long time.

And that made her far more dangerous than any enemy he'd ever face in the field. Because her weapon was hope.

CHAPTER 4

D iana tossed her basket on the ground and dove into the plants with angry gusto. She popped leaves off, tearing them far more violently than she would normally do. But she couldn't help it. That man was a stubborn ass. Pompous and brazen and... and *rude*.

Despite all that, she was drawn to him. Intensely. Last night she'd wanted to kiss him. This morning she hadn't been able to look away when he stood up, all male power and naked desire. This was a weakness in her, one she had succumbed to once before with dire consequences.

Consequences that had sent her to the country. Ones that had kept her alone. She had rejected all the advances of bumbling country fools who came sniffing around her.

But the Duke of Willowby was no bumbling country fool.

"Idiot," she admonished herself as she returned her attention to tearing leaves from plants.

"Me, you, or that poor plant you're destroying?"

She froze at the drawled question. Damn the man—could he not leave her in peace? It seemed not. Slowly she turned and caught her breath. There he stood, leaning heavily on the back of a bench in the middle of her garden. He had dressed himself. Poorly, of course. Perhaps because he was accustomed to the help of his valet. Perhaps because his injuries made it difficult.

The result of his being a bit undone was anything but to make him less attractive. He was roguish with his shirt half-untucked, his hair tangled around his face and his cheeks peppered with the dark beginnings of a beard. He looked like a pirate, not a duke. A pirate prince out for whatever treasure he could steal.

"What are you doing?" she asked, her tone sharper than she wished it to be. God's teeth, but this man brought out the worst in her.

He met her gaze and gave a half grin. "I'm doing whatever I please. Isn't that what you accused me of earlier?"

She dropped a tangle of herbs into the basket and folded her arms. "No, it was not. I said you are accustomed to everyone doing as you say. Though I assume it follows that you also do whatever you please without a thought to others."

"Oof," he said with a shake of his head. "I am truly a bastard, it seems. And you want to help me?"

He was smiling. Teasing her. And she caught her breath. When he smiled he was even more handsome than when he brooded, damn him. And his words, playful or not, hit her in the gut. Although she had been dragged into this by Stalwood, the fact was that she *did* want to help this man.

She drew in a long breath to calm her racing heart. "I was…sharp with you," she said. "Perhaps that was unfair."

He laughed once again. "On the contrary, I think it was entirely fair. I deserved it."

She wrinkled her brow, for now she was uncertain of him again. Was he playing so that she would lower her guard? He was a spy, after all, trained to manipulate. "You are entirely frustrating."

His grin broadened and the expression took years off his face. It brightened everything about him and made her wonder what kind of man he'd been before his injuries. Before the War Department. Just...before.

"Thank you," he said.

"It wasn't meant as a compliment," she said, but she found herself laughing despite it.

He let out his breath and leaned heavier on the bench. "In truth, I *do* owe you an apology," he said, now serious. "I have not been easy since my arrival, I know that. I just don't like to be...weak."

She could see how hard that confession was for him. She understood it. Even after being inactive for months, no one could deny that the man standing before her had enormous strength. She could only imagine how easy everything physical had always been for him. Men were taught that was their greatest asset. Losing it had to crush some important part of him.

She moved forward and held out her hands. "Sit, won't you?" she asked, motioning to the bench where he was leaning.

He nodded and let her help him into place. She bent, grabbed her basket and set it in his lap with a smile. "Hold this. At least you will be useful."

He laughed, but she heard the strain in his voice as he said, "Useful was never something I had to work for in the past."

She turned away, knowing that these admissions could not be easy. It was best to receive them with quiet, not to make too big a fuss.

"You are not weak, you know," she said as she crouched and examined a few flower buds on the plant before her. "You are injured. I swear, you men."

"Men?" he repeated as she set a few buds into the basket beside the other herbs she had selected before he came out. "Is this a problem with my entire sex, then?"

"Indeed, it is," she retorted. "You tend, as a whole, to equate not being able to do something with weakness. It does you no good."

"You're so certain?"

She glared at him. "Setting aside their ability, think of those other men who tried to help you since your injuries. I would assume you argued and demanded and forced even before you came to be under my care."

His sheepish expression told her everything before he said, "Well, er, yes, I suppose I did."

She shrugged. "And that is part of why you're not further along in your recovery. You cannot accept help because help is weakness. But you keep yourself injured and 'weak', as you put it, by not allowing someone else in to come to your aid."

"I thought the problem was untalented surgeons," he drawled.

"Stubborn patients are also an issue," she retorted with a smile.

He held her gaze and her heart fluttered a bit. This connection she felt whenever he looked at her like that was disconcerting to say the least. As a result, she forced herself to look away, but the burning of her cheeks had to be as obvious to him as it was to her.

"I traveled the world, you know," he said. "In service to my king, I learned new languages, saw things I couldn't even imagine. I pretended to be what I was not. It was all a grand adventure. A pleasure as much as a duty."

"It must be hard to lose that," she whispered.

He was quiet a moment, and then he said, "You told me there would be pain if I do as you say."

She swallowed hard and forced herself to meet his eyes. "Yes."

His lips pressed harder together. "But will I heal? Will I ever be anything like the man I was before?"

She caught her breath, moved once more by the hint of pleading in his voice. The desperation that drove his worst behaviors was clearer to her now. Everything he was had been tied up in what he could do. How he could protect. Where he could go without difficulty.

Losing all that had changed him.

She understood that.

"I will never lie to you, Lucas," she said, leaning in to touch his chin, turning it so that he met her eyes and could see the truth of her. "And I will not promise you what I cannot deliver. I don't know if I can bring back that man you once were. But if you let me look at you, help you, I promise you I will do everything in my power to try."

His eyes narrowed, like he was reading her, hesitating to trust her, but at last he nodded slowly. "Very well. I will give you your month."

Relief flowed through her, stronger than she'd thought it would, considering she hadn't wanted to do any of this in the first place. His refusal would have made her life easier. His acceptance made her happy, though.

"Good," she said.

He held up her basket. "Now, will you tell me what these herbs do?"

She smiled as the tension between them bled away a fraction. "Well, some are to ease pain. Others are to help with healing. This one makes chicken taste better."

He tilted his head back and laughed. "Best not to get them confused then."

"Never," she said, and took the basket, sliding it over her forearm. "Why don't we go upstairs and we can begin, this time in earnest? I want to look at your injuries more closely. Only then can we truly know what to do next."

If he wanted to hesitate or argue or refuse, he did not do it. He merely drew in a long breath, then got to his feet and took her offered arm as they slowly made their way back to the house and to the tortures she knew would come.

Lucas drew in a deep breath and tried to calm himself. When this woman touched him, it was mesmerizing. He'd never experienced anything like it with any lover he'd taken over the years. Being near her was like sunshine waking him in the morning or the warmth of alcohol buzzing through his system and addling his brain.

And yet, as she opened the door to the house, his anxiety about what would happen next rose in his chest. He'd been trained to handle pain, of course. A spy needed to be able to bear torture.

But the past six months had pushed him to his limits. He did not relish the idea of doing it all again, and especially not in front of this woman who seemed to be able to see into a man's soul, whether he used his training against her or not.

She tightened her arm around his waist as they began to climb the stairs together. "I will get you a cane," she mused, almost more to herself than to him. He stiffened, and she glanced over at him with a knowing look. "Let me guess—you shunned the idea of a cane because it made you weak?"

He pursed his lips at the censure that marked her tone. "When you say it like that, it sounds foolish," he drawled, hoping to cut the tension with a bit of self-deprecation.

She paused at the top of the stairs, her breath labored as she panted, "It *is* foolish. Great God, would you not feel better if you could wrangle yourself up the stairs or through a room without needing someone to support your weight?"

"I...suppose," he admitted slowly. "Does it trouble you?"

She cast him a side glance and began to maneuver him toward the bedroom. "Does what trouble me?"

"Always being right," he finished. "Does it keep you up at night?"

There was a second's pause, and then she laughed. The sound was like music and he drank it in while she helped him into the chamber and toward the bed. As he collapsed back onto the mattress, she buckled over him and landed across his chest. Pain shot through him, as it always did. But it was tempered by something else.

Something he hadn't felt in a very long time. Pleasure. Her body against his was a pleasure, and he found he didn't want to let that go quite yet. Her laughter faded and she stared down at him, watching silently as he lifted his arms to fold them around her. To hold her like he'd done the night he comforted her.

Only he hadn't comfort on his mind in this moment. No, he wanted something else from her and he was not going to be denied. He glided his fingers into her hair, cupping her skull to lower her mouth to his. She didn't resist—she only let out a tiny sigh, and then her lips were pressing against his.

It was like someone had relit the world after months of darkness. Electric desire flashed through his rusty body and he dug his fingers into her skin to draw her even closer. She obliged, opening her mouth to him and darting her tongue to meet his with hesitation that faded as he sucked her deeper.

For a moment, everything else in the world disappeared. He forgot his physical pain, he forgot his frustration and his guilt, he forgot the life he'd lost and the one he hadn't saved. He forgot everything and drowned in how sweet she tasted and how erotically she moved against him as her breasts flattened to his chest and she lifted against him with a deep moan in her throat.

And then, just as swiftly as she had surrendered, she pulled away. He let her go, watching as she staggered back, turning as she lifted her hand to her lips like she could still feel him there. He knew he could feel her.

And he wanted to feel so much more.

"Going to run again, Miss Oakford?" he asked as the time stretched out between them and he felt her readying to do just that.

She spun toward him, her cheeks flushed and her pupils dilated. She stared and then shook her head. "N-no," she stammered, her voice shaky and unfocused. "No, of course not. I'm to help you. It's time I did just that. Will you remove your shirt?"

He nodded as he sat up and slowly began to unfasten the buttons along the front of the fabric. She watched him for a beat, then shook her head as she knelt to begin helping with his boots.

His heart all but stopped at the sight of her on her knees before him. And when she looked up, apparently utterly unaware of how fucking tempting she was, it took all his control not to drag her back up his body, flip her on her back and just have her until he couldn't take anymore. Until she was sated and soft beneath him.

Until her voice was hoarse from crying out his name.

She tugged his boots off and set them aside. As she rose, she turned away and he watched her as she moved to where she'd left a tray earlier in the day. She picked up a few bottles, some bandages and a needle and thread, then returned.

"Here, let me," she said softly, setting the items on the bed beside him before she moved to help him pull the shirt over his head. He grimaced as he lifted his bad arm enough for her to pull the fabric away. After she tossed it aside, she leaned in, examining the scarred flesh as she clucked her tongue. "How often did they reopen it?" she asked.

He shut his eyes and shoved aside memories of those horrible experiences. Tried to forget the pain that had brought him to unconsciousness more than once. "I lost count after eight."

She turned her face, as if his pain affected her physically. "I'm sorry," she whispered as she traced the mark with the edge of her fingernail.

"You have to do it again, don't you?"

She jerked her gaze up to his. "How did you know?"

"I hear it in your voice," he said as he lowered himself back to the pillows. "And every healer does it, don't they? You have to make your own mark on me."

Her lips parted. "Stalwood should hire better men. I have no desire to mark you, Lucas. I do not take any pleasure in the pain that I will cause. But I hope you'll...you'll..."

He met her eyes at her hesitation. "What?"

"Trust me," she said. "I realize you don't know me. You have no reason to do so."

"I do," he said softly. "I do have a reason."

"And what is that?" she asked, even as she lifted a thin scalpel from the bed and dipped it in liquid.

"You're his daughter," he said, gripping the sheets with both fists as she lowered the instrument to his already burning skin and made a delicate slice.

She didn't look at him, but kept her focus on his injury. "That is a high standard to live up to," she said softly.

He bit his lip as she probed his wound, examining the damage that made him so damned broken. Then she clucked her tongue and set the scalpel aside. She picked up her mortar and pestle and began to throw dried herbs and a different, thicker liquid into the little bowl. As she mixed it, she met his eyes.

"Almost finished and then I will never reopen it again," she promised.

He gritted his teeth. "That's what they all say."

"I'm not them," she said, holding his stare.

He almost laughed, but couldn't quite when the pain was making his vision blur and his voice strangled. He tried to focus, tried to find levity in this moment so she wouldn't see how desperate and vulnerable she was making him. "You're certainly much prettier than the others."

The world began to spin around him. He could feel his pulse in the hole in his shoulder and that throbbing made his knees shake.

"Well, I should certainly hope so," she said, her tone still calm and soothing and he could hear the smile in it. "I've seen some of those louts my father trained. Prettier isn't exactly the hardest mountain to climb."

"Christ," he managed as he turned his head on the pillow.

She stood and leaned over him. A lock of hair he'd loosened when he kissed her fell from her plain bun and brushed over his skin. He focused on its silkiness, the way it tickled his chest.

"This will help," she promised, slathering the mixture she'd made over his wound.

He lurched at the cold of the medicine. The way it made his flesh tingle as it sank into the gash she'd created. But within a few seconds, he felt a blissful numbness that worked its way through the flesh.

"There now," she whispered as she reached up and began to unfasten his trouser flap. "Better?"

He stared at her, his body torn between pleasure and pain as she touched him. He felt dizzy as he whispered, "What are you doing to me?"

She smiled. "I must remove your trousers to look at your leg, Lucas. I promise it is only for the purpose of treating you."

He closed his eyes as she tugged the fabric away and left him naked. "You can do whatever you'd like, Diana. You must be able to see that."

She said something, but it sounded far away. He focused on the way her fingers brushed over his leg. He had no idea how much time passed and then she was next to him, her lips brushing his temple as she whispered, "Rest now."

He thought he should respond, but there were no words he could come up with. None that made any sense, at any rate. So he let his drooping eyes close and surrendered to the unconsciousness that his body demanded.

CHAPTER 5

Diana stood in the kitchen, pulling chunks of meat from the bones of the chicken she had just taken from the spit over the fire. She had always liked to cook and had done so for her father for years. The science of it was very similar to the science of poultices and tinctures, so the act felt familiar and soothing.

Not that it was working at present. Despite the occupation, her mind kept taking her back to thoughts of Lucas. It had been twenty-four hours since she had reopened and cleaned his wounds. He'd been sleeping ever since, a deep sleep of powerful pain and, she hoped, healing at last. He deserved that after the nightmare he'd been through over the past six months.

She'd checked on him nearly every hour. Told herself it was her duty as a healer, but that was only half the reason. The other half was the thing that kept her staring up at her ceiling in her bed. He had kissed her. Deeply and thoroughly and with all the experience a man of that type would have. She should have turned away, but she hadn't. She couldn't.

It was deeply disconcerting to admit that, even just to herself. But she'd felt a strange and powerful draw to Lucas from the moment she saw him. Something unlike anything she'd ever felt before.

She'd *wanted* that kiss. More and more with each passing hour she spent with him. Worse, she wanted another. *That* was why she came in to check on him. To study those surprisingly full lips. To consider what they would feel like if they touched hers again. If they brushed over her skin until she came completely undone.

"A very hazardous path," she muttered as she speared the carcass and tugged more steaming chicken from the bone. "One you've traveled before, to your detriment."

The Duke of Willowby was dangerous, full stop. There was nothing more to be said on the matter.

Except her mind kept saying a great deal more. Dangerous but so handsome. Dangerous but undeniably charismatic. Dangerous, but when he looked at her she wanted things she knew were wrong. Things that could destroy her entire world.

She shook her head, trying, for what had to be the hundredth time, to remove those wicked thoughts from her head. In her distraction, she moved her hand and grazed it along the side of the hot metal tong that was sticking out of the chicken's middle. "Ouch!" she barked, lifting her hand to her lips to suck on the red flesh.

"Let me help."

She turned and started at the sight of Lucas standing in the entryway of the kitchen, leaning on the doorjamb, his face pale. His clothes were wrinkled, his hair wild from sleep, but her body began to tingle nonetheless at the sight of him.

"What are you doing?" she asked, rushing forward to help him and forcing herself to focus on her role as healer, not wanton. "God's teeth, you should sleep another day after what you endured."

"*Another* day?" he repeated, his eyes going wide. "How long have I slept already?"

"Twenty-four hours, a little more, actually," she said.

He tensed and his lips thinned. "What did you give me? Laudanum?"

She helped him to a seat. "Something like it, mixed into the poultice to help with the pain."

"I don't like laudanum. It makes me out of control," he said softly.

She frowned as she lifted her hand to her mouth again. He caught it before she could reach her lips and turned it over to look at the minor burn that abraded the skin of her palm.

"You must have some magic for this," he said, lifting his eyes to hers.

Once again she was captivated by his expression. Once again she lost the ability to think clearly and rationally. What was it about this man? What was it about herself that opened her to such thoughts and desires?

"I can make a quick mixture," she admitted. "That will help it heal."

"Let me," he suggested, waving at the seat next to his. "Just tell me what to do."

She pursed her lips but decided against arguing. After all, she could see that he would not allow her to do so. This man was accustomed to getting his way, just as she had suggested before. So she drew a long breath, then began to give him orders about which herbs to use and how to mix them for her. To her surprise, he followed her instructions to the letter, without so much as an argument.

She stared as he crushed the items with her mortar and pestle, his muscles working in his good arm as he ground them together. He was very focused on the work, his mouth drawn into a deep frown, his gaze on the bowl. She could see the spy in him then, motivated, driven, undeniable.

Entirely undeniable.

"Now what?" he asked.

She jumped, drawn from those unexpected, unwanted thoughts. "Er, we—we put it on the burn," she stammered.

He turned toward her and smirked. "Well?"

She blinked. "Well, what?"

"Hold out your hand, Diana," he said, leaning in close enough that she felt his warmth.

"Yes, yes, of course," she breathed, and turned her hand over to show him the injury.

He spread the greenish paste he'd made across the burn. "Do you have a cloth to cover it?" he asked.

She nodded. "In the cupboard there."

He moved away and she took the opportunity to suck in a few deep breaths. The tension, the spark between them…God, it was powerful. She felt like she was losing all control and it terrified and thrilled her all at once.

He returned, soft flannel cloth in hand. He met her eyes as he gently wrapped her palm. He only looked away to tie it off. She followed his gaze and frowned at the knot he had used. It seemed familiar somehow.

"Some would call that witchcraft, you know," he said, plopping down next to her and stealing a piece of chicken from the plate where she'd been stripping the meat away.

She smiled, though his words made her stomach clench. "Indeed, you are right, even if you tease. Not that long ago I might have been accused of just that. Burned for it in some parts. Even now it isn't as if people trust a woman in such a vocation."

He examined her face closely, too closely, and she swallowed hard under his regard. What was he thinking?

"The female spies I've known over the years have said much the same," he said at last. "Their talents are unseen. I suppose it would be just as difficult to gain the respect *you* deserve."

She bent her head. "It is. But those who mattered gave it to me."

She felt him still watching her, and his voice was strained when he said, "Your father, you mean."

She caught her breath and stood, motioning to the chicken. "It's good you came down, actually. You need some nutrition. It will help your body heal."

"I'm so very glad you're in the business of protecting my body," he said, his voice suddenly rough.

She thrilled at the tone, knowing full well what it meant. Feeling her body call back to him no matter how wrong it was. To maintain some distance between them, she pivoted and found two plates. Quickly she dished out the chicken she'd been preparing, alongside carrots from the garden, which she had roasted in a wine sauce.

"Simple, but it is filling," she said as she set the plate in front of him and one at her own place, which she took.

He arched a brow and took up a fork. He speared both a slice of chicken and a carrot at once, and his eyes lit up as he chewed them. "Excellent," he said.

She laughed as she took her own bite. "You sound mightily surprised."

"I am," he admitted with a laugh as he all but poured the food down his throat. "I don't know any ladies who can cook."

She stiffened. "Well, I am not a lady."

"You were a gentleman's daughter," he said softly. "And a gentlewoman yourself. Anyone with eyes can see you are a lady."

"Hmmm."

She'd hoped the noncommittal answer would veer him to other subjects, but of course it didn't. He was focused now, driven, as spies tended to be when something struck them as odd.

"Where *did* you learn to cook?"

"Our housekeeper didn't mind showing me when I expressed an interest. I suppose she hoped it would keep me off my father's path. She was wrong, of course," she said with a sigh. "In truth, Father liked me cooking, for it is very much like making medicines. There's a recipe, a precision, a science."

He chewed thoughtfully. "I can see that would be true."

"When Mrs. Smith died, I took over in her role as housekeeper and cook for my father," she explained. "And assistant, when he needed it."

Lucas stared at her in what was clearly confusion. "He didn't want...more for you?"

"More?" she asked, feigning a lack of understanding when she knew full well to what he referred.

"A life outside of his world," he clarified. "A husband. Children."

She flinched as she set her plate aside and broke her gaze from his. "I doubt my father thought of me in that way. To him I was a tool. To be trained and used as needed."

"Didn't *you* want more, Diana?" he asked. "Don't you want more now?"

She pressed her lips together. He was dancing perilously close to an edge she could not risk gliding along. So instead she moved to take his empty plate. "May I get you something else?"

He shook his head and caught her wrist, keeping her from backing away. His hands were remarkably strong and she could see there would be no point in fighting. Worse, she didn't want to fight. She liked the weight of his fingers against her skin. She liked the intensity in his stare as he looked up at her.

She liked the dance between them, even if she knew the outcome could be nothing good.

"I don't want more. I'm not hungry."

She swallowed hard. "I cannot imagine that is true, Lucas. You ate so quickly and—"

He tugged her a bit closer. "I'm not hungry for food."

"Lucas," she whispered, though she offered no resistance as he drew her down, slow as molasses, into his lap.

She settled there carefully and now they were face-to-face. His breath stirred her lips, and he never broke eye contact.

"You want what I want," he whispered. "Or do you deny it?"

"What do you want?" she asked, her voice cracking.

He tilted his head, his expression challenging her, telling her he knew full well what she wanted. That she knew what he wanted too.

Which of course she did. There was no denying what he wanted. It was evident from the heavy length of his cock that pressed against her thigh as she sat in his lap. Evident by his dilated pupils and the way his hands clenched against her.

But he didn't say those things. He didn't say anything at all. He merely cupped the back of her head and drew her closer. And just like in his bedroom earlier in the day, she did nothing to resist him. In fact, she tilted her head, granting him greater access as his mouth met hers.

For the briefest of moments, the kiss was gentle. But then it shifted and suddenly she found her arms around him, she was lifting against him, his mouth was open, devouring her with passion that had been bubbling beneath the surface for days now. Finally it overflowed and she felt no desire to fight it or him.

She wanted this. After years of loneliness and grief and pain, she wanted something…good. And she wanted it now.

As if he sensed that, he pulled away. He was panting as he said, "Come upstairs with me, Diana."

She swallowed hard. This was her opportunity to regain purchase over herself. To deny him, to deny herself, and do what any other person in good society would consider the right thing.

And yet, she didn't do that. She stood, holding out her hand to him, and he took it. Slowly they made their way up the back stairs, down the short hallway. At the door to his chamber, he stopped and faced her.

"I need to be very clear, Diana—I want you. I want to make love to you. And under normal circumstances, I'd take the lead until you were begging beneath me. But such as I am—"

She lifted up on her tiptoes and pressed two fingers to his lips to silence him. "I know what to do," she whispered as she reached around him to open the door.

His eyes grew wide, but he didn't question as she backed him into the room, across it to the bed. He stopped there and winced as he reached up to remove his shirt. She stepped up to push his hands away and did it herself, unfastening and sliding the fabric gently from his shoulders until it fell behind him on the floor. She followed with his trousers, thankful that he was barefoot so they wouldn't be impeded by her removing his boots.

And then he was naked, standing before her, and she stopped breathing.

She stared at him, just as she had every time she'd seen him this way. The first time she'd tried, and perhaps failed, to look at him with the eyes of a physician. Tried to see him as a body she was meant to repair.

Tonight she stared at him as a woman was meant to stare at a man she would have as her own. She drank him in slowly, enjoying every inch of toned flesh, even the damaged ones that were hidden behind the bandage she had wrapped earlier. Her gaze flitted to the flat stomach, the narrow hips, and at last she settled on the hard cock that flared up in desire.

"I have not been touched by anyone but those meant to heal me in a very long time, Diana," he whispered, his voice rough with emotion as well as desire. "Please."

She swallowed, for his words struck far too close to the core of her. She, too, had missed the touch of another person. A touch of love or desire or pleasure. She hadn't realized how much she'd missed it until the night he held her while she wept and reawakened all the desires she'd tried to pack away.

There was more than one way to heal, wasn't there?

She moved forward, holding his gaze as she placed her hands flat against his chest. He hissed out a sound of pleasure, tracking her movements as she glided her fingers down his flesh, letting her thumbs flick at his flat nipples before she stroked them over his stomach.

"God's teeth," he grunted, dipping his head back as he used his good hand to balance himself on the bed.

She swelled with feminine power at the reaction. She liked

making this powerful man tremble as he trembled now when she stroked just one fingertip along the length of his hard cock.

His eyes came open, spearing her with his gaze once more. As she teased him, he lifted his hands and unbuttoned her gown in a few deft motions that gave her a glimpse, once more, of what this man had been like before injury. She shuddered as he pushed the gown open and tugged it over her arms until it collapsed on the floor beneath her feet.

Her undergarments were simple, a short chemise over a pair of drawers. For once in her life, she wished she collected pretty underthings, but the plain cotton that separated her from him seemed not to bother him. He just stared at her, his pupils dilating until there was almost no brown left, his hands shaking as he slipped them under the straps of her chemise and pushed it down, lower and lower until her breasts were bared.

"Diana was a goddess," he whispered as he bent his head and blew warm air against her nipples. They hardened, and sensation rushed through her as she thrust her fingers into his hair and tangled them into the unruly curls.

"Y-yes," she said, her voice breaking.

"You are aptly named," he murmured before he darted his tongue out and traced the hard peak of her nipple. He swirled his tongue around and around, and her knees nearly buckled at the pleasure. She found herself tugging him closer, holding him against her in a silent demand for more. For everything.

He chuckled against her flesh and looked up at her. "Shall we continue this on the bed?"

She nodded and watched as he took his place against the pillows. He lay on his good arm, propping himself up as he left a spot for her to join him.

She drew a long breath. Here was another of those chances to run away from this. From him. But she didn't. Instead, she shimmied her drooping chemise away. He sat up a little more, stalking her with his gaze as she untied the bow at the waist of her drawers and slowly slid them down around her ankles, as well.

She was naked. *They* were naked. Once she got onto that bed with him, there would be no going back. He would touch her and she would touch him and everything would become moonlight and foggy pleasure. It would change everything about what she had agreed to do to help him.

And she wanted to do it despite all that.

She wanted to do it *because* of it. And because she had been alone and hurting for so long. Didn't she deserve the pleasure this man promised with every turn of his head and blink of his eyes?

"Changing your mind?" he drawled.

She blinked and realized she'd been standing naked before him, musing on what would happen next. He didn't look perturbed, though.

"Not that I don't enjoy the view," he continued. "But I do not take what isn't fully and happily given, Diana. Once we do this, it cannot be taken back. And I can make no promises along with it. Not with my profession."

She drew in a long breath. "I appreciate that honesty, Lucas. But I do not hesitate because I want promises. I would not ask for them, nor would I accept them if they were made."

He examined her for a moment, then held out his hand. "Then we are of a mind."

She nodded, and her own hand shook as she took his and joined him at last on the bed. She settled onto the pillows on her back beside him. For a moment he did nothing but look at her.

"I was not entirely honest," he said at last.

She tensed. Dishonesty was to be expected but it terrified her nonetheless. "About what?" she forced herself to ask in a calm tone that belied her inner turmoil.

"I do make *one* promise."

"And what is that?" she whispered.

"Pleasure," he murmured, and then he placed his warm hand on her stomach, spreading his thick fingers across her flesh as she arched slightly against him out of pure instinct and desire.

"That's all I ask from you, all I want," she choked out.

She cupped the back of his head and drew him down, drowning once more in his kiss as he stroked those fingers lower, lower, to her hip, to her thighs, and finally he pushed her legs open a fraction and rested his palm against her sex.

She broke the kiss with a gasp. She had forgotten what it was like to be touched so intimately. To feel the rush of desire flow through her and to want so much more than just the brush of fingers. In that wild moment she wanted those fingers inside of her, she wanted his tongue, she wanted his cock. She wanted everything, and she shuddered with the power of that unfettered desire.

And also unbridled terror.

"Doesn't this hurt, using your bad arm to—" she began, struggling to sit up and bring reality back to this wild fantasy.

He laughed softly. "Stop being a healer for the next...half an hour," he said. His smile widened. "Or hour. If there's pain, it's worth it."

As he spoke, he parted her folds and stroked his finger across her entrance. He was gentle as he did so, almost teasing. She collapsed back at the touch and arched, almost against her will at the sensation. When she glanced up, she found him watching her face. Watching her surrender.

"More," she groaned, because she couldn't resist anymore.

His eyes widened. "I don't want to hurt you."

She caught her breath. He assumed she was untouched. That she was offering her virginity and he was trying his hardest to maintain control when he took it.

Her hands were shaking as she reached down and covered his hand with her own. She pressed him hard against her, feeling his finger breach her a fraction.

"There is nothing to hurt or to steal, Lucas," she promised, her cheeks flaming as she whispered that confession. "Just *touch* me."

He stared at her a moment, his eyes wide and filled with questions. She prayed that spy part of him, that part that investigated and prodded and examined, would be silent. That he would let her have her secrets and just give her what she wanted in return.

And her answer was given when he drove two fingers deep inside of her. She bore down against him with a gasp of pleasure. He grunted his own and began to stroke deeply within her. He curled them as he pressed his thumb against her clitoris. She was writhing now, taken instantly to the edge of madness. To the edge of pleasure.

He took it with his skillful fingers, drawing her to the brink and then dragging her over the cliff. She arched her back, digging her heels hard into the bed as wave after wave of pleasure tore through her. Changed her. Reminded her of all she wanted and all she'd lost. She cried out his name as she shook and clawed and pled for more and for less.

At last the spiraling sensation eased and she flopped back against the pillows with a sigh of relief. He removed his fingers, held her gaze and lifted them to his lips, where he sucked her essence from the tips.

She shuddered as desire flowed through her again. She wanted more. It was obvious he did too.

She sat up and cupped his cheeks, kissing him deeply, tasting herself on his tongue for a brief moment. Then she pushed him back, taking the pressure off his battered body and rolling him to his back.

"The goddess takes control?" he teased, though his voice was thick with wanting, not anything playful.

"If you want to be in control, consider it incentive for you to do as you're told and heal," she said as she straddled him, shivering as his cock slid against the apex of her body, but not yet positioning herself to take him inside.

"Incentive, indeed," he growled as he sat up a fraction and tugged her down for another kiss. His fingers tugged tight on her head, leading her despite his precarious position.

She shifted, sliding a hand between them. She stroked his cock from base to tip once, then twice, feeling him twitch with pleasure against her. Then she maneuvered him to her slick entrance and glided down over him in one slow stroke.

He broke the kiss with a wild cry as she fully took him. His hips bucked, forcing her to thrust, and she gripped the pillows on either side of his head as she began to ride him hard and heavy and fast. He dragged her back into the kiss and she lost herself to passion she'd never thought she'd ever experience again. She pushed harder, grinding down against him, seeking the release she'd already had again. Wanting it with greedy, miserly desire.

He reared up beneath her, and that crash of their pelvises gave her what she desired. She cried out, driving her tongue into his mouth as she came for what felt like a blissful eternity. He caught her hips and kept her moving, drawing out her pleasure.

When she could refocus at last, she saw how his neck strained, how his breath was ragged. With a yelp, she moved away from him, caught the length of his cock and stroked him, keeping up the rhythm that had been created until he jolted out a cry and his essence spurted from him in heavy bursts.

She collapsed beside him, tucking herself into his good shoulder as he wrapped his arms around her. He did not speak or ask her questions, she did not offer explanations or discussion. It was peace and quiet and gentle pleasure. And that was how she fell asleep, in his arms and in his bed.

CHAPTER 6

Lucas jolted awake with the same jarring suddenness that he had in the past six months. Today, though, something was different. And he realized with a start that it was the pain. It was there, yes, still burning and clawing, but it had lessened. He did not want to wrench his shoulder from his body, at least.

And that was a positive thing.

There was something else that was different too. He could smell Diana's perfume on his pillow, that sweet vanilla scent of her hair that made a man mad. That proved their night of passion had not been an addled dream brought on by laudanum and pain.

It had been real.

And yet he woke alone. That scent was the only indication she had been in his bed.

Slowly, he sat up, bracing for increased pain. It came, but it was still less than usual. "She truly is a witch," he mused aloud, then threw off the covers and gingerly stepped from the bed. He wanted to find her. To talk to her. To make certain she was not troubled or pained by what they'd done.

And that required putting on his clothes. Always a challenge.

He moved to the wardrobe in the corner of the room and

opened it. At some point Diana had placed his few shirts and trousers in the closet, folded neatly. When did she have time to do the laundering with all the other things she did?

He lifted the shirt and stared at it. His old nemesis. It required moving in ways that did not make his shoulder happy. But he gritted his teeth and slowly put his arm through the hole. Reaching back made the pain double, and he let out his breath through his nose with a low moan of discomfort.

"Would you like some help?"

He pivoted and found Diana at his door, tray of food in her arms. She was wearing a simple gown and her hair was half down around her shoulders, framing her face and making her even more beautiful than normal. He found himself wondering what she'd look like in a ball gown, done up like the queen that she was.

Of course, that would never happen. They would never go to a ball together, that wasn't possible. He shook away the errant thought.

She was looking at him. She'd looked at him before, but now her gaze swept over his nearly naked body and her eyes lit up with knowing pleasure. Suddenly dressing didn't seem all that important.

And yet having her help him felt like a loss. A surrender.

"I hate being so useless," he admitted as he looked at the shirt hanging from his arm.

She set the tray down by the door and moved to him. She took the shirt from his arms and pulled out a pair of trousers. He balanced on her to step into them and held his breath as she began to fasten the flap.

"Useless again, is it?" she said softly. "You will relearn these things. Though I would think, as a duke, you would be accustomed to having help. You have a valet, don't you? In some other life?"

"Another life." He pursed his lips. "That is the way to put it. Yes, I did have a valet then. Very long ago. I have not had help dressing myself since I was...God...nineteen? Twenty?"

She glanced up at him. "That was when you joined the War Department?"

He nodded. "I'd been an officer, too, in the army. Briefly. But I did have a valet there."

"A duke in the army," she said. "Most do not pursue such things."

He looked away. "I had my reasons."

She returned her attention to what she was doing. He was pleased for that. He didn't want to talk about the past.

"I want to look at the wound," she said, unwrapping the bandage on his shoulder. He steadied himself on the back of a nearby chair as she did so.

"It feels...better," he admitted. "Though perhaps that is wishful thinking."

She looked at the now uncovered wound, wiping away what was left of the salve she'd put on it. Although he was untrained, he could see the injury appeared less angry.

"It looks better," she said with a nod. "We've a long way to go, but I think there's progress. Let me get my bandages and I'll redress it. Sit in that chair, will you?"

He did as she asked, watching as she gathered her materials. She returned with them and with a cloudy drink that she handed over to him. "Drink this."

He eyed and smelled it. It seemed benign enough. Smelled a bit floral, but nothing terrible. He took a sip. "Good God, that's awful," he said, glaring up at her.

She laughed, the music of the sound filling the room and warming his heart in ways he did not particularly like. "It is that," she admitted. "But it's an old recipe meant to help you regain your strength. Drink it all, please."

He made a face, but downed it in a few long gulps. As he made little sounds of displeasure, he set the glass away. "How do I know you're not trying to kill me?"

Her laughter increased as she began to rewrap his shoulder. "If I were trying to kill you, I assure you, you'd be dead."

He wondered at her bright tone, at how easy the teasing was and how much lighter it made him feel. He'd spent half a year wallowing in physical and emotional pain and here…here it was different.

And he was just as taken aback by the fact that she was not mincing or simpering about what had happened between them. And yet it was a subject that needed addressing. He watched as she caught up his shirt and shook it out, then came around behind him to help him slide his arms into the holes. With her assistance, there was far less pain, though he still gritted his teeth against it.

"Diana," he managed to grind out as a way to distract himself from the discomfort. "Are we going to talk about what happened last night?"

Diana froze, her body suddenly unsteady. Being near this man was hard enough, thinking of every moment that his hands had been on her skin and their bodies had been joined was distracting to the furthest degree.

And now he wanted to analyze those moments out loud. Like a good spy would.

She let out a long sigh. "I-I suppose we should," she said.

She could feel him watching her as she walked away to open the curtains and let some light into the dim room. The view of the garden below helped a little, so she focused there and tried not to let her emotions swell up too high or too far. It wasn't that she regretted what they'd done. She refused to be judged for something they had both participated in equally.

"Did I take advantage?" he asked softly.

She swung around in shock at that question. It was not what she'd expected, especially considering her lack of virtue had been clear in so many ways.

"*You* are the one who is incapacitated," she said.

A little smirk lifted one corner of his distracting lips. "Am I?" he teased, and some of the tension left both the room and her body.

57

Still, she felt heat flood to her cheeks. She was not one to blush often—her vocation had hardened her in some ways. And yet her cheeks burned like an innocent hardly out of the schoolroom. "You're teasing."

His smile widened. "I am. But my question is a genuine one."

She swallowed hard before she whispered, "You didn't take advantage, Lucas. I could have stopped what happened between us half a dozen times last night, but I didn't, because I wanted it as much as you did. Wanton as that sounds."

He held his gaze on her, his expression unreadable once again. And she hated that. Hated his ability to turn off emotion, to withhold it with such ease. It brought back such memories and such pain to go with them.

"And now?" he asked at last. "In the cold light of morning, do you feel differently about what we did?"

She turned her back on him again, clenching her fist against the cool surface of the window. This was harder than it should be. "I know the dangers of such a thing. The *consequences*."

"So do I," he said, and she started because his voice was right behind her now even though she hadn't heard him rise from the chair or hobble over to her. He touched her arm and she turned toward him, staring up into his eyes. "But that wasn't what I asked. What do you *want*, Diana?"

She could not say those words, express what she wanted out loud. Want had gotten her into so much trouble in the very recent past. This felt different, though. She was older, wiser. And Lucas was not like the man before. He was not like *anyone* she'd ever known at all.

He reached out and took her hand. His fingers were rough on her palm and sent a shiver through her that likely made her continued desire for him very clear. He smoothed his thumb over her flesh gently, rhythmically. "If you cannot or will not say it, then I will. I wanted you like I've never wanted another person, Diana. It's disconcerting, actually, to feel so much physical draw to someone hardly more than a stranger to me. But that want is far from sated. I *still* want you."

She jolted at the confession, so plainly and gently said, without false promises or manipulations that she would expect of a man trying to get his way. Especially a spy.

"And what does that mean?" she asked, her voice shaking.

He lifted a hand to cup her cheek, and it took everything in her not to lean into it with a sigh of pleasure and surrender. He had too much power. Power in general. Power over her. She should run from that, but she didn't.

"I don't know," he mused. "But...you asked me for a month, Diana. Could I not ask you for the same?" he asked. "There is more than one way to heal a wound, and I think we could both benefit from it."

She paused, for that phrase—*more than one way to heal a wound*—was exactly what she'd thought to herself the previous nights, when she was trying to justify a night of pleasure. Now he was using the same logic to offer a month of it. A month in this man's arms and in his bed. Without promises or strings attached. Without anything but pleasure.

It was shocking, of course, to be made such an offer. Scandalous, even, though she did not feel scandalized as he looked down at her, very patiently waiting for her response.

"Unless you don't feel the same draw I do," he said, his tone unreadable.

She swallowed hard. "I think it's clear I do. I...do. I'm just not...sure."

"I understand," he said, and touched her cheek again, this time tracing it with his fingertip. "It's not something a gentleman should ask a lady. Not something I ever would have pictured asking you, but here we are."

She nodded. Oh yes. Here they were. "If we're going to do this... this thing," she whispered at last. "You must make me one promise and one promise only."

He nodded slowly, his expression not changing so that she could tell how he felt about her demand.

She drew a deep breath that felt like it shook through her lungs. "You must do everything in your power to make certain I *never* get with child."

Now he could not control his expression. Shock flowed over his features before he said, "I assure you, I would never be so careless as to do such a thing. Though you must know that I would take responsibility if you did—"

"No!" she interrupted sharply, disinterested in hearing his lies on a subject that cut her down to the very heart. "No child, Lucas."

He examined her face for a beat and then nodded slowly. "I'll be careful."

She tensed, for his curiosity about her request and the strength with which she demanded it was evident on his face. He had questions, ones she had no intention of answering now or ever.

"Diana," he began.

She silenced him by lifting to her tiptoes, cupping his face and kissing him. It worked, because of course it did. He was a man before he was a spy, and need would destroy curiosity every time. He slanted his mouth over hers, opening and claiming as his arms came around her and held her close.

She found her tension fading as the kiss swept her away. Thoughts and memories melted, leaving only sensation and desire. She slid her hands up to his chest, still bare, for neither of them had fastened his shirt after she helped him with it. She bunched her fingers against the muscles there, tracing light patterns on his skin with the edge of her short nails. He grunted in the back of his throat and his hands traveled down to her backside to grind her against him.

She moved to unfasten the trousers she had just helped him with when there was a sound from the lower floor of the house. Banging on the door. They broke apart and their eyes met. His were lit with concern, and he backed up.

"Will you fetch the pistol I have under my pillow, please?" he asked, calm despite the horrifying question.

Her eyes went wide, but she did as he asked, moving to the bed. "You keep a pistol under your pillow?" she asked.

He stepped to the window. "I do, I must since—" He stopped and turned to her with a hand lifted. "You may put it back. It's Stalwood."

Diana's eyes went wide and she lifted a hand to her loose hair. She felt like last night had branded her somehow. That this bargain they had just struck to continue the passion between them branded her even more. Stalwood would see, wouldn't he? He was too clever not to.

"Are you going to answer it or should we hide until he goes away?" Lucas teased, but Diana saw the steadiness in his stare. The gentleness she didn't expect but that drew her in whenever he revealed that side of himself.

"Hiding does sound lovely," she said. "But I should let him in. I fear he'll break down the door if I do not. Can you manage the rest of your dressing yourself?"

He nodded and waved her toward the door. "Go ahead, go ahead."

She drew a few long breaths as she hustled down the stairs. Stalwood was knocking again, this time more strenuously. She rushed to the foyer and threw open the barrier, her breath coming short as she did so.

Stalwood stood there, of course. His face was lined with concern that gave way to relief as he looked down at her. "Good morning, Diana. I was beginning to get worried when you did not answer."

His gaze flitted over her, and Diana could not help a blush as she stepped aside and ushered him into her parlor. "I apologize. When one keeps no servant, sometimes one takes a bit longer to respond."

Stalwood nodded. "I see. Does that mean you would like a servant? I could find someone trustworthy to—"

"No!" Diana interrupted, perhaps a bit more strenuously than she should have if Stalwood's delicately raised eyebrows were any indication. But the idea of having someone else come into this little bubble she had created with Lucas was not a pleasant thought. "I only mean that I manage well enough. I like the cooking, the wash is sent out. There is no trouble."

He inclined his head. "As you wish."

She shifted. "My manners, I'm sorry. Will you join me in the parlor?"

Stalwood followed her to the little parlor. She stirred the embers of the fire and threw on a log to warm the room further. Drawing a long breath for calm, she pulled open the curtains to let more light into the chamber.

"How is your patient?" he asked as he settled himself into a chair. He was watching her. She felt it with every movement.

She forced a bright smile as she faced him once more. "Well. Improving with each passing day."

"He has settled in then. Not giving you too much trouble?"

Diana almost laughed as an image of Lucas flashed through her mind. He was leaning over her, his fingers pressing deep inside of her, coaxing out intense pleasure as she cried out his name over and over.

"None," she croaked out.

"I am shocked," Stalwood said with a shake of his head. "The others who worked with him complained endlessly about his moods."

"They were not as talented as Diana."

Both Stalwood and Diana glanced to the door as Lucas eased inside. Stalwood was on his feet in an instant, examining his employee with eyes of concern. Diana smiled. She had always liked Stalwood despite it all. He truly cared about those who risked their lives for the safety of king and country.

"Good to see you, Willowby," Stalwood said, and held out a hand.

Lucas shook it with his good arm and then made his way to the settee. He sank down, and Diana could see that finishing his toilette and coming down here had been taxing for him. But he wiped the exhaustion away and smiled at Stalwood.

"Come to check up on me and warn Diana about my poor attitude?" he asked.

Stalwood glanced up at her and motioned her to sit next to Lucas. She hesitated before she acquiesced. Sitting next to him seemed dangerous. Stalwood was a spy, too, after all. He could see signs as well as anyone could.

But she couldn't exactly go against his request without making a scene so she sat, trying to keep a proper distance between herself and her lover.

"Diana will see enough of your attitude, even if she is too polite to complain to me about it," Stalwood said with a falsely stern tone. "But it is good to see you with a bit of color in your cheeks."

Lucas nodded and sent Diana a bit of a knowing look that made her blush. "It's good to feel a bit more alive again."

"Well, I hope I will see continued improvement. I would very much like to have you back in the field when you are able."

Diana watched as Lucas's entire demeanor shifted. He leaned forward, his face hardening, his body going to a ready position. Gone was the gentle lover or the broken man attempting to heal. Here was the spy. She shivered at the shift. She quaked at how much it affected her when she knew it should not.

After all, Lucas wasn't hers. They had both made their boundaries very clear. Even if they shared pleasure for the next few weeks, his destiny would not be tied to hers.

And she needed to remember that so she would not become too involved and risk her heart. That was the one thing she could not lose. Not again. Not ever.

CHAPTER 7

Lucas stared at Stalwood. He could see his spymaster had trouble on his mind when he said he wanted Lucas back in the field. The idea of it made his palms itch and his heart race.

"If you want me back after denying me all these months, you must have something you need my particular skills to work out."

Stalwood glanced past him to Diana, and Lucas jolted. He'd been so excited about the prospect of being back in the field, he'd almost forgotten her presence. Now he looked over his shoulder and found her pale, her expression one of deep concern.

He winced at that look. He knew it. It was loss, something he had felt so many times in his life. She was thinking of her father. Of what this profession had taken from her. What he had allowed to happen even before he burst into her life and her home.

"Perhaps you two would like to be alone," Diana said, rising. "I will...I'll go make some tea for us all. See if I have anything resembling a biscuit even though it's early for it."

She didn't wait for the response, but left the room. When she was gone, Stalwood shook his head. "Perhaps I should not have involved her in this."

Lucas arched a brow. "I tend to agree, actually."

"Questioning authority? That sounds like the old Willowby returned at last. She has worked some magic on you," Stalwood said, his tone dry as firewood.

"She has lost a great deal."

Stalwood wrinkled his brow. "Yes, she has. She loved her father deeply."

"And I'm the reason he is dead," Lucas said, pushing to his feet and limping to the window. "How that woman doesn't despise me speaks to the sweetness of her character. I do not deserve her help or…or anything else."

Stalwood was watching him. Lucas could feel his stare boring into his back. Feel him putting pieces together from the little moments he'd seen with the two of them together.

"Oakford made his own bad decisions that day. Your foolhardiness is not all that is to blame. I didn't send you here to prostrate yourself for punishment over whatever wrongs you have or haven't done," Stalwood said softly. "Nor did I send you here to corrupt her."

Lucas turned slowly and met his superior's eyes. Stalwood knew. But of course he did. The tension between him and Diana was palpable. Sex hadn't released any of it, only made it stronger. Only gave him knowledge of what he would do to her later to make them both feel better.

Stalwood's disapproval wouldn't change that, even if it should have.

"I don't want to corrupt her," he responded.

"Good, she deserves better." Stalwood folded his arms. "But that isn't what we need to discuss."

Lucas straightened. "You have news."

Stalwood nodded. "Carter Mackany was killed last night. Murdered."

Lucas's stomach turned, and he stumbled back to the settee and stared at his superior. Stalwood's expression was heavy with grief and anger, emotions he was sure his own reflected. He'd known

Mackany for years. He'd trained Lucas on the intricacies of different accents so he could take on whatever role came to him on a case. They'd even worked together in Scotland when the queen's jewels had been stolen, Lucas's first successful case.

"Murdered," he repeated when he could speak.

"He was on a case in France. It involved the running of weapons past the blockades."

"Deep cover?"

Stalwood frowned. "The deepest. No one should have known his whereabouts unless they were in our organization."

Lucas stared at him as that news sank into his gut and sat there, cold and heavy. "Our traitor."

"He's been silent for months, since the attack. I think killing Oakford and injuring you must have put him off for a while. He knew there was heat on him. But he seems to be functioning still within our organization."

Lucas focused on the crackling fire. "I want him. I want to catch him and punish him for what he did to me. To Oakford. To Mackany. To how many others?"

"I understand." Stalwood reached into his coat pocket and withdrew a stack of folded pages. "This is the full report about the day you were attacked. It contains not only your account, but those of the others who came after, the remaining witnesses and details of the investigation we've done since that day. I want you to look at it, if you're up to it. See if you can weave any of the pieces together or see anything we've missed."

Lucas took the papers with shaking hands. It had been months since he'd gotten to do anything useful. And while this was not exactly heading to the field to lead the chase, it was something.

He would take something over nothing any day.

"Be careful of Diana with those things," Stalwood said softly, drawing Lucas from his thoughts.

He looked at the papers again. "Yes, of course. She needn't know every bit of her father's last moments. And she's too clever not to involve herself if she knew I had these." He stood. "Help me back to my chamber. Tell her I got tired. It will give me time to hide the paperwork. I'll go over it later when she is busy."

Stalwood nodded and followed Lucas from the room. But as they moved up the stairs, Lucas couldn't help but feel guilty for the subterfuge. Diana was doing everything in her power to help him and now he was going to lie to her.

That didn't feel good as her friend, her patient or her lover. He could only hope those lies would lead to the revealing of the man responsible for her father's death. At least he could give her that peace. But only if he withheld the truth from her now.

D iana stood at the door with Stalwood, saying her farewells after the two had shared tea. When she returned and found Lucas gone to bed, she'd expected the earl to depart right away. But he'd stayed for over an hour and they'd chatted of nothing at all.

It had been nice, actually, not to have the dark cloud of her father's loss hanging between them.

But now he held one of her hands and was examining her face far too closely. The cloud was back. "You are not sleeping well."

She blushed. That was true, though the cause for her current state of unrest was not the unpleasant one he assumed. Her night had been spent with Lucas. And she intended to repeat that night. She longed to do so, if only to forget everything else in her life that troubled her.

"I'm fine," she reassured him.

Stalwood shook his head "I'm no substitute for your father, Diana, I know that, but I do feel some responsibility for your well-being. As his friend as much as his superior."

"You were always his friend," she said softly "And I appreciate that. As did he. But you needn't worry."

He was silent a long moment before he asked, "Did I make a mistake, asking you to help Willowby?"

She stiffened. "No," she said. "I can already see improvements in his condition. I have no idea how far they can go, but considering that my father cared so much for the man, I see it as my duty to do whatever I can to help. I don't regret taking on his care, my lord."

Stalwood held her stare. "He is a good man, Diana. I would never have exposed you to him had I any doubt about that. But he is a spy. You know what that means. So be...wary."

She blushed again. It seemed Stalwood had sensed some level of connection that had formed between them, even if she doubted he had guessed the whole truth. If he knew Lucas had bedded her, she had a feeling there would be a much larger explosion.

"I'm always wary, I assure you," she said, then squeezed his hand and pulled away. "I'll send an update on his condition in a week. Good day."

"Good day," he said, touching his hat to her before he returned to the fine carriage that was waiting for him in her small drive.

She shut the door and turned toward the stairs behind her. She'd promised Stalwood that she was always wary, and it wasn't entirely untrue. She knew better than to trust Lucas with her heart. With her soul.

But her body was something else. She longed for his touch. Longed to finish what had been interrupted when Stalwood arrived.

She longed, and that was undeniable. She shook her head as she went up the stairs. Lucas's bedroom door was closed and she hesitated a moment before she knocked lightly.

There was a sound of brief movement before he called out, "Come in."

She stepped inside. He was propped up on the bed, still fully clothed, though Stalwood had apparently helped him with his boots.

"He is gone?" Lucas asked, his gaze flitting over her from head to toe. She shivered at the intimacy in that stare. At the intensity.

"Yes," she said. "I wish you had called for me when you got tired. I could have helped."

A brief flash of emotion moved across his expression, but then it was gone. "I did not want to interrupt you in whatever you were doing. Stalwood was up to the task of assisting me."

She stepped closer. "I have a hard time picturing the very proper Earl of Stalwood being up to such a menial chore."

Lucas's brow wrinkled. "Do not mistake him. His title has never made him soft. He once worked heavily in the field before he took over as leader of the spies."

She nodded slowly. "I suppose I should know more than any other not to judge a spy by his outward appearance. They are rarely what they seem or claim to be."

She winced the moment the words were out of her mouth. She'd said far too much, revealed it to a man who was always finding deeper meaning in what was said. It was in his nature. And she saw him doing it now, examining her like he was collecting evidence.

"Come here." He held out a hand to her.

She swallowed hard before she did as he'd ordered. She came to him and slipped her hand in his. There was an instantaneous reaction through her body. Heat and tingling desire and...comfort.

It was the last that made her want to jerk her hand away. She did not want to seek, nor find, comfort in this man. That was the most dangerous trap she could fall into.

"We were interrupted earlier," he said softly, lifting the hand that wasn't holding hers and gliding it into her hair. He massaged her scalp gently and she let out her breath in a long exhalation of pleasure.

"Yes, we were," she murmured, letting him tug her in.

"I'd like to finish what we started," he said as he drew her across his body and pressed his lips to hers.

She melted into his heat, happy he had chosen not to pursue anything but the desire that coursed between them. That was all she wanted, nothing more. Remembering that was paramount to her own safety.

But all those thoughts faded as he drove his tongue between her lips, swirling it around and around her mouth, tasting her and softening her and making her weak with wanting him. She shifted to move beside him on the bed and lifted against his body, rubbing against him like a cat as the kiss deepened and spiraled and went on forever.

She was lost in him and she loved it. She never wanted to be found if the pleasure and peace she experienced in his arms was what she could have forever.

The thought of forever jolted her, and she pulled back, staring up into his face. Not forever. There were no forevers for her. None that she wanted and none that were offered. Getting caught up in any thoughts otherwise was an exercise in pain and foolishness.

"I do not like that look," he drawled, pushing her onto her back gently. "You are thinking…overthinking."

She smiled despite her thoughts. "Am I so obvious?"

"Only to a keen observer of the human experience," he said, sliding a hand down her body and catching the edge of her skirt. He began to slide it up inch by inch. "Which I am."

She pursed her lips. "You forgot to mention modest."

"I would never lie and say I was that," he said. The skirt was at her knees now, and he skated his fingers over the flesh there until she arched up with a shiver of pleasure. "I know my…talents. Why should I not be proud of them?"

She could hardly think now. The skirt was around her thighs and his fingers were warm against her skin when he parted her drawers and touched her.

"What talents exactly?" she gasped as he left her skirt in a pile around her waist and placed his hand flat against her sex.

He lifted his gaze to her face and grinned. "I'm so glad you asked."

He inched down her body, making his movements carefully so he did not create any more pain than he had to. He settled between her legs, lying on his stomach so he didn't have to support much of his weight on his bad arm.

"Lucas," she whispered, but hardly got his name past her lips when he leaned in and blew a gust of warm air against her sex. Her body was so ultra-sensitive that she bucked at the sensation.

His eyebrows lifted. "Oh, very good," he murmured, then ducked his head and licked her.

She fisted the coverlet in her hands with a mewling cry at the sudden and unexpected feeling of his mouth on her so intimately. At the very unexpected electric pleasure that he created. Experience or no, she'd never felt anything like it. Never imagined a man doing such a thing or that it would create such a sudden, immediate and volcanic reaction through her entire trembling body.

It was magic, pure and simple.

And it was relentless. Because of course—it was Lucas driving it. He stroked his tongue over her in long, even strokes, swirling the tip around her clitoris every time.

"Please," she gasped out, her fingers coming down into his hair, pulling him close, pushing him away, uncertain how to get more and yet lessen the intensity of what she was experiencing.

He glanced up. "All in good time, my dear," he whispered, then returned to his work.

She collapsed back, her eyes fluttering shut and her world becoming nothing but sharp sensation. She found herself lifting her hips to him, meeting the rhythm of his tongue over and over again as pleasure built within her.

And as it did, his focus changed. No longer did he lave her entire sex. Now he focused entirely on her clitoris. That sensitive nub of nerves sent shockwaves through her. She was on the edge and she wanted to fall and fly.

He sucked her and she got to do both. Wave after wave of intense pleasure rocked through her. She arched against him, her hips slamming out of control as he drew the sensation out further and further, past the point where she felt she could bear it, past the edge of what felt like sanity and safety. It was everything, and it pushed out the boundaries of her small world until it felt like she could do anything.

Slowly, the pleasure faded. Eventually, he lifted his head, smiling up at her with feral, male confidence.

She couldn't even move, but it didn't matter. He inched back up her body, unbuttoning her dress, shoving it down her arms. She lifted her hips to let him glide it away. He left her chemise, but removed her drawers.

"Roll over on your side," he said.

She did so, facing away from him. He lay on his good side next to her, his mouth against the back of her neck, his breath hot and steamy against her skin. The hard thrust of his cock pressed to her backside and he spread her open, smoothing her wet entrance before he speared her body in one long, heavy stroke.

She ground backward against him, burrowing into the crook of his body as his arms came around her. He rolled his hips as he thrust, probing deep inside her sex, pressing her body in ways she had never felt before. She met him stroke for stroke, that pleasure she had only just abandoned returning in rapid and even more powerful succession. She came a second time, moaning his name as he increased the power and pressure of his thrusts and finally, as he grunted out her name, he withdrew and she felt the heat of him pump between their bodies.

She shivered and he drew her closer, his mouth brushing her skin, tattooing her with his whispered, empty words of desire. And she drifted off to sleep with all that in her head. And nothing else that normally troubled her.

CHAPTER 8

Lucas scanned the document he had pressed between the pages of a book Diana had loaned him, trying to find some hidden meaning or clue within the words. It had been four days since the visit from Stalwood, and finding time to review the documents he'd been given was not easy.

Not that he was complaining about how his time had been spent. Diana was a skilled lover, responsive, and never one who simpered or played games with his desire.

Of course, she was also a taskmaster who insisted on working on his healing too. That was their relationship now. Pain and pleasure. Sometimes one immediately following the other.

But he was feeling better. Stronger than he had in a long time.

The door to his chamber opened and she entered. He shut the book immediately, hiding the document he didn't want her to see, and smiled over at her. She was wearing a plain gown with a striped skirt and her hair was half up, as usual.

"You left bed far too early," he drawled. "Why in the world do you insist on dressing?"

She laughed at his question but didn't stop at the bed. Instead,

she moved to a panel that was in the corner of the room. Carefully she drew it aside and revealed a tub there.

He blinked. "Some spy I am—I never even noticed that."

She smiled as she turned toward him again. "My father was of the controversial notion that washing helped inspire healing. And while I have very much enjoyed our sponge baths, I think you are recovering well enough to allow you to use the tub if you're up for it."

"I'm up for anything that has to do with you," he said, tilting his head toward the half-erect cock that tented his sheets. A permanent state of being when she was around.

She rolled her eyes. "You are a cad, Your Grace. I'm off to start bringing up the water."

"Let me help," he suggested, moving to throw the covers back.

She shook her head and held up a hand. "You will injure yourself carrying buckets," she said.

He pursed his lips. She was right, of course, but that truth still stung. She didn't allow him to address it, though, but disappeared from the room, leaving him alone with his feelings of ineptitude.

She returned a few moments later, bearing a heavy bucket laden with steaming water. As she poured it in the tub, he shook his head. "I do not like being useless."

She faced him. "You are not useless, Lucas. But if you rip open the injury on your shoulder or harm your leg, you could very well be."

He folded his arms. "Would you at least ask Stalwood's lackeys to help you?"

She pondered that. "Yes, very well."

She waved him back to his comfortable position and disappeared from the room again. He heard her open her door, heard her talking to whichever spy was guarding the house at present. Within moments, a tall, strapping man Lucas did not recognize came into the room carrying not one but two buckets of water.

The man inclined his head before he dumped each into the tub. "Your Grace."

Lucas winced. Though he had grown accustomed to the times Diana gently teased him with his title, hearing it from this stranger still made his stomach clench.

"Thank you," he ground out as the man left. It was a few moments before he returned. Lucas had to assume Diana had more water to heat before the buckets could be filled again, and how that strapping man must enjoy the opportunity to engage with her. Why wouldn't he? She was lovely and bright, sensual and kind.

Lucas *liked* her. He'd been trying not to like her. Trying not to feel any more than he ever had for any temporary lover. But it was impossible to view her as such. That feeling set him on his heels and he struggled to deal with it as the young man returned and dumped water in the tub once more. It was more than halfway full now, only a few more buckets would do the trick.

"What is your name?" Lucas asked, desperate to keep him here rather than allow him to stay with Diana while she prepared the water for the tub.

"Logan, Your Grace," he said, facing Lucas once more. His gaze flitted over him and Lucas felt his discomfort—his *pity*. Lucas's stomach clenched. "Geoffrey Logan."

"How long have you worked for Stalwood?" he asked.

"Less than a year." The young man settled into a military at-ease stance naturally.

Lucas nodded. "This must be one of your first assignments."

"It is," he admitted.

"Not exactly exciting, I fear." Lucas watched him closely for any reaction. There was one, the boy hadn't trained himself not to give it yet. A flash of frustration. A hint of restlessness.

"I'm happy to do it, I assure you, Your Grace. You are well thought of in the department. Many who trained us spoke of your abilities, referenced your exploits. You did so much for the country during your time in the field."

Lucas shifted. His accomplishments were being spoken of in the past tense. Something from a bygone era that was over, a reminiscence by friends he had worked with on cases. His own fears, spoken in plain words by a man who was hardly that. Anger rose in his chest and he carefully tamped it down as best he could.

"At least the company is fair," he drawled. Logan arched a brow and shook his head as if he didn't understand. Lucas glared at him. "Miss Oakford."

Color filled Logan's cheeks. "I—er—yes, sir. She is very lovely."

"All of them think so?" he pressed.

"Only three of us, Your Grace," he explained. "On a rotating schedule. But yes, she does occasionally...come up."

"Mr. Logan, I'm ready for you once again!" Diana's voice came from downstairs, and the young man saluted before he hurried off to help her.

Every fiber in Lucas's body itched with anticipation. Annoyance. Frustration unlike any he'd ever experienced. He hated every part of this, and then add Diana to the mix and it was impossible. He didn't need to be jealous, for God's sake. She wasn't his—she was only a temporary distraction. If she wanted to allow this or that or any young man to court her, that was her right. She could bed the entire War Department and he had no place to judge her. She was owed pleasure and happiness and a future.

He could only give her one of those three things. His shortcoming, not hers.

Logan returned with Diana at his heels. He had two buckets and she one. He dumped his two, then smiled at her as he took the last one and added it to the steaming tub.

"Is there anything else I can do, Miss Oakford?" he asked.

She reached out to touch his arm. "No, you've been a great help, thank you."

He nodded to her, then to Lucas, and left them alone. Lucas moved to stand and she held up a hand. "Not yet," she said. "One more thing."

She departed the room again and he flopped back on the pillows in increasing frustration. Being out of control was not something he enjoyed. It reminded him of…

Well, it didn't matter. He wasn't going to think of that time, of that life he had abandoned and why.

Diana returned with a small bowl filled with herbs. She lifted it in his direction before she moved to the tub. He had to smile as she sprinkled them into the steaming water.

"Are you going to boil me like a finely seasoned chicken, then?" he asked, his frustration fading in exchange for the teasing that had begun to feel so easy and comfortable between them.

She set the empty bowl aside and turned to him with a laugh. "More like a tea, and you shall be the biscuit dunked in it. But right now the water is too hot and the herbs must steep."

"What will they do?" he asked.

"You are always so curious, Your Grace."

"I am," he admitted. "Especially when a lady is attempting to make a meal of me."

She laughed again, the music of that sound touching every part of him. "They will help you relax. They will soothe some of the pain. Nothing to harm you."

He watched her closely. "I don't think you'd ever harm me, Diana. Not on purpose."

She drew back at the intimacy those words created. He was rather shocked, himself, that he'd said them. He hadn't meant to. There was just something about this woman.

She cleared her throat. "You may feel differently in a moment. While the bath cools, I would like to try massaging your muscles."

He blinked in surprise at the notion. "Rubbing me down, you mean. Like a prize horse?"

She shook her head and shot him a playful look that told him she was only barely tolerating him. "I suppose that is a step up from being a chicken or a biscuit."

"If you think it would help," he said. "I'm not adverse to the notion of you rubbing your hands on me."

"I will try very hard not to become distracted. Thankfully you did not make the same mistake you accused *me* of earlier and dress, so if you would roll over on your stomach and remove the pillows you've built into a fortress behind your head, that would be helpful."

He did so and lay flat on his stomach, turning his head away from her. He heard her moving around, then her hands touched him. They were slick with a fragrant oil that smelled like cinnamon and something exotic he couldn't place. He hissed out pleasure at the erotic sensation of flesh gliding over flesh.

"Oh, I should request this treatment every day," he groaned.

"You might not like it as much as I go deeper," she said. "Pleasure is not always the first reaction, but pain."

He opened his eyes and stared at the other side of the bed. Her words reminded him of a realization that had been troubling him a few days. One he had not discussed with her, but now it sat in his head, a jealousy amongst other unwanted jealousies.

"Were you married?" he asked at last.

Her hands hesitated on his back, and then she went back to her work. "You mean because I was not...was not *untouched* the first time you made love to me?"

He turned his head to look at her as he said, "Yes."

Her cheeks tuned red and she turned away for a moment. He set his jaw. Perhaps he'd gone too far, been too blunt. His friends used to say he could be, a long time ago.

She looked back at him and he saw her exhaustion. He leaned up on his stomach, ignoring the shot of pain through his shoulder, and caught her hand. "You don't owe me any explanation, Diana. I know that. I want you to *know* I know it. Despite that, I'm asking because I'm curious. And because I want to know more about you."

She stared at their intertwined fingers. Then she pulled away and motioned him back to his original position. Her hands came back to his skin and she sighed.

"When my mother died, my father only knew medicine. He had no idea how to raise a child, certainly not a daughter."

Lucas thought of his own parents. His father who had always despised him. His mother who could hardly look at him. He doubted Oakford had ever been that harsh, but that didn't mean he'd been a good parent or given Diana what she needed.

And *that* he wholly understood.

"It must have hurt you," he said softly.

Her hesitation was the only answer she gave to that question for a moment. Then she whispered, "Sometimes. Eventually he began to teach me about his vocation. Of course, I quickly learned that he taught me what he knew because it was all he understood. And that meant we had long talks about the body and all its processes." She drew a long breath. "I am not like the ladies you were raised with, Lucas. I was *never* a tittering innocent."

"Not in mind, perhaps. But the body is a different thing," he said.

"Yes." Her voice cracked, and it took everything in him not to lift his head and look at her. Not to roll over and pull her closer. He fought those urges, not just for his own sake, but because he doubted she would continue if he did so. He could sense her reluctance.

"You don't have to tell me," he said again.

"I know. But I suppose you deserve the truth given the...the nature of our relationship." She sighed again. "I was innocent until I met *him*."

"Him," he repeated.

Her fingers dug harder into his muscles and he tensed against a rush of pain. For a moment, she just worked at it and slowly the muscles relaxed and the pain lessened.

"I'm sorry," she said. "I know that hurts."

He knew she was trying to distract him on some level. That she was reluctant because her story was obviously painful. He didn't want to hurt her, but this drive inside of him, the spy's tenaciousness, it didn't relent.

"Who was he?" He pushed and rolled over at last so he could look at her when he asked it.

Only he did not see pain in her expression. At least that wasn't all he saw. There were much deeper emotions in her stare. Anger. Resentment. Loss. And grief. Something deeper and more potent than mere fleeting pain.

He saw it all and he wished he could take back the question. Not because he didn't want to know the answer, but because suddenly the answer felt far too important. Far too intimate. The answer would bind them, and he feared that as much as he had ever feared anything in his life.

But he was about to know it. There was no going back.

CHAPTER 9

D iana could hardly breathe, but she managed to keep her voice
calm as she said, "You are tenacious."

He smiled at her, but she saw the falseness of it, heard it in his
voice as he said, "It is an investigative prerogative."

She pressed her lips together. She liked his teasing most of the
time. It made her comfortable. In this moment, it felt false. A way to
make the tension fade, to get whatever it was he wanted from her.

"Am I being investigated?" she asked softly.

His gaze grew hooded and heated as he reached out to touch her
leg through her skirt. "Most intimately."

She frowned more deeply. If he was using what they'd shared
against her, that cut her to the bone. And yet she still felt driven to
tell him the very truth he sought. If she did, it might make him
understand who she was on some level. And perhaps to drive him
away a little too.

After all, a person like him would not want a woman who had
given herself so easily. That would put a wall between them, and
perhaps that would keep her from being so needy when it came to
this man.

"He was a friend of my father," she said, and hated how her voice shook. "He came to our country home as a visitor. Or so I was told."

Lucas sat up a little, resting on his elbows. She saw pain on his face, but not as intense as it had been days before. They were making progress.

"What do you mean, so you were told? That wasn't the truth?" he pressed.

"I think he was…" She hesitated, for she had never felt comfortable with this part of her story. "He was part of a case my father was working on."

Lucas stared at her, his expression hard and suddenly cool. "Oakford told you he worked on cases?"

"From time to time, yes," she said. "I know he was mostly meant to be a surgeon for the men, but he had a brilliant mind, and sometimes he worked on other things."

"I see." Lucas was quiet a moment. "So this other man came as part of something your father was working on. For the War Department."

"They had their heads together quite a bit and always suddenly grew silent if I entered a room unannounced. I was helping my father with his household by then, and he barred me from his study and told me not to review his paperwork while his visitor was there." She shrugged. "I'm not a fool. I understood what was happening. Does that surprise you?"

"That you are not a fool?" he asked. "Not at all. I *am* surprised to hear your father worked on cases. I did not know he took them on. But I can see how his mind would be a good fit for the work. As you say, he was brilliant. I often turned to him to help me problem-solve."

She drew in a long breath to keep herself from the tears that inevitably rose in her when she considered her father too long. "I'm sure this man was doing the same."

"Who was he?" Lucas asked.

She turned away, fists clenched at her sides. "No, I will not tell you that. I will not have you discussing me with your cronies, comparing experiences."

"Diana!" he said, his sharp tone forcing her to look at him. He was sitting up now, staring at her. "You cannot think I would ever disrespect you or what we've shared in such a manner."

She lifted her chin. "I don't want to think it," she said. "But what do I know of how you talk when you are alone with the others?"

"Not like that, I assure you," he said, his tone laced with disgust at the very thought. It was so real that it actually gave her relief.

"His name doesn't matter," she said, and moved to the tub to test the water. It was almost perfect now and it gave her an excuse to stay away from him, to stare off so he wouldn't see her face when she continued her story. "In the end, I cannot even blame him completely for what happened."

"How can you say that? You were an innocent, he was a visitor in your father's home."

She shrugged, like it didn't matter. The biggest lie she'd ever told. "I was lonely and foolish. I took flirtation for something more. And when he kissed me..." She trailed off as she remembered that moment in full detail. Then she had been thrilled. Now she felt empty. "Well, I felt like a light had been turned on inside of me. One that had always been there, but I'd never known it."

"How long ago did this happen?" he asked, his voice rough.

She forced herself to look at him. He was unreadable as always. "Two years," she whispered. "I was not quite one and twenty. That probably sounds so foolish to you, as most women have more sense at such an age."

"It is not so old," he said softly.

"To me, it certainly wasn't. I had not gone to balls or had suitors. In some ways I was naïve about the ways of men and women, of love, of...*matching*. He offered me an...an illusion. And I let him have what he wanted because I thought it meant love and a future."

His cheek twitched. "And once he had it?"

She bent her head. "Everything changed. I discovered he was

married, for one. That broke my heart. And then my father found out the truth about our tryst. He was angrier than I'd ever seen in all my life. I thought he might kill his friend. But he didn't. The other man left and..."

She stopped. There was so much more to the story, but it was impossible to say those things out loud. She never spoke of them, she certainly wasn't about to start with a man who'd already told her he offered her nothing but pleasure.

"And?" he said.

"And now I'm here," she said, her tone falsely bright. "And you know what happened. Now, why don't you get into your bath? It is the perfect temperature to help those muscles loosen. It will relieve your pain."

He held her stare for a long moment and she felt him reading her. Felt him analyzing as he'd been trained to do. She knew in that moment that he sensed there was more for her to tell and she held her breath as she waited for him to accuse or demand she give him the whole story.

Instead, he got up, silent and slow. As the sheets fell away, she found herself looking at his body. She couldn't help it. He moved toward her, and when he reached her he caught the back of her head and drew her in for a kiss.

She sighed, flattening her palms on his bare chest and reveling in his taste and how he washed away all the pain that had been burning inside of her during her confession.

When he pulled away at last, he looked into her eyes. "I am not using you, Diana."

She caught her breath. "I know," she said. "I know that. This time I am entering our arrangement with eyes wide open. No one can be hurt if there aren't any lies."

"Diana—" he began, but she shook her head.

"Get in now," she said, offering him a hand to balance himself as he did so. "That's enough seriousness for the moment, I think."

He pursed his lips, but didn't argue. Instead, he sank beneath the hot water with a shuddering sigh and his eyes fluttered shut with his head rested back on the tub edge. She let out a sigh of her own. The subject had passed. At least for now.

And if she was careful, they would never have to broach the topic again.

L ucas had no idea how long he had been reclining in the tub. Long enough that the water was beginning to bleed out some of its heat. He had been seduced by the bath. By the warmth that seeped into his body, by the sweet, soft fragrance of the herbs Diana had added, by the way his muscles had begun to relax and the pain that was his constant companion eased.

And yet he wasn't fully comfortable. His mind still turned, running over what she had confessed about the man who took her innocence. She had been very honest about a remarkably painful subject. To have been seduced and discarded by a friend of her father, another spy...it brought up an anger in his chest that was far more powerful than it should be.

And questions. It brought up questions. He had known George Oakford his entire life as a spy. He'd never known the surgeon to work a case, nor to assist in one. That day Lucas had been injured had been an aberration, a moment of opportunity when he needed backup and Diana's father had been there.

Oh, he'd talked to the man about thorny problems, of course. Oakford had a mind like a steel trap and was quick to offer advice or solutions. But he could not picture a scenario where he would have actually gone to Oakford's home, where he would partner with him in a case. The idea seemed...off.

"Here," Diana said, her soft voice breaking through his thoughts.

He opened his eyes and took the soap she now held out toward him. "Ready for me to be finished, are you?"

She smiled. "The water is cooling and you should wash before we get you out. Sitting in the cold water will be no good for your injuries."

He nodded and began to wash himself. He was keenly aware of her watching him as she retook her chair a few feet away. Watching him with erotic interest that set his body on edge in a most pleasant way.

Wanting her was easy. Knowing her? That was another story. Her confession had brought him a bit closer, of course, but he still felt her withholding. There was more to her past. More to the man who had hurt her.

But right now wasn't the time to push. Perhaps it never would be. After all, he wasn't here to get to know this fascinating woman. He wasn't going to be with her long. She said it over and over—they both knew what this was. An affair, meant for pleasure.

Nothing more.

"Your father was a good man," he said.

She shifted in her seat and her eyes darted away with discomfort at the intimacy of that statement. "Yes," she said at last. "He was that."

"He spoke of you sometimes," he continued, and then questioned himself on why. Didn't this go against what he'd just decided with himself? That this was a temporary affair that did not require any deeper knowledge or connection?

She bent her head farther. "Did he?"

He could not read her tone, didn't know if that information he'd provided hurt her or helped her, was a surprise or something that inspired anger.

"Yes," he continued, despite all the things telling him to stop. "He always said how clever you were. How proud he was of you."

To his surprise, her expression grew suddenly harder. Slowly, she stood up and paced away, her hands clenched at her sides. "Yes," she said through gritted teeth. "I know all about how he valued my *usefulness*."

He shook his head, sitting up in the tub and setting the soap on the edge. "It was more than that, Diana," he breathed.

She pivoted, and now she speared him with a look. "He talked about you, too," she said, clearly trying to change the subject. "The Undercover Duke, he called you, though I never knew your real name. He teased about it and told me you were a member of a very prestigious duke club, but that somehow you were still good at what you did."

Lucas turned his face. His club. He tried so hard not to think about that. About them. His friends. The ones he hadn't talked to since...well, *since*...that was all. "They are the best of men," he said softly.

She tilted her head, and there was a moment of silence before she said, "Well, my father considered you a...a..."

He looked at her, wondering why she struggled to find a word that was so simple. "A friend?" he suggested.

She nodded. "Yes, that, of course. But it was more than that. He made it very clear he saw you as a—a son, I think. Sometimes I was actually rather jealous of your bond with him."

"A son," Lucas repeated in shock. "That means a great deal to me."

He said no more, he couldn't. But that didn't stop Diana. She stepped forward, her bright green gaze focused on him. Reading him as only she seemed capable of doing. As always, it made him uncomfortable because it felt so damned vulnerable.

"What is it?" she asked.

He clenched his teeth and shook his head. "It's nothing."

"It's more than nothing," she whispered. "After all, I told you about my past—you cannot tell me one thing in return?"

He sighed. That was fair. And what he would say would reveal nothing important. At least not anything she would *understand* the importance of.

"My own father didn't view me as a son," he said, every word stinging as it came out of his mouth. "In fact, he could scarcely stand the sight of me. So your father's acceptance on that level, it means more than you could understand. I...I'm sorry I failed him. So sorry."

She moved closer, and now those bright eyes snapped. "Stop saying that. My father was involved with spies and their duties for decades, Lucas. He knew the risks."

"As do we all," he said. "Some of us are destined to die for our country. I just didn't think that was your father's destiny."

Her face twisted in horror. "Are you saying it is yours?" She swallowed hard. "Is *that* why you avoid taking on the mantel of your title?"

"Partly," he admitted, and that one word felt like a thousand-pound weight dropped on his damaged shoulders.

"What is the other part?" she pressed.

He shook his head and then slowly pushed to his feet. The water ran down his body and he watched as her attention shifted from his face to his chest and his stomach and his cock.

"I don't want to talk anymore, Diana," he said softly.

She held his gaze for a long moment, and then she closed the remaining distance between them. She reached out and pressed her palm to his stomach, stroking her fingers over the firm muscle there.

"I see," she whispered as she reached back with her opposite hand and caught up a fluffy towel from the table behind her.

She shook it out and handed it over, but he didn't cover himself. He just steadied himself on her shoulder and stepped from the tub. He caught her, cupping her backside and drawing her firmly against him. She squealed as his wet body molded to hers, but any playful protest was lost when he dropped his mouth to hers.

As always, she responded. He loved that about her. Her body was made for his. Made to be touched. Made to be worshipped, and he was up to that task, although sometimes touching her made him want to be whole again more than anything else. Whole so he could take her and hold her and pleasure her in a dozen new ways. Ways she hadn't even thought about before.

But for now, this would be enough. He backed her toward the bed and they fell together. He reveled in how their bodies fit, even as he struggled to keep himself perched on his good arm as he kissed her and kissed her until everything else faded away.

She arched beneath him, little sounds of pleasure already escaping her throat as she drove her tongue against his in needy, powerful desire. His cock ached, his body ached, he needed to be inside of her. Now.

"Roll over," he grunted as he pulled away.

She did so, sprawling onto her stomach on the bed. He grabbed her hips and tugged her until she was bent over the side, her delectable backside giving him the perfect view of pleasures to come.

Slowly he fisted her skirt in his hand, tugging it up and up her body, over her calves, her thighs, up over her hips and bunched it against her back. He reached around her, rocking against her gently as he untied the waist of her drawers. They dropped around her ankles and left her in just garters and stockings and gorgeous bare skin.

He cupped her backside and she shuddered beneath him. His name escaped her words in a soft breath and she lifted up, offering him everything.

He wanted to take it. He massaged the firm flesh there, tugging her back so he could slide his cock into the crease. She gasped at the shock of him against that forbidden place, but she didn't protest. She just looked back over her shoulder at him, uncertain.

"I could," he drawled, holding her stare as he stroked his cock over the rosebud entrance to her entirely distracting bottom. "And you'd like it."

She bit her lip. "Would I?"

He nodded. "I'd make sure of it. But I have nothing here to ease the way. So not today. Not this time. This time I'll take..." He trailed off as he slid his cock down, around to the entrance of her sex. When he touched the tip to her, he found her wet, hot, ready. "...here," he gasped.

She pushed back and he slid in an inch. One inch of heaven as she gripped him like a well-fitted glove. He'd been with many women in his day. He'd always liked pleasure and had done nothing to deny himself.

But this was different. When he thrust into her, filling her from base to tip, it was different. It was unique. It was everything. He entered her body, and there was part of him that felt like he was coming home. To a place he'd never really had. That he belonged with her, joined with her physically and perhaps more than that.

The thought jolted him and he thrust again to erase it. Pleasure skirted up his cock and it did make all these musings fade. He gripped her hips, digging his fingers into her skin, denting the flesh there, probably leaving little bruises. But she moaned in desire and he didn't stop. He just began to pound against her.

She met him stroke for stroke. Her body clung to him, making him work for the movement, work for the release. And it came, hard and fast and heavy. He focused hard to keep it at bay, for he wanted her to milk it from him with her orgasm.

"Touch yourself," he grunted.

She looked over her shoulder at him a second time, and he nearly came undone at the sensual expression, the glazed passion and naked longing on her face.

She didn't say anything. Just held his stare as she snaked a hand between her legs and began to rub her clitoris. He felt her bearing down against her fingers, against his cock and he shut his eyes. She would unman him and he couldn't wait.

He felt her jolt beneath him and she let out a gasp, a groan, and then her pussy was gripping him in wave after wave of release. He thrust through it, reveling in the rippling pull that urged him to release.

When it came, he nearly spent inside of her. Only barely did he withdraw, letting out a cry as he poured himself out against her skin and felt her shiver beneath him.

Then he fell against her, tucking her to his side and letting the connection warm him, the release heal him, and her presence soothe him, even though he knew full well that it wouldn't last.

CHAPTER 10

Slowly Diana woke through a cloud of comfort and pleasure. She was warm and safe, and as she cuddled into the blankets she felt strong arms fold tighter against her. This was heaven, there was nothing else to it, and she didn't want to wake up from it.

Except she did. Reality crept in at last, and she opened her eyes to find hazy sunlight filtering into the room behind the curtains. She was on her side, facing Lucas. His arms were around her, but he was still sleeping.

In this rare moment, she drank in the sight of him. He was truly beautiful, and never more so than when he was relaxed like this. It made him look younger, less jaded by the world, less affected by pain.

But she wasn't fooled by the look. Yesterday he had used passion against her. They'd been talking, she had requested he share a little about the life he'd once led, and he had cut her off by bedding her.

She'd let him because his touch was too perfect not to surrender to. She wanted it, she wanted *him*. So she'd taken him, over and over, until night came, until sleep came.

But she couldn't ignore that he was perfectly willing to turn the desires of her wanton body against her.

Was that for the best? Well, that was another question entirely. Sharing secrets with him was dangerous. It led to a sense of closeness, which was false, a trap. If her walls came down, that could be devastating, especially considering the anniversary that would soon approach. A week more and she would be fighting to keep herself distant from him so he wouldn't see her weakness and her heartbreak.

Perhaps she needed to start practicing that distance now.

She rolled away slowly and pushed at the covers, moving to extract herself from his arms, but he tightened them around her and suddenly she was flush against him. Her back flattened against his broad chest and the hardness of his cock pressed against her as he placed a kiss to the place where her neck and shoulder met.

His voice was deep and sleepy as he murmured, "You told me to rest, Diana. Stay in bed with me today."

She couldn't help but smile, even though the pure temptation of those words was dangerous beyond belief. Stay with him for today? It was too easy to begin picturing staying with him forever. In his bed, in his arms, in his life.

"We'll starve," she protested, trying not to sigh as he continued to kiss along her skin.

"Worth it," he breathed.

She shivered, searching for an answer that would free her from the prison she adored. "Stalwood is coming later this morning," she finally said.

"It's not later yet," he argued, and began to flick her nipple with his thumb until she could not find her breath.

But she did find her resolve. She pushed against him. "Lucas, honestly, we don't have time."

He released her immediately, and she stumbled from the bed and searched the floor for the robe she had discarded late last night when she went on a search for food after the third time he made love to her.

When she was covered and somewhat calm, she turned back to

him. He was staring at her, his gaze hooded and analyzing and judging. Like he could see through her if he focused hard enough. In truth, she feared he could.

"Come, I'll assist you as you ready yourself for the day," she said, turning to efficiency to cloak her deeper emotions. "Let me look at that wound and then I'll help you dress."

For a moment she thought he might refuse. Confront. Seduce her back to his arms, and then she would tell him everything she'd spent a lifetime keeping secret. He would have all of her and when he left he'd take it all with him.

But he didn't. His face was still unreadable as he drew out of the bed and inclined his head. "As you wish, Diana. Whatever you'd like."

She motioned him to the chair by the fire so she could check his wound, but this acquiescence felt nothing like a victory. It felt like a move in a chess game.

And it was one she didn't think she was winning.

All morning Lucas had felt the distance Diana put between them. It was evident in the cool way she assisted him. In the way she avoided conversation beyond polite questions and answers. The way she put him in the parlor for his breakfast, rather than in their...*his* bedroom or the kitchen, where they sometimes broke bread together.

She'd even refused his offer of help when she got ready. There had been no playfulness to it, nor seductive teasing. She had just left him alone and not returned for nearly an hour.

He had no idea what had set off the change in her. They'd made love for hours the night before and it had been magical. And yet today...

Well, today she was building walls. Walls that were for the best, of course. He knew full well they were getting too close, and yet he felt a desperate desire to claw those walls down, to gather her against him and demand that she give him more. Give him everything.

Utterly unfair.

She entered the parlor where she had put him some time ago. A tea service was balanced in her arms. While he watched, she set it on the sideboard and quietly went about arranging it.

"Stalwood will be here momentarily," she said without looking at him. "I know you two have much to discuss, so I'll leave you alone once you are situated with drinks."

He arched a brow and moved toward her a step. When she stiffened, as if she had sensed his intentions, he stopped and stared at her. "What is this game, Diana?" he asked softly.

She jerked her gaze to his. "Game?"

"You are not a servant to me nor to him, yet you are playing at it. What is going on? Have I done something wrong?"

He found himself holding his breath at the answer, waiting for her to reveal some way for him to scale this wall between them. But she merely smiled at him, an expression that was utterly false, and shook her head. "Of course not. Everything is fine."

"Don't sport with my intelligence, Diana," he said, his tone a bit harsher than he wanted it to be. "I don't appreciate it."

Her lips parted and then she swallowed hard. He saw her fighting within herself, trying to find the words to say whatever had spooked her. He leaned forward, desperate to hear them, but then there was a knock at her front door.

She looked relieved. The expression lasted just a flash of a moment, but he saw it. He recognized it. It hit him in the gut like a punch.

"Excuse me," she said, not meeting his eyes as she scurried from the room. He shook his head as he listened to her open the door, greet the earl, then guide him back to the parlor.

"Lord Stalwood," she announced, once again like she was Lucas's maid rather than his lover. His—his *friend*, for that was how he had begun to think of her in the time they'd been together.

He didn't want to lose that.

"Great God, but you do look better," Stalwood said as he came into the room, hand outstretched.

Lucas still chose to shake with his good arm, but felt more strength in even that. "Diana has worked wonders," he said, looking past Stalwood to her. She was still not meeting his gaze.

"I should send all my injured to you, my dear," Stalwood said with a brief smile for her.

She stiffened at the suggestion and some of the color went out of her cheeks. "I-I would not dare to take my father's place, my lord. Now I will leave you two to your discussion."

She said nothing more, but pivoted on her heel and all but fled the room. Stalwood stared after her and then looked at Lucas. "I did not mean to offend her," he said. "I did not think that she would take it that I was trying to replace her father."

Lucas motioned him to the settee and moved to pour the tea himself. "It isn't you who offended her. I seem to have done that all on my own."

Stalwood arched a brow. "Have you now? How?"

He shook his head. "I am not entirely certain. We were getting along fine and then—" He cut himself off and shrugged, wincing at the pain in his shoulder. "She is a riddle."

Stalwood was staring at him with even more focus now. "I've known her since she was a girl, you know. Oakford worked with me and for me for years."

Lucas straightened with true interest. "And what kind of child was she?"

Stalwood hesitated and then said, "Bright. Quick to laugh. But with a vein of sadness that ran through her. She missed her mother, I think."

"And now her father." Guilt washed over Lucas as he said it.

"Yes. She is...she's more fragile than perhaps she looks."

Lucas considered that statement. It didn't ring true. Fragile was not the word for Diana, for she had a core of steel that ran through her. Fragile meant weak in some way, and she was not that.

"Vulnerable," he suggested. "She is vulnerable beneath that façade of confidence and strength. Perhaps I...I did not honor that."

"Do I need to intervene?" Stalwood said softly. "Remove you from her care?"

Lucas's stomach tensed at the very idea that he would be separated from her at this juncture. He pushed back at the feeling. That was silly. He was confused by her behavior and that turned everything upside down. He only wanted to be well and she was helping with that. There was no other reason not to want to walk away.

"I think she could still do me good," he said. "Ten days with her and I am already feeling closer to whole again."

Stalwood leaned back in his chair. "Just have a care."

Lucas ignored the warning and handed over his superior's tea before he took a place in a chair across from him. "I've been looking over the case files."

Not as much as he wanted to, of course. Diana had been a distraction, but he'd taken the time where he could find it. The thrill of the hunt had returned immediately.

Stalwood leaned forward, his eyes lit up with interest. "And?"

"I have some questions and some observations," he said. "First, did...did George Oakford ever get assigned cases?"

Stalwood blinked and the confusion on his face answered the question even before he stammered, "Oakford? He was a surgeon— why in the world would I put him on a case?"

Lucas drew a sharp breath. "So I thought."

"Why would you ask about that?"

"Diana said something about her father having a visitor. She believed the man to be a spy and she thought they were working on a case together." He said no more about her confession. That was a line he would not cross.

"No," Stalwood said. "I *never* assigned him a case. Of course, he put himself in the middle of your mission six months ago, so I cannot say for certain that he hadn't done the same in the past. But he never confessed as much to me. Could she have been mistaken?"

"I suppose so. After all, it was an impression she had, not something her father actually said to her. Still, it stood out to me. Made me wonder..." He trailed off. He had a nagging feeling in his chest. Something that felt incomplete.

"I can look further into it," Stalwood suggested. "Check my records. When did she say this occurred?"

"Two years ago," he said. "I don't know more specifics and the story was not relayed to me in a fashion that would allow me to press her."

Stalwood's gaze narrowed. "Very well. I trust your instincts on that. I'll investigate further. What else?"

"The more I look at the case file, the more I think that not only was the man on the estate that day our traitor, but that he might not have worked alone."

Stalwood jerked. "You think I might have more than one bastard in my ranks?"

Lucas nodded. "Perhaps. Though this man's partner may have been of lesser rank. When he killed Oakford and injured me, probably believing I would also die, it spooked him. That is why it has taken so long for him to return to his wicked ways. But now that he is..."

He stopped himself. He'd been pondering something in the past few days. Now Diana's change of attitude made him think even more about it.

"What?"

"I've been hidden for months, protected so that I could not be found by this person, yes?" he asked.

Stalwood nodded. "I felt you might be in danger. You still likely would be."

"I agree. But that could be just the way for this man to be drawn out." Lucas stood and paced the room slowly. "Think of it, Stalwood. Returning to the field in the shape I'm in would be out of the question—I know that, even if I hate to admit it. But there is nothing that says I could not return to some kind of public life."

"As bait?" Stalwood asked.

Lucas faced him, unable to keep the excitement from his voice. "Bait is one way to put it. Torment is another. Think of this man, feeling he's in the clear, uncertain what the one potential witness to his crimes is capable of doing. Then I return. He might not be able to resist me."

Stalwood pressed his lips together. "It's not a bad idea, really."

"You sound surprised," Lucas said with a chuckle. "My good ideas are exactly why you brought me the case files in the first place."

"Modest, as always," Stalwood said, his tone dry as dust. But his smile belied any annoyance his tone might have conveyed. "We'd have to tread carefully, though. If it is known you are staying here with Diana—"

Lucas shook his head. "No, I've thought of that too. This place is too isolated, too small to be safe if my location is made public. It would be better if I...if I returned to the ducal home here in London. Took up my duties as Willowby."

Stalwood lifted both eyebrows in surprise, and Lucas couldn't blame him. He had never had, nor expressed, any interest in the title. Quite the opposite, though no one knew why he had pushed his dukedom and all that went with it so far away. Not his friends, not his colleagues, no one.

"You *are* driven if you are willing to be Your Graced for a case," Stalwood said softly.

Lucas lifted his chin. "George Oakford is dead because of me and Diana deserves justice. Answers. So do I. I'm willing to do almost anything for that."

"Your mother is staying in the London home, you know," Stalwood said, holding his gaze. "Will she be a problem?"

Lucas tensed. "My mother. I'm certain she'll be a problem for me, but for you, for the case...no."

"If you think it for the best, then I approve," Stalwood said. "I'll arrange for guards for your estate, ones I trust implicitly. Is there anything else you need?"

Lucas shook his head. "Not at the moment, though if that changes I'll inform you. I'll just need to tell Diana and arrange for her to move with me."

Stalwood's eyes widened. "You intend to take Diana with you," he repeated.

"Of course," Lucas said. "She is helping me greatly with my recovery. But it's more than that."

"More."

Lucas's lips parted at the knowing tone of Stalwood's voice. "Yes," he grunted. "More. Diana will have to come and go if she is not staying with me. She'll be seen and that could put her in danger if the man who did this to me, to her father, is watching. And we want him to be watching. If she is with me then she'll be under the care of your guards, as well as me."

Of course, there was so much more to it than that. He had no intention of saying so to Stalwood. Perhaps he didn't need to, if his superior's pinched expression was any indication.

"And how will you explain her?" Stalwood asked. "This beautiful young woman who has come to stay with you unattended?"

Lucas froze. He hadn't actually thought that far ahead. Here their arrangement had not been public. In his home...well, he knew he was considered a bachelor—a catch, thanks to his fortune and his title. The traitor to their cause would not be the only one watching his home, his every move.

"I'll talk to her," he said. "And let her decide how she'd like things presented."

Stalwood rose. "I agree that is the best way of it. Let me know what you two come up with and if there are any additional things you need. I will speak to you after you are settled."

"Very good," Lucas said, and motioned his superior into the

foyer. They shook hands and he watched as Stalwood headed out the door and into his waiting carriage.

Now that they had a plan, Lucas's mind was racing. This wasn't quite back in the field, but it was working a case, truly working it.

And he couldn't wait to get back into the thick of things and remember what his life was truly about.

Diana moved about Lucas's chamber, tidying up. That was all she could think to do while Stalwood and Lucas talked downstairs. She had no place there with them. She had no place with Lucas at all. Yet reminding herself of that was somehow difficult.

"You are being so utterly foolish," she bit out, letting the words hang in the air around her. She heard them, she knew they were right. They still stung.

With a quiet curse, she yanked a pillowcase from the pillow, tossing it into the basket on the floor beside her. When she did so, a book fell from within the folds of the fabric, bounced off the edge of the bed and clattered to the floor, sending folded sheets of paper sliding across the wooden surface.

She sighed and bent to retrieve the items. "Spies and their secrets," she muttered, thinking of the pistol she had already carefully set aside when she stripped the other pillow of its cover.

Lucas certainly had enough of those secrets. Things he hid about his past, his life, his vocation. She knew what it was like to live with a man like that. Her father had been much the same. Close-lipped and careful, steering her away from anything that mattered to him. The last time she'd seen him, he'd been angry with her for coming into his study at their country estate and reorganizing some of the items on his desk.

That was their last conversation, for he'd left soon after and never returned.

She winced and turned over yet another paper. She was ready to stuff them all back into the book and put it on the side table for Lucas when she caught a glimpse of her name, written in a shaky hand on one of the sheets.

She frowned and held the paper to her chest. These were Lucas's private things. No amount of sex or whispered secrets from the past gave her any right to go rifling through them.

But it was her name, on this paper he had placed in a book and then hidden in a pillow. How could she not be curious?

She glanced at the door. Although she could not hear the men talking in the closed parlor below, she had not yet heard Stalwood leave either. Until he did, she was safe to…to…

"Snoop," she said out loud, completing the sentence in her head.

But as much as she hated the description, and the fact that it was entirely apt, she still lowered the paper and stared at it. This was Lucas's hand, she would bet her life on it. His injury made it shaky, but there was still a flourish that fit him.

What was on the paper was far more interesting. It appeared to be a long series of notes, bullet-pointed and neatly organized. He was writing about her father's murder, listing off a long line of facts about the case.

She staggered to the chair before the fire and sank into the cushioned seat. Her heart was pounding, her hands were shaking. She knew a little about that day. Bare skeletons of facts, told to her by Stalwood and Lucas. But this was detailed. This was horribly detailed. Lucas had written down every moment of that day, including exact words that had been said, and the collection of them swam before her eyes as they filled with tears.

"Diana."

She jolted and jerked her gaze up to find Lucas standing in the doorway. His face was hard, lined with anger and betrayal as he limped to her and snatched the page from her hand.

"What do you think you are doing?"

CHAPTER 11

Lucas winced as Diana stared at him, her green eyes dark with grief and pain. Her hands shook as she lowered them into her lap, and she let out a sigh that seemed to shake her all the way to her very core.

But when she stood up, the pain was gone and it was replaced by an anger he had not expected. "What am I doing? What are *you* doing?" she snapped.

He drew back, surprised by the power of her raw emotions and by the reaction they inspired in him. It was sudden and formidable, a combination of wanting to rail at her for interfering and also wanting to hold her and comfort her in her pain.

He shoved all of it away and struggled to be controlled and measured. "You are asking *me* when I walked in to find you going over my private papers? I did not think you'd take the time you had while I talked to Stalwood to rifle through my room."

Her lips parted on an outraged, huffy sigh. "How dare you! That is not what I did. I was tidying up your chamber while you were busy, changing your sheets so the laundry could be sent out."

She motioned to the bed and he noted that it was, indeed, half unmade and his room was less cluttered. Things he should have observed immediately upon entry to the room. Noticing details was engrained in him, the first thing he'd been trained to do as a spy. Yet he hadn't because he'd been distracted by Diana.

"So when you found something hidden, you decided that gave you a right to look at it?" he asked.

She folded her arms. "No. The book fell and the pages folded inside scattered. I thought you were being ridiculous hiding so much, just a spy so obsessed with his secrets that he thought everyone else was, too. But when I was picking up the papers, I saw my name on them."

She pointed to the one he held in his hand. He slowly turned it over and winced. Of all the things for her to find, this was one of the worst. It was an accounting of every detail he had gathered or gleaned from the case. Her name was in it because she was part of the case for him now, tied to it and to him in a way that would never be undone.

But he would never have had her read some of it. Like how her father had looked lying dead on the ground. Like the details of their last conversation or the sound of the shots when Oakford was gunned down.

From her face, she had read it all. And now it would never leave her mind, just as it would never leave his.

"You have been investigating this case all along," she whispered. "And you hid it from me."

"Since the last time Stalwood came here," he admitted as he folded the paper and put it into his jacket pocket. "And I wasn't hiding it. I didn't tell you what I was doing because it has nothing to do with you, Diana."

Her face crumpled at that statement and she backed away from him like he had struck her physically. "He may have loved you more, Your Grace," she whispered, her voice shaking. "But he was *my* father."

He recoiled at not just her words, but at the emotion laced in them. He moved to her in three long steps and caught her hands.

She struggled against him, but he refused to release her. Indeed, he tugged her closer.

"He loved you, Diana, of that I have no doubt. And when I say that my investigation has nothing to do with you, I meant that you should not have to think of your father this way. That you should not think of his last moments, but of what you shared with him while he was alive."

"You think I didn't think of his last moments long before I read the details of them?" she gasped, yanking free at last. Tears had begun to stream down her face and her breath came in painful hiccups. "I wonder if he was afraid. I wonder if he was in pain. I wonder if he knew that these were his last moments and if there was any peace for him. I wonder if he...if he thought of me."

Lucas stared at her, this woman made of intelligence and kindness and iron. This woman who was utterly alone in the world now that her father was gone. How well he knew that feeling.

He stepped forward and gathered her into his arms. This time she didn't resist him. She let him pull her against his chest as he smoothed her hair gently. She shook as she wept, a pouring out of all the grief she had been holding back.

When her tears had slowed a little, he whispered, "Diana, yes, I am investigating his death. We all deserve justice. Him, me and *you*."

She lifted her face toward his, and he was struck with the thought of that first night he'd been here, when he'd held her like this and comforted her in similar grief. Now he knew her better. Now he wanted even more to soothe the wounds she carried so quietly and bravely. The ones the world didn't see.

He wanted to soothe the ones she hadn't shared, too. The ones he sensed below the surface, where she so jealously protected them.

"If I deserve justice, then I also deserve the truth," she whispered. "And I want it, Lucas."

He hesitated. "You want to know about my case?"

"I don't expect you would agree to that," she said, pulling away from him. Leaving him cold. Bereft in ways he didn't want to analyze. "But stop hiding it from me. This is too small a house for you to do so."

He jolted. Here he'd come upstairs, ready to give her the news of their move and he'd forgotten it all when faced with her tears. Yet another example of how deeply she distracted him.

He bent his head. "I'm...sorry."

She wrinkled her brow. "You're actually apologizing to me?"

He nodded. "Yes. Not for investigating. That is my nature and my duty and I will not change for anyone. But perhaps I should not have been so secretive. You are right that Oakford was your father—no one has been more affected by his death. To investigate under your roof, behind your back, was wrong."

"Thank you," she said, though her tone was still stunned. He wondered if apologies were so rare to her that she hardly recognized one when she heard it.

"And that brings me to the subject I wanted to broach with you when I came upstairs," he continued. "It has to do with the investigation."

She tilted her head. "Very well. What is it?"

"Stalwood and I agree that I could do more on that count if I were to move to my own home here in London."

Her lips parted. "What? Why?"

He hesitated. Here he had just promised not to keep her locked out of what he was doing. But he didn't want to endanger her, either. At least no more than he knew he would just by being in her presence.

"Please, won't you be honest with me?" she said, exhaustion lacing her tone. "I'm so *very* tired of all the lies."

Yes, he could see that in her face, in her eyes, her posture. She was on the edge, ready to fall. He didn't want to be the one who pushed her, even if he didn't think he could be the one who caught her either.

"I'm going to tell you the truth," he said. "With the understanding that it is not something you may repeat to anyone at any time."

She nodded slowly. "Very well, though who you think I would tell, I don't know."

Her words reminded him once more of how alone she was, and he winced before he said, "The man who was responsible for your father's death, the traitor...he is back at his old ways. There's been another death."

Her knees buckled and she just caught herself on the back of the closest chair as she stared at him in horror. "No. No!"

"I'm so sorry, Diana, but yes. This man, he no doubt knows I'm still alive, but Stalwood has done a very good job hiding me these past six months. We think if I come back into the public eye, it might push this bastard to a breaking point. It might make him do or say something that would reveal him for the coward he truly is."

"You want to use yourself as bait."

He smiled. "That was what Stalwood said, as well. You really do have the mind of a spy in some ways."

He expected her to smile back, but instead she stepped toward him with eyes flashing. "So you're going to make it obvious where you are. You're going to all but tempt him to you, open your doors to him, allow him into your home to threaten—"

"Diana," he interrupted. "I would not let you be in danger."

She cupped his cheeks. "I'm not talking about me, you fool! I'm talking about you. This man already nearly killed you! How can you consider putting yourself in his path? Teasing him with your presence? What if he comes after you again?"

He tilted his head. She was truly only concerned for his well-being. His heart throbbed at that fact. It was not one many people in his life had shared. No one on any deep level since he'd pushed his friends away after entering the service of the War Department.

And yet here she was, fearful not for herself, but for him.

He turned his face and kissed one of her palms. "Stalwood will arrange protection. For us both."

"Both?" she repeated.

"Yes. I want you to come with me. To continue helping me there as you have here."

She drew back, her hands dropping away. "You want me to come to your home in London. Your ducal home. As what? Your servant? Your physician? Your—your lover?"

He sighed. "That is part of what we must determine. If you came to my estate here in the city, it wouldn't be like it is here on the edge of the city. People would see. They would know, Diana. I could protect you from many things, but not gossip. Stalwood could arrange for some kind of chaperone, of course. Someone to make it look less untoward, but—"

"I don't want a governess," she said. "That would make my work harder." She got up, pushing past him to pace across the room. She paused at the window where she looked down at the garden.

"Then what do you suggest?" he asked.

"My being there would help you," she whispered.

He pulled himself into the chair she had vacated and nodded. "Yes. I am much recovered in the time we've spent together. And to be honest, I would feel more comfortable having you close. I have no idea who this person is. I have no idea what he knows about your father. About you. But I don't like the idea of your being alone until he's in custody or dead."

She flinched, as if she hadn't thought through the possibilities of what would happen to the man responsible for all this pain that had come into their lives.

"Your mistress," she said softly.

He jolted as he looked at her. "I beg your pardon?"

She faced him. "The way I will have most access to you, Lucas, is if we call me what I am. That is, your mistress."

"You are not my mistress!" he burst out, moving toward her so quickly that he nearly fell over from the sudden movement and the pain that followed.

"You are bedding me," she said, keeping her gaze even. "That is what a man of your stature does with a mistress."

"That kind of suggestion would utterly ruin your future," he snapped.

She tilted her head back and laughed, though there was no hint of pleasure in the sound. "Dear man, what future do you assume I have? I am the daughter of a man of no title, no fortune, hardly anything to recommend him. I am no virgin. I bring nothing to the table for marriage to a man of rank or privilege. Even if I did, I have no such desire for that kind of match. Or any type of match, really. I was spoiled to that sort of thing long ago."

Lucas stared at her. She was talking about that man, that spy who had taken her innocence. *He* was the one who had spoiled her to the thought of love or family or a future that was more than a lonely existence where she helped everyone but herself. That the loss of that person had inspired such bitterness had to mean she had loved him.

And a spike of jealous pain and rage jolted through Lucas with that thought. He straightened and speared her with a glare that he hoped kept his true heart hidden.

"It's unfair to you, Diana," he insisted.

She shrugged. "Life is unfair, Lucas. I would think you know that better than most. It is decided. I will play the role of your mistress and I will go with you on this move so that I may continue to help you."

He set his jaw. He did not like this, but she was not wrong. The easiest way to make this work was for her play that role. Play it? Hell, it wasn't far off from how he treated her. The only difference between a lover and a mistress was the financial support a mistress got.

Perhaps he owed her that as much as he owed her anything. But now was not the time to think about those things. She would be safe in his house, she would no longer have to fuss over cooking or cleaning or anything but her work. And since he was getting better by the day, even that wouldn't be as taxing for her as it had been upon his arrival nearly two weeks before.

This was for the best. Yes. The niggling feeling in his stomach that it wasn't was only excitement over being allowed to continue his work.

"Well, I may not agree, but I suppose it is settled," he said. "I'll send word to my servants here in Town that we will be arriving in twenty-four hours. Does that give you enough time to prepare?"

She swallowed, and then her face transformed. No longer was she his lover—there was a sense of distance there. That wall she had tried to put up in the morning, but higher now. More formidable. "Certainly, Your Grace. Though it will likely mean that I will be quite busy until we depart tomorrow."

She nodded in his direction and then turned to go. At the door, she turned. He held his breath as she struggled with whatever she was going to say.

"I want to help you, Lucas. I will in any way you see fit. But please, don't lie to me again or hide what you're doing. Please."

The second please lilted out, shaky and more emotional than he thought she might have wanted. It spoke volumes about her. Revealed more than she had even when she made love to him.

He nodded. "I may not be able to tell you everything I'm doing. I won't, in fact, but I won't lie to you about that. I won't hide it."

That seemed to satisfy her, for she left the room. And left him feeling that nothing between them would ever be the same.

CHAPTER 12

Lucas stared across the fine carriage that had been sent to retrieve him. Diana was looking straight ahead, her gaze inscrutable and her hands clenched in her lap. She looked as though she were being led to the gallows, not to his fine home a mere hour's drive across the city from her own.

Of course, that was how he felt about this shift, too. He had no interest in returning to the ducal home and the ducal life. That was what he'd been avoiding for years. Almost a decade, actually. A decade since the moment that had blown his life apart and exposed the lies beneath.

"Are they accustomed to you bringing home a mistress from time to time?" Diana asked, her soft voice cutting into his thoughts.

He jerked his head up. "I..." He hesitated. To tell her the truth was to reveal some of that exposed nerve that was his family and his past. But he had promised not to lie anymore. "In truth, I do not go here often," he admitted.

She tilted her head in surprise. "Even when you are in Town?"

"I have a townhouse near Piccadilly," he said. "I prefer to spend my time there."

"But you are coming here because it is—"

"More public," he said. "It will make it look to our traitor as though I have given up my life as a spy and shifted to the life duty dictates."

"After the extent of your injuries, I suppose that makes sense," Diana said. "Have you ever thought of doing it in truth?"

"I have no interest in being Duke of Willowby," he said, his tone far harsher than he had intended.

She did not recoil from it, though. Instead, she leaned in, reaching out to take his hands in hers. "But you *are* Duke of Willowby."

He almost laughed. Almost let the whole story fall from his lips as she massaged his hands. Luckily, the carriage turned into his drive and then pulled up to a stop. It silenced any foolish confession that might have fallen from his lips.

He straightened and tugged his hands away. "And now we play our roles."

She was slower to sit up, and her expression was troubled as the door to the carriage opened and revealed a footman. She went out first, smiling at the servant in thanks before she turned back and helped the man as Lucas eased his way down the short stairs. He saw the servants who were lined up outside to greet him exchange looks, and his cheeks flared.

Whether they were wondering at why the prodigal son had returned or marveling at his fall from physical prowess, either option was difficult. He didn't like their whispers and their judgment.

Diana slid her arm through his and whispered, "Steady on."

He glanced down at her, surprised that those two little words had cut through the anxiety and emotion. Suddenly he cared a little less about the others. There was her and that was enough.

She guided them up the stairs, careful to make it appear that he was bearing all of his own weight rather than leaning slightly on her as he quietly greeted the servants. When they reached the top step, his father's butler, Jones, awaited them. Lucas pressed his lips together. He and Jones had never seen eye to eye.

But to his surprise, the butler actually seemed pleased to see him. "Your Grace," he said. "How good to have you home, sir."

Lucas stepped into the foyer and looked around with a sigh. Home. This place had never been home. Nor had any of his father's estates. He had never spent a moment of his life feeling wanted there. Feeling loved. He'd hardened himself to the reactions those facts created, but he recalled them well. Recalled the pain of being so young and knowing he was despised by a man who was supposed to care for him.

"Jones," he forced himself to say. "May I present Miss Oakford."

The butler's gaze slid to her, and Lucas felt her shift under the scrutiny. Of course she would. Being labeled a mistress was something she claimed to be able to handle, but that did not mean she would enjoy the exercise.

Still, Jones managed admirably. He bobbed his head in welcome. "Miss Oakford," he said. "We shall endeavor to do all we can to ensure your comfort during your stay."

"Thank you," Diana said, her voice very small and even meek.

Lucas didn't like it, but he pressed on. "I do apologize for deciding to come so suddenly. I hope it did not create too much work for the staff."

"No, Your Grace," Jones said as he took gloves and hats from them. "Since your mother was already staying here, it really required nothing."

Lucas stiffened. "Ah, yes. The duchess. Is she still in residence?"

Now the butler looked uncomfortable. "Er, yes, Your Grace. She is packing up for a move to the dower house, but she is still here. She wanted to see you when you—"

"I see her. You may go, Jones."

Lucas glanced across the foyer as the butler left and found his mother standing there. He buckled just a fraction at the sight of her. The last time he saw her, it had been at his father's funeral. When she'd stood at his casket, snow and rain swirling around her furs, her dark gaze narrowed on him. He'd never felt so lost in his life.

And he'd run.

"Mother," he said, pulling from the warmth of Diana's presence and toward the coldness of hers.

She flinched at that one word. Turned her face away a moment before she refocused on him. "Back to do your worst, are you?" she asked, her voice trembling.

He stopped moving. "To do my duty," he answered, for that was not untrue. It just wasn't the one she would think of when that word was said.

"Duty," she hissed. "What would you know about duty? You'll drag this title and all it stands for to the ground before you're finished."

Lucas did not respond, for what she accused was often exactly what he'd wanted to do over the years. Burn it all down. Leave nothing behind of the name or the title or the prestige that was part of it.

Now it was different. Somehow it had changed. He might not want to be Willowby, but he had no desire to destroy what Willowby represented.

"I assure you—"

"You're bringing your whore to the ducal estate."

Behind him, Diana gasped, and he glared at his mother. "You might want to be very careful who *you* call a whore, *madam*."

She swung on him. He could have dodged it, but he didn't. He let her hand crack against his cheek, felt the heat of it, the sting, and did not move or turn away.

"Lucas!" Diana cried out.

He lifted a hand so she would not come to him or interfere. If this was what his mother needed, he would not deny her.

"Why couldn't you just stay away?" the duchess whispered, her tone harsh though there were tears in her eyes.

He held that teary gaze and saw everything she'd been through in her life. Everything she'd put him through, as well. He inclined his head. "I'm sorry," he said, softly but firmly.

Her lips parted, almost in surprise. Her expression relaxed just a fraction and she whispered, "I suppose we all are. Now I'm going to the dower house. Goodbye."

She strode past him then. Past Diana, without even looking at her. Out the front door to the carriage that had just been emptied. She shouted an order in a trembling tone and it took off.

For a moment, all was silent. The only sound was the ticking of the large clock in the foyer, counting out the unending seconds since his mother struck him.

Finally, Diana stepped forward. "Oh, Lucas," she whispered as she gently took his hand.

He looked down at her. There was no pity on her face, not like many would have shown, or the gossipy interest that the aristocrats of his acquaintance would have expressed. There was only understanding, much deeper than before they came here.

There was only empathy.

Part of him wanted to lean into that. To let her wrap herself around him, bleed out the anguish like so many less talented healers had tried to bleed out his injury and pain. He wanted her to fill up the holes in his heart and his soul.

But he couldn't. He extracted his hand from hers and said, "I have some letters to write. Jones!" The butler appeared before Diana could reply. "Take Miss Oakford to the chamber I requested in my letter. Thank you."

Then he turned and left before either of them could comment or see how deeply he had been affected. And how much he had to regret.

D iana paced the room she had been given, but it did not help her burn off any of the nervous energy she felt. There were too many things going on in her mind to feel calm or rational.

First off, the chamber was a palace. It was almost the same size as her entire cottage. She felt as though she had shrunk down and now there would be no escape. It was also too fine, even for the mistress she was pretending to be. Everything was sterling silver and gold flake and fine muslin and silk. She was so accustomed to plain and serviceable that anything more felt almost foreign to her.

What was also foreign to her was the fact that Lucas's room was connected to hers through an antechamber. She'd discovered that fact the moment she'd been left alone in this museum of a house. When she'd opened the door, she'd found two maids putting away his things. The way they'd stopped talking the moment she entered the room made it clear what they'd been gossiping about.

She sank into the closest chair and covered her eyes. She'd told him she could handle all this, but now she questioned that statement made with all the bravado of a woman who didn't know what she was getting into.

But could she tell him that? No, of course not. Firstly, because she would have to admit he'd been right. Secondly, because he had much larger issues to deal with.

She shuddered as she thought of the scene with his mother in the foyer. She had few memories of her own mother, but they were all warm and soft and gentle. Watching as the Duchess of Willowby swung at full force at her son, that Lucas had let her do so, had hurt her heart in a deep and powerful way. The woman hadn't even asked about his limp, as if she didn't care that her only son was injured, had almost died.

Diana's hands shook with empathy and anger on his behalf. There was so much about the man she didn't know, couldn't understand because he locked her out of his life and his secrets. His body? Oh, that was hers. She had no doubt she could have his body any time she crooked her finger.

But his mind? His soul? His heart? His secrets?

Those were off limits.

"I suppose a mistress *is* the best way I could be described," she muttered. "Or what his mother called me: a whore."

The idea stung, for when Lucas touched her she felt so much more than that between them. But she pushed that aside. She was here to help him. Right now he had to be hunched over a desk, his muscles getting tight and painful.

So she had to go to him. That was all there was to it. Not to ask him to share with her. She knew better than to do that. But just to... help. She just wanted to help.

She left the chamber and wove her way through the estate. Somehow she found the stairs, but she was soon lost in the twisting and turning hallways and doorways that seemed to lead to nowhere.

How in the world could anyone get accustomed to this life?

She had no answer to that, but didn't need one, for as she turned yet another corner she discovered an open door ahead. She saw the flicker of firelight reflecting on the wood and sighed as she moved toward it.

What she found was a study. As she entered the room, she was hit with the scent of old cigars and long-burned fires. The room was pompous and stuffy and *nothing* like the man who sat behind the huge mahogany desk in the back. Lucas was hunched over, scribbling a note with a massive feather pen that he dashed in and out of the ink beside him with little care to drips he dragged across the page.

"Lucas?" she said softly.

He jumped and jerked his head up to look at her. For the first time since she met him, he had been stripped of his boundaries, his walls, of all the training he'd received as a spy that kept him safe and separate from anything unpleasant around him. His pain was clear on every angle of his handsome face. It went deeper than mere physical injury and she understood it down to her very core.

It was the same as her own pain. Mirror images brought on by what she assumed were far different circumstances.

"I don't want to talk about anything," he said as he warmed a stick of wax over the candle beside him. He sealed his letter and quickly stamped it shut, then stood.

"No?" she asked, tracking his every restless move as he came around the desk, letter in hand, toward her. "That's good. Neither do I."

He drew in a few breaths and some of the energy went out of him. He slowly began to turn back to the man she'd known, the one she'd given herself to. Not the reluctant duke anymore, not the unwanted son. Just Lucas.

"Then what do you want?" he asked, and from his tone he knew full well the power and double meaning of those words.

She hesitated, for the idea of having him, making love to him, was tempting indeed. Especially since she had spent the previous night in her own bed, separated from him because she knew this thing between them was spiraling out of control.

But right now she wasn't certain that sex was what he needed. At least not the only thing he needed.

"I want to walk," she responded.

His face fell so quickly it was almost comical, and she had to hold back a giggle at the expression. "Diana," he began.

She held up a hand. "On orders of your physician."

She saw how he wanted to argue with her. How he wanted to refuse what she suggested. But then he just sighed and threw up his arms, almost in surrender. "Very well."

She drew back. "That's all? Very well? You aren't going to give me some treatise on how that isn't what you want to do?"

He shot her a look. "I've never given a treatise in my life."

Now she couldn't help but smile as she folded her arms. "Never?"

"Fine." He shifted his weight. "Once or twice. But to argue with you? I've learned that is a fruitless endeavor. Let me ring for Jones and give him this to deliver, and then to the Willowby gardens we'll go."

She noted that he said "the Willowby gardens", not his own, separating himself once more from the title he held. But she made no comment as he moved to the bell by the door. To her pleasure, he rang it not with his good arm, but with his injured one. And though she saw that he flexed his fingers and shook them out a little after he did so, his reaction was nothing like the pain he had exhibited just two weeks before when he first came into her care.

Part of her was happy for that fact, of course. To ease his pain even a fraction was a victory and one that she would savor for the rest of her life.

But the other part felt something darker and sharper and deeper. Part of her felt a great terror at seeing him function so well physically. Because soon she would have no reason to be by his side.

Soon, she would lose this thing between them, this connection that was so tenuous and sometimes perfect. And that was something she had to come to terms with, or risk losing more than she wished to consider.

CHAPTER 13

Lucas turned Diana down yet another path in the vast garden behind his home, but he was not pondering the beauty around them. No, there was something far more pleasant that intruded into his mind. Her warmth against his side, the feel of her fingers on the inside of his elbow as she pressed them there, the scent of her hair, something warm and sweet that wafted to his nostrils and brought him…peace.

And then there was the wide-eyed wonder on her face as she stared at everything around her. She could almost make a man not hate a place anymore.

"It is magnificent," she breathed at last, her words almost uncertain, like they were not the right ones.

He forced himself to look around, and then he shrugged. "Not as wonderful as your garden," he said.

She pulled her arm from his and turned on him with a look of pure shock on her face. "How can you say that?" She moved forward a few steps, her hands clasped. "The fountains, the trees, the flowers…is that hedge trimmed in the shape of a little rabbit?"

He couldn't help but smile at her enthusiasm. "Yes, a little rabbit.

I think there are squirrel hedges and stag hedges and bird hedges, as well."

"Marvelous!" she said, and clapped her hands together with all the wonder of a child.

"Have you never been to a garden like this?" he asked. "I am rather astonished considering your father's predilection for plants."

She glanced at him. "Firstly, my father's interest was in purely medicinal plants. He thought these sorts of things were foolish. Beauty or other frivolous notions didn't appeal to him much."

Lucas inclined his head. "I admit, Oakford was very pragmatic."

"As far as coming to a place like this, how would I be invited? My father may have known very important men, but I had no place with them. Neither did he, truth be told. He was a merchant, in a way, providing a service for his betters. We were not exactly invited to garden parties."

Lucas wrinkled his brow. He had been so separate from this kind of life for so long, he had almost forgotten the snobbery involved. He sighed before he spoke. "I suppose you are correct."

"Of course I am." Her gaze darted away. "We belong in very different worlds, Your Grace."

He bent his head as those words sank into his body in ways he doubted she had meant. "Oh, Diana, you have seen my mother. After bearing witness to that little scene between us, do you think I *ever* belonged here?"

She caught her breath and turned to face him. There was her empathy again, fully on display. As warm and healing as the sun above them.

"I'm sorry, Lucas," she said as she approached him cautiously. Her hand lifted and she settled her palm on his cheek. He leaned into it, reeling in her warmth and her kindness and her strength. He needed it all in that moment, and she didn't disappoint.

"As am I," he said softly.

He thought she might question him, but instead she slid her hand back through his arm and guided him forward again, past the huge Zeus fountain his father had so loved and farther into the garden.

They were quiet for a while, but it was a comfortable silence. Finally she glanced up at him. "Who were you writing to? If it does not reveal secrets of the empire, of course."

He smiled at the teasing tone that was back in her voice. He found he liked it when things were easy like this. Far better than when they were fraught with pain or betrayal.

"No state secrets, except that I obviously need to spread the word that I am back in Society and recovering from my injuries."

He felt her hesitation. Anxiety seemed to float between them in an instant. But her voice was steady as she said, "I see."

"I wrote to my friend Simon. Er, the Duke of Crestwood," he said. "One of the members of my duke club you were asking about before. He is our social butterfly. If he knows, then everyone else will soon know."

"Your duke club," she said with a small smile. "I admit I have been interested in that subject ever since my father first mentioned it. You must be the youngest amongst a stodgy group of middle-aged and old men."

"I *am* the youngest," he said. "But they are not stodgy. There was an odd set of years where all the dukes, old and young, seemed to have children, heirs, at the same time. We are all within a five-year gap of each other."

She shook her head. "The group of you must cause quite a stir with the ladies."

He chuckled. "Truth be told, I don't really know. I went into service when I was eligible and then into the War Department. My experience as a Society duke is limited. But I assume they are breaking hearts, though several of my friends are now married. Even having families."

"I suppose you are of the age," she said, her tone suddenly far away. "How did you form this group?"

He turned his face slightly. Here she was focusing on a subject that she surely thought would be easier on him than discussing the terrible relationship he shared with his mother. But in some ways, this one was just as hard.

And yet he found his lips moving regardless of his long desire to keep his secrets locked away. Diana just inspired honesty. "Almost all of us had...bad fathers," he said softly. "And so we vowed to help each other navigate the waters of our future duties. We became fast friends, and I know I could depend on any one of them for anything I asked."

When he was silent too long she said, "But?"

He stopped in the path and faced her. "You assume there is a but?"

"I can tell there is."

His shoulders rolled forward in the defeat and shame he felt in his heart. "They could not say the same about me. I am not a...good friend. I cut myself away from them. I could hardly be called one of their number anymore. In truth, I have no idea if Simon or any of the rest will even want to see me."

"You were friends since you were children," she said. "I'm certain this man will be thrilled to hear from you, especially if it has been a long absence. And you can always turn back to them, Lucas."

"I don't know," he said, and stared off away from her across the garden. "It is complicated."

"I'm certain it is. *You* are, I've learned that in the short time we've shared." She smiled gently. "But nothing is permanent, until it is. And regrets are hard to bear when there are no amends to be made anymore."

The pain was obvious on her face and in the shaking of her voice. He took her hand and smoothed his thumb over the soft flesh there. "You are thinking of your father."

She nodded. "Yes. There were things we should have said, I think. Now I never will."

Lucas took a deep breath. Yes, he had things he wished he'd said

JESS MICHAELS

to Oakford himself. "I would like to visit him. Was he buried here in London?"

She caught her breath, and he saw how difficult this was. How much it cut, burned, destroyed her from the inside out. Once again, his guilt rose, more painful than any injury he'd endured.

"No," she breathed out painfully. "There was a service here, for those in the department, private and small. But his body was taken back to our country home. I wanted to...see him." She turned her face. "But Stalwood wouldn't let me."

He drew back. "Why?" he asked, and already could see how terrible the answer was.

She swallowed. "Stalwood didn't tell you?"

He shook his head slowly and could barely draw enough air to whisper, "No."

"His body was...mutilated, Lucas."

Diana watched as Lucas recoiled, staggering back with a look of pain on his face that cut her to her core. It made her relive her own horror and pain when she'd been told that she couldn't see her father's face one final time.

"No!" he cried out. "No!"

She caught his arm and guided him to a bench, where he sat down hard and put his head in his hands. For a long time he was silent. So silent that she sank down beside him and placed her hand on his back to slowly smooth circles across the muscled plane.

"When?" he choked out.

"I don't know," she whispered. "Stalwood wouldn't tell me much about it. I assumed he had been struck in the...in the head."

He pursed his lips. "No. No, he wasn't. That bastard did this to him, damaged his body. But why? Why would he do such a thing? And only to Oakford when there were so many others who he could have destroyed."

124

He seemed to be talking to himself now, and she shook her head. "What do you mean, others?"

Lucas jerked beneath her hand and looked up, his face blank. "I shouldn't tell you," he whispered. "If you didn't see it on my account you found at your home, I shouldn't leave you with that image."

"I want to know," she said.

He cleared his throat. "Our traitor shot all the servants, anyone who could identify him."

She flinched at that brutal news. "I-I didn't know that."

"I was told afterward." Lucas shook his head. "I was lying there, dying next to your father. There were a hundred other things that man had to do before he fled the scene. Why would he stop to mutilate Oakford?"

Her stomach turned. "I don't know."

He jolted, like he was realizing, once again, how horrible this was for her. "Oh, Diana. I'm so sorry. You've had so much taken from you already and now this."

She shivered. Sometimes it was hard not to have that same reaction. Not to count the cost of the life her father had lived, in all the ways it had destroyed or altered her own. But today she felt none of those things. Today she just looked at the man beside her and wanted to ease some of his guilt.

"There *is* a small memorial at our home here in London," she said. "In the very back of the garden. And of course his body is back home. I try not to think about what was done to him. Instead, I focus on where his spirit is. His soul. Free and, I hope, with my mother."

"That is a good way to think of it and if it gives you peace then I urge you to hang on to that notion," Lucas said. "But it takes away none of my guilt or my pain. Nor should it."

"Lucas," she began.

He pushed to his feet and paced away. When he ran a hand through his hair, it ruffled the long locks, giving him that rakish, pirate air.

"I'm sorry," he interrupted. "I'm so sorry, Diana. And if you hate me, then I deserve no less. I certainly do not deserve and have not deserved the care you have shown me."

She gasped and moved to him in three long steps. "You stop that! You stop that right now."

"I—"

She lifted her hand to cover his lips, smoothing her thumb over his mouth gently. "I have listened to you talk about your responsibility in this matter over and over during the two weeks we've been together, Lucas. And I've said it to you before, but I want you to truly hear it now: my father made his own choices."

"And if I—"

"Stop!" she insisted. "Please. If you hadn't, if he hadn't, if I hadn't…there are a thousand other things that might have happened to us if we'd turned left instead of right or gone somewhere a moment later or sooner. You'll drive yourself mad if you live in a world of possibility instead of facing what actually happened. He chose to help you. He died. And I hate that. I hate it." She realized tears were beginning to collect in her eyes and she blinked fiercely to clear them away. "I hate that he is gone. But I'm coming to terms with it. So should you."

He stared at her for a long moment. Long enough that she shifted with discomfort at his focus, especially when she had no idea what the thoughts in his head were. She had been harsh with him, pointed. He might turn her away now that he was settling back into the role of duke who did not have to take that from anyone below him.

But at last he reached out and touched her face. "You are a far better person than I could ever be, Diana Oakford. I am lucky to know you."

She drew in a breath at that unexpected compliment and the warmth that rushed through her. He could set her aflutter with just a few words, a look, a touch. He could make her feel like she belonged even though she didn't, couldn't, wouldn't ever belong in his world. *Any* world that he inhabited, duke or spy or both.

"Come inside with me," he whispered.

The roughness in his voice was undeniable. The way he looked at her was even more so. The emotions of the day began to slide away, replaced by something warm and dark and wicked and passionate. Something she wanted to ease her pain and to ease his.

"Come inside," he repeated. "But only if you wish."

"Are you going to touch me if I do?" she asked, feeling her cheeks darken with color as she did so.

He nodded slowly. "Oh yes, I'm going to touch you, Diana. Because I need you. And I want you. And I think what we both need right now is to forget. Will you help me forget?"

He held out his hand and she took it without hesitation. "Yes," she whispered.

CHAPTER 14

Diana looked down at Lucas's hand, his fingers threaded through hers, and shivered as he opened the door to his chamber. He led her inside and watched as she pulled away from him.

"When I came in earlier, I was so embarrassed by the knowing expressions of the servants that I didn't look around," she said as she did just that.

Lucas shut the door behind himself and leaned against it. "You came in earlier?" he asked.

She nodded as she glanced at him. "Yes. I-I didn't realize our rooms were connected."

He arched a brow. "That is one of the finest benefits of your pretending to be my mistress. I asked for us to be put in adjoining rooms. So what do you think of the chamber?"

She shrugged. "It is fine, of course. But it isn't really...*you*, is it? It's so stuffy and formal and...and..."

"Blue," he said, looking around and at the cornflower explosion that surrounded them. "It's very blue. And no, it is not me. But none of this house truly is. My mother decorated it after her marriage to my father. She likes frippery."

She frowned at the mention of his mother, her mind turning to that horrible scene in the foyer once more. She'd never seen a parent so cruel to their own child. She had to wonder what had caused it.

He smiled slightly, but the expression was laced with sadness. "Please don't ask me about her," he whispered. "Not now."

She shook her head slowly. "I won't. Right now I want this…"

She trailed off as she moved to him, cupping his cheeks as she leaned up into him and pressed her lips to his. His arms came around her, pulling her up tightly against his chest. She melted at the warmth of him drawing her closer. Drawing her in, making her safe and whole.

He angled his head, slanting his mouth against hers, driving his tongue inside, tasting her and emptying her mind of every thought except for getting him into that bed.

She dropped her hands to his jacket and swiftly unfastened it. When he shrugged it off, she smiled, for the expression of pain that always accompanied the action was far weaker. He was healing and that made her heart soar.

But it was her body that took over when he slid his hands into her hair, his fingers bunching against her scalp as he threaded down the bun she had hurriedly made that morning. Hairpins scattered around their feet and she shivered at the intimate touch that was so innocent and so wicked all at once.

"I love your hair," he murmured, pressing his face into the locks. "I love the look and the smell, I love how it feels on my skin. Like silk."

She blushed and caught his hand, leading him back across the impossibly huge room toward the even more impossibly big bed on the back wall. He smiled, indulging her lead in this moment, though she saw in his eyes that he had no intention of letting her control continue.

She looked forward to the moment when he stole it from her at last.

As they reached the bed, he began to unbutton her gown. He did it slowly, holding her gaze as he looped each button through its hole and then gently parted the coarse fabric of her plain gown. His fingers brushed her collarbone, her chest, as he did so and she couldn't hold back a small sigh of pleasure at the feel of skin on skin.

It had only been one night apart, but it had felt like an eternity. And *this* was coming home.

He pushed the dress from her shoulders and down her arms, then stood back and looked at her. His eyes were wide, like he'd never seen her like this before. She blushed beneath the attention, turning her face away so that he wouldn't see how much his regard moved her. Changed her. Made her want more than would ever be possible for her in this life.

"I am forever struck by you," he said softly as he hooked his thumbs through the drooping fabric of her gown and pushed it away, leaving her in only her chemise. "Struck by how perfect you are in every way."

She shook her head. "Not perfect, I assure you."

"There is nothing but perfection here, Diana," he whispered, cupping her chin and tilting her face toward his. His eyes were dark and intense, dilated with desire, but also focused in that heavy expression that he only had when he was focusing on something he wanted.

Today it was her.

She lifted on her tiptoes and pressed her mouth to his. Words fell away then. His slow seduction ended and the kiss deepened with a sudden urgency and intensity. Want took over, need ruled, and she shivered as he stripped away her underthings with much more quickness and purpose than he had used on her gown.

"Get in my bed," he ordered, suddenly the lord of the manor, suddenly the duke.

There was no denying that order, for it *was* an order, not a request. She took her place on his pillows and watched through a hooded gaze as he undressed himself. It took longer than she thought he wanted it to, but he did it on his own and finally stood before her naked.

She stared as she always did. He was a specimen, that was something no one could deny. From his broad shoulders, marred by that terrible, misshapen, raised scar that was slowly healing, to his narrow hips to his strong thighs, scarred again by the horrors he'd been through. He was as perfect as he'd claimed she was. Perfect and delectable.

She wanted to taste him.

He smiled as she crooked her finger and beckoned him over. He took a place beside her and she immediately rolled over to cover him. He arched a brow. "You think you can control this?" he teased.

She reached between them and stroked his already hard cock. "I know I can."

He shut his eyes and arched against her as she continued to stroke him. Over and over, gentle but firm. And as she did so, she slid down his length until she could lower her mouth and take him inside.

His eyes flew open and she met his wild gaze without hesitation as she sucked him.

"Diana," he gasped, his hands coming down to her. She thought he might push her away, but as she took him deeper his fingers tangled in her hair instead and he let out a low, long curse.

She smiled against him and began to pump her mouth slowly, reveling in the hardness of his cock against her tongue. In the taste of him, the smell of him. The way his hips flexed against her, pushing himself farther into her throat. She added her hand to the torment, stroking the part of him she could not manage with her mouth as she began to establish a rhythm that would bring him to completion.

She wanted that. To taste that moment when she stole his control and claimed him in a way that could not be changed or forgotten, even when they were no longer together. She moved toward it with an increasing drive and felt him start to tense with the movements of her hand and mouth. His legs stiffened beneath her, his feet flexing as she sped up, rolling her tongue around his girth with every downward stroke.

He was close to release and she found herself grinding against the bed as she took him, her body set on fire by the power he was allowing her. By the feel of pleasuring him. By the taste of his body as he got closer and closer to completion.

"Diana, I can't...I'll—" he stammered, his fingers moving to push her away.

She ignored them, sucking harder and faster instead, and he let out a heavy cry before he exploded. She took every thrust, greedy in her desire for his salty-sweet taste. And only when he flopped back, his breath hard and uneven, did she allow him to pull free.

She smiled at him, spent with pleasure. Her own body still hummed with throbbing, wet desire, but seeing him brought to his knees was oh-so very worth it.

She moved to lie beside him and his eyes came open. "Oh, you think you're finished, do you?" he asked, his tone utterly wicked.

She cocked her head. "I think I finished you, Your Grace."

"Not by half," he said, and caught her arms. He drew her up as he inched down until he lay flat on the bed. She expected him to pull her to a kiss, but he didn't. He moved her farther up his body, until she straddled his chest.

"What would I..." she whispered, understanding at last. "Won't I crush you?"

"Oh, what a way to go," he drawled, and tugged her farther until she was positioned over his waiting mouth. She gripped his headboard with both hands and gasped as he parted her folds and licked her gently. Then not so gently.

She ground down, riding his tongue, finding pleasure with every taste, every stroke, every moment that proved he knew her body and what it wanted and needed. The fact that he did made it easier for her to let go. To let him, and when she did, the pleasure that had begun to build the moment he pressed his tongue to her exploded and she convulsed over him, jerking as she clung to the headboard and moaned his name over and over.

Finally she collapsed to the side, rolling into him, feeling his arms come around her as she continued to feel the ripples of sensation fading through her entire body.

He said nothing, at least at first. Instead he just combed his fingers through her hair, a gentle, rhythmic motion that helped her slowly come down from those heights of release he inspired every time he touched her.

She had no idea how much time had passed when she propped herself up on her elbow and looked into his handsome face. "You're doing so much better, Lucas."

A shadow of a smile crossed his face. "Judging my performance, and with such...enthusiasm," he teased. "Makes me think I have to prove myself to you again."

She laughed and swatted his chest lightly. "It was not a judgment of your performance," she said. "I meant that I can see how much more easily you are moving, how much less pain reflects on your face with some actions you take."

He shrugged his good shoulder. "I know you're right. I cannot say that I am not still frustrated by what I cannot do. I do see that there is more and more that I can. But it is hard not to...not to be the man I once was. Not to know if I ever could be again."

She nodded and reached out to trace his jawline with her fingertip. "I can only imagine how difficult that is."

"But my recovery is due entirely to you," he said.

Heat flooded her cheeks and she turned her face. "I don't think entirely."

"Well, I take full responsibility for *your* recovery," he said.

She glanced back at him. "My recovery? What are you talking about?"

"You burned yourself almost two weeks ago, and look." He caught her hand and lifted it up, showing that the little burn was long gone. "It is all thanks to me and my magnificent doctoring skills."

She couldn't help but laugh, though the fact that he had brought up the topic made her mind turn to that day in her kitchen and how he'd mixed the poultice she had required, then wrapped her sore hand. "I have actually thought of that day often," she said. "But not because of your superior skills."

"You wound me, madam," he said. "I hoped I had a future and you have dashed my hopes."

She shook her head. "You tease, but I'm certain if you applied yourself to study that you could become a good physician. A surgeon's duty is all about detail and you pay attention to those in spades. Which leads me to a question."

He nodded, and the teasing was gone from his demeanor. "Of course. What can I answer for you?"

"That day you tied the wrap on my hand in a very special way."

He nodded. "Yes. It was special."

"How did you learn that technique?" she asked.

A shadow crossed over his expression, and he leaned back on the pillows and stared at the ceiling for a moment, like he was gathering his thoughts. Like this answer was more complicated than she'd thought it would be.

"When I woke from my injuries, it was almost twenty-four hours after the attack," he explained slowly. "I wanted to get up and get to work, but when I tried I was crippled with pain and unable to bear even a little weight to stand."

She bent her head. "Of course you would try, despite nearly being killed."

"We are who we are, yes," he said with a wry smile. "The surgeon insisted that I could not rise, and for a month I didn't."

"It must have been so frustrating for you," she said softly. This man, this vibrant, exasperating, active man would not have handled being confined to a bed. She could only picture how terribly he must have behaved.

"I thought I might run mad," he admitted. "They kept trying to give me things to entertain me, but I was half wild with laudanum and God knows what else. And all I could think about was that day. Your father. The sound of shots cutting through the air."

He stopped, and she reached out to cover his hand with hers. "And the knot?" she encouraged, steering him back on course with as much gentleness as she could muster.

He shook his head. "Of course, I'm sorry. That first day, when they changed my bloody bandage, they left it there next to my bed. All I could do was stare at that knot. It was...intricate. So I began to practice tying it, over and over. Until I could master it."

She pressed her lips together and tried not to let her thoughts run away from her. It was almost impossible when this information led to more questions than answers.

"Your surgeon, was he trained by my father?" she asked.

Lucas sat up slightly. The lazy sensuality that had flowed through them before was now gone. He was focused again, looking at her with sharp, hawkish interest.

"No," he said slowly. "Not that first one. He was your father's contemporary, but not his student. Yates, I think his name was."

Diana made a face, for she knew the man. "You are lucky he didn't kill you. My father thought very little of him. But how would he know?"

"Know what?" He leaned in. "What has brought this interrogation on?"

"The knot," she explained. "It's likely nothing, but I've only ever seen my father tie it. It was a bit of a...signature for him, if that makes sense. Even I had a hard time learning it, for it is, as you say, intricate. But you tied it with ease. I just wondered how you came to know it. Still, I suppose Yates might have picked up the practice from my father."

Lucas continued to stare at her. His eyes were a little wide, his jaw set. There was the spy again. Her lover was gone.

"Yates didn't tie the knot I learned from," he said softly. "The injury to my leg, it was deep."

"Yes," she said with a shiver. "It's evident from the scarring and your remaining limp. It healed beautifully, though, unlike the shoulder that the doctors could not leave alone."

He nodded. "That's because when they found me, my leg had already been bandaged. It's been a bone of contention on how that happened. Perhaps the first men to arrive did the bandaging, perhaps it was someone else. But the knot I learned from was on my leg before a surgeon ever examined my injuries, Diana."

Her lips parted and she drew back. "But if that's true…"

"Then whoever did it knew the special and advanced techniques used by your father to treat the injured." He climbed out of the bed and paced across the room before he turned back and speared her with a stare. "Whoever did it once trained under him."

CHAPTER 15

The color had gone out of Diana's cheeks as she stared at him from his bed. The hand that held a sheet over her body shook as she processed what Lucas had just told her.

In truth, he was having trouble processing it, himself. The bandaged leg had been an unanswered question from that day, of course. But it had been chalked up to something that had happened in the chaos of that horrible afternoon. Something a kind servant might have done, or a fellow spy when they came upon him after the guard had been called in.

Now, though, this new information slid into the puzzle of his mind and fit in to a blank space. Only it created more questions than answers.

Answers Diana had begun to provide in unexpected moments.

"How or why would someone know my father's methods?" she pressed. Her voice was shaking.

"A very good question," Lucas said. "He did have acolytes. Trainees. But if one of them was there, then it would mean…"

Her lips parted. "That they were the traitor?" she burst out.

He shrugged. "It's a possibility. One I hadn't considered. Only, if they were the one who attacked your father and me, why would that person then bandage my leg? It saved my life, I've been told that multiple times in the past six months. Why would the man who attacked me want to *save* me?"

He asked the question and the moment he did, an answer came to mind. A terrible, horrible answer that he'd never even considered until that moment.

An answer that had nothing to do with anyone else in the world but Diana's father. Only he couldn't believe that George Oakford would be involved in the attacks on the War Department.

Not Lucas's friend. Not Diana's father.

"What is it?" she whispered, her bright green gaze snagging his. "Please tell me why your expression is like that."

He stared at her. She had already gone through so much. Lost so much. He couldn't tell her about this niggling feeling that now took root in his chest. He refused to do that to her.

Not until he knew for sure that he was right.

"I've shut you out," he said softly. "I know that hurt you."

She folded her arms now and he saw a lonely flash of anger across her lovely features. "I do understand it on some level, even if I hate it," she said.

"What if I didn't shut you out?" he asked just as softly. "What if I...what if I needed your help? Would you be willing to provide it?"

She opened her mouth, and he saw the emphatic *yes* in her eyes even before she spoke. Still, he raised a hand to hold off her answer. "Before you reply, you must know that you'll get details, Diana. Information that may greatly pain you."

She lifted her chin, and that core of iron that ran through her had never been so obvious. "I have felt pain greater than you can imagine," she whispered. "I can face it again, especially if it means finding the truth and bringing whoever did this to you, did this to my father, to justice. If you think I can help, then let me."

He nodded slowly. "Let's get dressed then. The full case notes are in my study. We'll go over them together."

. . .

D arkness had begun to flood into Lucas's study, and Diana looked up to find him lighting lanterns and stirring the fire to make her reading easier. In his chamber back in her cottage, she hadn't gotten to read quite so much of his materials. Now she'd read them all and her chest hurt as she shoved the papers aside and drew a ragged breath.

"I'm sorry," Lucas said as he sat in a chair beside hers. He was studying her face closely. "Is it too much?"

"No," she said, though in her heart she didn't completely feel that it was true. "Yes, it's hard to read these things. To picture my father lying dead, cut down by an assassin's bullet, likely fired by a friend to you both. But it isn't only that. It's the high emotion of the past few days. It's the time of year..."

Lucas tilted his head. "The time of year?"

She pushed to her feet and paced away. She had not meant to say that out loud. Something in him brought it out in her, though. Something that told her to whisper her darkest and most painful secrets.

Even though he gave nothing back in return.

She pushed her shoulders back at that self-reminder and faced him. "It's nothing. Have you ever created a timeline for the events leading up to that day, the day itself and after?"

He nodded. "Certainly, but it never hurts to do it again. I can write it down if you'd like to give me your impressions."

He pushed from the chair and moved to the desk, where he pulled out parchment and laid it out across the width of the desk. He dipped his quill into the ink and looked at her in expectation.

"When were there first suspicions that a traitor was in your midst?" she asked. "The papers were not clear on that."

"Three years ago," he said, scribbling down the date at the far end of the paper. "Some information went missing and our enemies had it. It was obvious it had been stolen, sold."

"And there had been nothing before that?" she asked.

He shrugged. "A few minor incidents here and there, but nothing too suspicious. We do not think our traitor was in action for more than a month or two before the first large incident."

"You say minor incidents. I assume it wasn't obvious at first that you were dealing with a traitor?" she asked.

A shadow drew down over Lucas's face. "You do ask the right questions. No. We recognized strange things were happening here and there, but it took us about six months to determine that we had a traitor in our ranks. The information stolen could have been taken by someone outside our universe. Infiltration from outside, rather than a turn from within. Even when the truth became clear, there were multiple agents working on multiple angles of the case. No one was working well together. That's why, two years ago, I was put in charge of the entire operation and took over regarding everything to do with our traitor."

He was adding dates to the timeline, and Diana moved to stand beside him and look at it. Her stomach turned. Here was the beginning of the end for her father. For herself. The point where a boulder had been positioned at the top of a very high hill and begun to roll out of control toward her life.

She could see it now. She could not stop it. It was horrifying to see it laid out as such, and she shivered as she paced away from Lucas. He caught her hand as she did so and drew her back. He was looking up at her from his seat, his dark eyes filled with understanding and empathy.

"Is it too much?" he asked.

She reached down and traced his cheek with her fingertip. His pupils dilated, but he didn't draw her closer. "No," she whispered. "Well, yes, but not too much to stop. It's just hard to see the path of destruction that led to my father's death. To your injuries."

He released her hand as he looked at the growing list of dates and events. "Yes. It's always been difficult for me to see it like this. To wonder what I could have done to stop it all."

She pressed a finger at the first date on the timeline and shook her head. "Only this man could have stopped it all," she said. "Only *he* could have turned back to the right path and kept that terrible day from happening."

He nodded slowly but his expression was incredulous. Like he understood but did not believe.

"Let's carry on," she suggested, moving away from him. "Were there any big moments in your case once you took over?"

"Yes." He shuffled papers around on his desk and then motioned to the one before him. "We look for patterns in cases, you see. And the first one I found in this case was here, right after I took over."

She looked at the paper he indicated and caught her breath. "The cases that led to shared information with enemies, the things that the traitor did, all came after cases were taken over by other agents."

"Every case was one where one agent had taken over from another. Now, the agents who came off cases and the ones that took over, there's no pattern there that I can find. Different men. But somehow our traitor was aware of the transition and used it to his advantage."

Diana glanced over at him. His face was lit up in the same expression she could feel her on her own. She smiled gently at him. "I can see why this is so thrilling to you. For the first time I understand it a little better."

He wrinkled his brow. "Well, there are times it is exciting, certainly. Finding a pattern like this one is a thrill unlike any other. Moving forward in an investigation and knowing you're one step closer to uncovering the truth, it's..."

"Intoxicating," she whispered.

He nodded. "Yes, that's the word for it. There is no other drink or drug or vice that I've found that feeds my soul like this one."

"It did the same for my father," she whispered as she traced her finger along the length of their timeline.

Lucas was quiet for a beat, and then he said, "Did he tell you much about what he did for the department?"

"He was a surgeon, of course. It's all I thought he did until he showed up with...with that man two years ago. It was obvious there was more to it. So I don't know, perhaps Stalwood put his mind in use when his hands were not."

Lucas looked away, and something in her heart dropped at the unexpected expression on his face. Like he had something to hide.

"What?" she asked.

He shrugged his good shoulder. "I never knew him to be assigned to cases. Stalwood said he didn't, either. It surprises me, is all, that he would...would be working on something neither of us knew."

Diana stared at him. There was a cautiousness in his demeanor now. She didn't like it. "You live in a world of secrets. I'm frankly shocked that you think you know them all."

"You're right, of course," he said after a long hesitation. "But—"

He didn't get to finish whatever thought was in his head. At that moment, there was a light knock on the door and then Jones put his head into the room.

"Your Grace, you have received a missive. You said you wanted it the moment it arrived."

Diana watched as all of Lucas's confident bravado faded, replaced by an almost boyish nervousness. He rose from the desk and crossed to his butler. Jones held out a folded sheet and Lucas took it, his hands shaking slightly. "Thank you, Jones. We will come in for supper shortly if Mrs. Cox is ready for us."

Jones inclined his head. "She will be within the half hour, Your Grace. Is there anything else you need?"

"No," Lucas said, still staring at the letter in his hand. "That will be all."

Diana shifted as the butler shot her a look, that same judgmental one he'd given her every time he saw her, then left the room. Once he was gone, she shoved her discomfort aside and focused on Lucas. "What is that?" she asked, taking a cautious step toward him.

He jerked his head up, like he'd forgotten she was there. "I-it's from the friend I wrote to today. Simon Greene, Duke of Crestwood. I didn't expect for him to respond so swiftly, but this is his hand. I would recognize it anywhere."

He made no move to do anything else, and Diana now took the remaining steps toward him. "Are you going to open it?"

He glanced at her again. "In truth, I am…I'm afraid to do so."

She drew back at the unexpected honesty of that response. There was an intimacy required for a man like Lucas to admit he was afraid to anyone, but certainly to her. She longed for more of it, for that connection she had been seeking all her life and yet knew was foolish to look for in him.

"Because you pushed them away for so long?" she asked, her throat suddenly dry.

He turned the letter over and over in his hands. "Yes. It wasn't always like that. I was the youngest of the group, some would say the most sober. But it never kept me from being included, cajoled, loved equally."

She smiled at the description. "That sounds lovely, to have such friends as that."

He swallowed hard, and she thought she saw a faint glimmer of tears in his eyes before he blinked them away. "It was. But it changed."

"How?"

He shifted, and for a long moment he was silent, fighting a battle within about what to say. She prayed she would win that battle. Win a glimpse into the truth of him.

"It started…oh, it started a long time ago," he choked out, his voice thick. "I was sixteen. Something happened."

"Something?" she pressed, wishing with all her heart that he could find a way to confide in her. He knew so much about her and she knew…nothing.

He shut his eyes, and pain flowed over his face like a waterfall. And then it was gone. Tucked away because he was a spy and capable of masking anything important.

"It isn't important what. It changed me, that is all. I started to push away from everyone then. My family, my friends, everyone. When I was eighteen, my father died. Instead of taking over my title, I enlisted in the military as an officer."

She lifted her brows in surprise. "A rare thing for a man of your station."

"My family was furious. I was the duke, damn it. I was not meant to risk my life and line for king and country." He shook his head with a derisive snort. "I didn't listen. Within two years I'd started at the War Department. I wrote to a few of my friends, but every year it was less often. Every year I pushed further. And now...well, I haven't written to anyone since at least a month before the attack."

She nodded slowly. She didn't understand the particulars of what had sent Lucas away from everyone he loved and that still troubled her. But she did perfectly understand the utter pain he clearly felt at the action. The loss and the grief at having no one.

That she understood perfectly.

"The distance cannot have meant as much as you think," she said softly. "Your friend has written to you now, an almost immediate reply. Surely that means something."

He stared at the letter once more and still didn't open it. "I fear it will tell me to sod off," he admitted. "I'd deserve no less."

She reached out and wrapped her fingers around his. She felt the warmth of his skin and the crunch of the paper, she felt the slight tremble of his hands. "I could look," she suggested gently.

He looked at her, holding her gaze for a moment, two moments, an eternity. Then he released the pages into her care and nodded silently.

She leaned up and kissed his cheek, then broke the seal on the back of the pages and opened the letter. It was two pages long, and she scanned the first page briefly before she smiled and began to read it out loud.

"*Willowby,*" she began, and Lucas flinched as he always did when someone used his title. She thought this time was also about his friend, his fear. Swiftly she continued, *"You do not know how long I have waited to hear from you, or how much fear our group as a whole has felt since you stopped writing months ago. To know that you are well and in London brings a joy to my heart that is only surpassed by recent happinesses in my own life, of which I long to share with you."*

With every word she read, she watched the tension bleed from Lucas's shoulders, the fear leave his face, replaced by relief and joy. She watched every twitch and change, reveling in seeing the hardness go out of him, replaced by something gentler. Younger. Something untouched by whatever had changed him that he refused to share.

"Shall I go on?" she asked. "Or would you like to read the rest yourself?"

He held out a hand and she passed the letter over. He read over it and let out a long sigh before he read it a second time. Like the first was not to be trusted. Like he wanted to be certain it wasn't a dream or a fantasy that his friend still cared.

"They are coming tomorrow," he said at last.

She blinked. She had not read that far in the letter herself. "They?"

"Yes. Simon, his wife Meg and another of our friends, Matthew. He's the Duke of Tyndale and was apparently visiting them when the letter arrived. They'll be here for tea in the afternoon."

"I-I should not be here for that," she stammered.

He stared at her. "Not be here?" he repeated, like she had spoken some foreign language. "Why in the world would you not be here?"

She wrung her hands and moved away from him. "I-I am not fit to meet two dukes and a duchess. Not before our arrangement, certainly not since I am being labeled as your mistress."

"Why would they care about that?" he asked.

She spun toward him and threw up her hands. "Don't be obtuse, Lucas, it is beneath your intellect. Your servants look at me like I am a whore. What would a duchess think?"

Lucas's jaw set. "If my servants dare to be rude to you, I will sack them at once. As for the duchess in question, I've known Meg nearly all my life. She has never been anything but kind, generous and accepting. At any rate, she'd be a hypocrite if she had anything to say about the matter. I may no longer be directly informed about the details of my friend's lives, but I hear enough. She and Simon were embroiled in a terrible scandal not a year ago. She would never dare to judge someone else."

Diana shook her head. Those words sounded lovely, but she knew they were likely untrue. Ladies could be cruel to one another. "I don't know," she whispered as she looked down at herself in her plain, serviceable gown. "She cannot like me."

"If she does not like you, I will give you a hundred pounds," Lucas laughed. "That is not Meg."

She paced away, still uncertain. Still emotional thanks to the difficulties of the past few days, thanks to the anniversary about to come, the one she kept trying to push away, though she couldn't fully do it.

"You are certain I should not just go...go home?" she suggested. "I could come back in a few days and give you privacy with your friends."

He moved to her, turning her gently before he took both her hands. "I would like you to be here," he said, holding her gaze. "Please stay with me."

It was the "please" that hit her in the gut, made all her arguments vanish on the wind. She slowly nodded. "Very well. If that is what you need, it would hardly do to withhold my presence."

He cupped her cheek. "Excellent. Now..." He drew her closer, molding her body to his as his arms folded around her. Her heart began to race, as it always did with him. "There is something else I require. And I think you require it too. Will you come upstairs with me?"

She hesitated for a moment, not because she didn't want what he was asking for, but because she did so very much. She had become addicted to him. To his touch, his taste, his comfort. And she knew how dangerous that was.

Yet she didn't resist him. She just pushed away her fear and her heart and let him take her upstairs where she knew she would feel nothing but pleasure once more.

CHAPTER 16

Diana stood before Lucas the next morning, staring in astonishment over what he had just requested. She blinked.

"Cut your hair," she repeated. "And shave you."

He nodded slowly. "Yes. I cannot quite meet my friends looking like a pirate, can I?"

She reached out, swirling one of his curly locks around her fingertip. "I'd rather miss the pirate, I admit."

A grin flashed over his features, and her knees went a bit weak. "A pirate is made up by deeds, lass," he said with a wink. "I promise I will never stop…plundering…"

She shook her head at the lewd tone of his voice and how her body reacted with both desire and a comfortable connection. Damn the man for making everything so…easy.

"You're a cad," she said with a chuckle, then swept up the scissors from the table where the servants had set them and began to examine his locks. She'd cut her father's hair over the years, so she was not unaccustomed to the act, but her father's hair had never been a fall of coarse curls.

"You can't be angry at me if I make a muck of it," she said, then snipped the scissors for the first cut.

He caught the lock as it fell and held it up. "A trophy, my lady."

She laughed as she took the piece of hair and shoved it into her pelisse pocket. Then she focused her attention on the job at hand. With a deep breath, she began to cut. At first, it was all businesslike, but as his hair grew shorter, she slid her hands against his scalp to shape it.

"Mmm," he said, nuzzling her forearm as she moved around him. "I would have asked you to do this ages ago if I'd known."

"You are distracting me and shall end up all lopsided if you keep that up," she said, but her breath was short.

"It might be worth it," he said, pressing a kiss to her arm and then winking up at her.

She tried to ignore him and at last stood back and stared at her handiwork.

"Mirror?" he asked.

She shook her head. "No, not until we're finished." She picked up a towel from the steaming hot bowl of water that had also been brought in. She squeezed some of the liquid out and gently wrapped his face. As they waited for his whiskers to soften and his pores to open, she examined the man before her.

She was transforming him back to the man he was before. Perhaps back to the life he had abandoned all those years ago. A man couldn't be a spy forever, especially when he had a dukedom to attend to. And with his injuries, a life in the field might never be possible again.

So he would go back to being His Grace. He would, eventually, take up those responsibilities. One of them would be to marry a lady of breeding, one who came from wealth and a titled family. He would create a family with her.

She blinked at the wayward path of her thoughts. None of those things were her concern, of course. She and Lucas had been clear from the beginning that an affair was all this could ever be. That he was not thinking of a future with her. That she could not think of one with him.

"Ready?" she asked, her tone falsely bright as she unwrapped the steaming cloth and set it aside.

She lathered his face gently, memorizing the angles of his jaw and the feel of his ragged whiskers. Remembering how they had brushed her skin so many times. She liked the intimacy of the act more than she should. He had to trust her with the straight razor in her hand. He seemed to do it effortlessly, as he kept his eyes shut even when she first scraped the blade over his skin.

She focused once more on her work, a godsend when her mind wanted to take her to such troubling places. Bit by bit, she smoothed away all the whiskers, trimmed his sideburns, and then set the razor aside and wiped his face and neck clean of all the little hairs that had fallen there during her duty.

She stepped back and couldn't help but gasp. He was almost another person, this freshly coifed and shaved man before her. But utterly handsome, utterly perfect.

"It can't be so bad as all that," he said, and held a hand out for the mirror.

She gave it over at last with a shake of her head. "Not bad at all. You are very handsome. You are...you're a duke."

His gaze flitted up to her. "No, I'm not," he whispered as he set the mirror aside and reached for her hand. She gasped as he gently tugged her into his lap. He nuzzled her neck with his freshly smooth cheek, and she shivered with renewed pleasure.

She turned her face into his and kissed him. His hand came up, fingers gliding along her neck, against the base of her skull as he angled her head for better access. The kiss deepened and she felt the swell of his cock begin to press against her thigh.

She drew back and smiled. "That won't do," she said.

He arched a brow at her teasing tone. "No, not at all," he agreed with a false earnestness. "Not when we have company coming. What should we do about it, do you think?"

She laughed and was once again struck by how easy this all was.

Too easy. And yet she reveled in it. Reveled in the pleasure of it and of him.

She slid her hand between them and kept her gaze focused on his as she wiggled her hand past the fold of his dressing gown. She pushed the fabric aside and glanced at what she'd revealed. His cock, hard and proud, curling up now that it was no longer confined by silky fabric.

She wrapped her hand around it, sliding her fingers up and down the length as he sucked in his breath through his teeth.

"That wasn't exactly what I had in mind," he ground out. "Not that I'm complaining."

"We have no time for anything else," she whispered as she pressed light kisses along his now-smooth jawline. "Not if you want to actually be dressed when your friends arrive."

He dipped his head back with a moan. Already he lifted into her palm, grinding against her. "Being dressed is overrated. I could come down in my dressing gown."

She pumped faster. "I don't think *that's* a good idea. Besides, this is far too pleasurable for me."

"Is it?" He let out a garbled curse. "How so? It seems you're not getting much out of it at all."

"No?" She leaned back and stared at him, tightening her grip, watching as his cheek twitched. "Right now you're on the edge of control and *I* put you there. If you don't think that holding that little bit of power over you isn't pleasurable, then...well, you're wrong. I want to see you lose your grip on that control, Lucas." She leaned in and gently sucked the column of his neck. "Now, please."

He made a rumbling cry from deep within his chest, and then she felt the ripple through his cock just before he came. She continued to pump him gently until he went limp in the chair. Only then did she wrap her arms around him and press a deep kiss against his lips.

He sighed as she pulled away, and said, "Christ, if someone

wanted to kill me, they ought to just send you. But I'd die a happy man."

She shook her head and slowly got up from his lap. "You shouldn't even tease about such things, considering."

He straightened a fraction and nodded. "I'm sorry. You're right. I didn't mean to make light of something so close to the truth. Blame it on an addled mind."

"Addled by…"

"You," he finished with a flash of a grin. She shivered. God, but he was even more handsome all pulled together as he was now. She'd have thought that impossible.

"So you blame me," she said, stepping away. The distance might help with her attraction. Another lie to tell herself.

He shrugged. "If the very skilled hands fit." He tilted his head and his smile fell. His gaze grew heated and heavy. "Don't think for a moment I don't realize I now owe you something just as spectacular after that."

She swallowed hard. "I didn't realize we were keeping score."

"When it comes to pleasure for pleasure…always." He winked.

She bent her head. "I look forward to it. Now, shall I call for your valet, or would you like me to help you dress?"

"You are my very favorite valet, Miss Oakford, I think you know that. But given the circumstances, I think it might be best to ring."

"The circumstances?"

He caught her hand and drew her close, pressing his mouth hard to hers. She wound her arms around his neck and melted against him. It was habit now, something she didn't even think of. He touched her, she was his.

"That if you touch me again, I don't think we'll make it downstairs to meet my friends," he growled against her lips. He gently turned her and then swatted her behind. "Now go before I change my mind."

She laughed as she left him, but after she'd gone into the

adjoining room and closed the door behind herself, she leaned back against it with a sigh. The connection she felt to this man was growing with every second she spent with him.

And she knew full well that she needed to sever it. Sooner rather than later if she wanted to maintain her sanity and her heart.

Lucas shifted as he stood at the window in his study, staring out at the gardens behind the estate. The tick of the clock on the mantel sounded like a shotgun blast in his ears every time it counted another second. One more tick closer to the moment when his friends would be here.

And he'd have to face everything he'd done to push them so far away.

Suddenly he felt Diana's hand slide into his own. He turned to find her staring up at him, understanding on her face. Empathy. God, but he wanted to lean into that. To take everything she offered until he could refill the emptiness inside of himself.

Only he didn't think he was capable of giving her anything in return. A fact that grew harder to take with every passing day he spent with her. He was using her. Using her to heal. Using her to find peace. Using her to investigate his case.

And her assistance was unearthing more and more questions he knew could possibly break her heart. He didn't want to do that.

"Don't be nervous," she whispered, and that calming tone seeped into him and reduced his anxiety.

There was a knock on the door, and he tensed as he turned to find Jones there, as expected. "The Duke and Duchess of Crestwood and the Duke of Tyndale are awaiting you in the purple parlor, as requested, Your Grace."

He nodded acknowledgment. "We will join them momentarily, Jones. There is no need for you to announce us."

The butler's lips pinched, but he bobbed out his own nod. "Certainly. There should be tea and biscuits being delivered there as we speak."

He left then, and Lucas managed to draw a full breath before he smiled down at Diana. "Here we go."

She slid her hand into the crook of his arm and let him guide her from the room. They walked down the hallway together, and there was a part of him that felt like he was being led to the gallows. Why, he could not say. He loved all three of the people in that room waiting for him.

But he had not shown his love very well. And despite Simon's kind letter, he still feared what he would find when he opened the door to his mother's hideous purple parlor.

They reached that door, and as he extended a hand, Diana squeezed his arm. "Don't expect the worst."

He nodded, but couldn't stop himself from doing just that as he pushed the door open. His breath caught as he entered the parlor.

Simon, Duke of Crestwood, and Matthew, Duke of Tyndale, stood together by his fire, examining one of his mother's horrible little miniature horse statues that she loved so well. Meg was at the sideboard, pouring tea. They looked…the same. And so different. He could see all the time that had passed since he last let himself near them.

It had only been a moment. And it had been years.

"Great God, he's here in the flesh," Simon said as he turned from the fireplace and made a straight line right to Lucas. Diana released him and Lucas found himself yanked into a strong embrace from one of his best friends. Simon pounded him on the back as he whispered, "You have been more missed than you could ever realize."

Lucas's knees almost went weak at that statement, and at the realization of how missed his friends had been too. He'd tried to pretend that wasn't true. That he could manage on his own, *deserved* to be on his own, but now he felt the lie of it.

Simon drew back and Matthew reached out to shake Lucas's

hand. He felt Matthew's careful gaze searching his face and finding the pain he tried to hide. Matthew had experienced so much of his own that there was no doubt he knew it when he saw it. "You look a fright."

Lucas couldn't help but laugh at the greeting, one the group had always reserved for each other when they'd been apart for more than a few weeks.

Meg had stood by while the men made their greetings, but now she stepped up and took both his hands. Lucas smiled at her, for he saw so much of her brother James, the leader of their group, in her. He also saw the unmistakable swell of her belly now that she faced him, and his gaze shot to Simon. He beamed and nodded slightly.

"Don't listen to them," she said with a laugh as she bussed his cheek. "Oh my, it is so good to see you. You don't know how difficult it was not to have an entire gaggle of dukes come raining down on your home when the group heard of your return. Simon insisted we not overwhelm you all at once."

Lucas couldn't help but picture that, all his friends here, like no time had passed. Like nothing had changed, even though half of them were married now and none of them knew the truth about him.

He shook off the thought and stepped back to take Diana's arm. "May I present my...my friend, Diana Oakford. Diana, the Duke of Tyndale and the Duke and Duchess of Crestwood."

His friends all turned to her, and he felt her stiffen a fraction at their regard. He couldn't blame her. There was no doubt what they would assume she was...and quite correctly.

"So lovely to meet you," Meg said, stepping forward to take her hand. There was slight hesitation in her voice as she said, "Any friend of Lucas is a friend of ours."

"Thank you, Your Grace," Diana said, but though she smiled, Lucas could hear the tension in her voice, see the falseness of her expression.

He'd grown so accustomed to her utter confidence that this hesitation hit him in the gut. She was truly uncertain around his friends and he wanted her not to be, even though he doubted this kind of meeting would occur often.

Because this was temporary. Nothing more. Though that was getting harder to think.

"You know, Lucas, I recall this house having a wonderfully fine garden," Meg said.

"Oh, yes, it's so lovely," Diana agreed, and her enthusiasm was not forced with those words.

Meg smiled. "Perhaps Miss Oakford and I could take a turn there. It will give you gentlemen time to catch up."

Simon glanced at his wife and a world of understanding flowed between them. Diana looked at Lucas, and he wished it could be so easy with her. It was and it wasn't, for there were walls there that did not exist between Simon and Meg. They'd torn down those walls a year or more ago.

"I would like that," Diana said slowly.

"Excellent!" Meg said. "I hope you know a bit about flowers, for I am terrible when it comes to horticulture."

Diana laughed as they exited the room together. "I know a little, Your Grace."

When they were gone, Simon moved to shut the door behind them and then he turned to Lucas with a shake of his head. "I keep thinking I must pinch myself—you are truly standing in front of me. How long has it been?"

Lucas bent his head in shame. "Years, I'm afraid."

"And over six months since anyone in our circle had a letter," Matthew added as he sat down and sprawled his long legs out in front of himself. "We have taken bets on what kept you away, you know."

"If I told you, you would not believe me."

Simon arched a brow. "Perhaps that's true. Someone will eventually wheedle it out of you, you know. Now that you're back."

Lucas stiffened. When he wrote to Simon, he hadn't been thinking so far ahead as to consider himself "back". He'd been thinking about what he'd lost by walking away from his friends, of course. He'd been needing to spend time with people who understood him. He'd also hoped they could help him make this strange reentry into Society that was meant to help his case.

But being "back"? That felt...so very odd.

"Don't give us that look," Matthew said. "That you're thinking of running. Meg was right when she said it was nearly impossible to keep everyone from crashing down your door to see you. If they think you're going to bolt, you may be kidnapped and hogtied."

Lucas shook his head. "I would not want to see how that turned out. No, I'm not going to run. But I'm so behind on everything that has happened. Will you fill me in?"

Simon shot him a look, like he knew Lucas was avoiding subjects that needed to be broached. But he drew a breath and began talking. Lucas leaned back, reveling in the stories of the recent marriages of James, Simon, Graham, Ewan and Baldwin. His heart hurt when he realized how ill their friend Kit's father was. He laughed when he heard how Robert was up to his old ways, wondered along with his friends why Hugh was in such an ill humor and stared at Matthew, who hid his pain well. But not well enough that he couldn't see it, even years after the death of Matthew's fiancée.

There it all was, laid out before him, and he felt an ache that he had been so separate from it all.

"You have been busy since I left," he muttered as he pushed to his feet and paced to the window.

"You too," Simon said. "Considering the limp."

Lucas faced him. He'd thought he'd hidden that fairly well. His leg had not bothered him as much lately—he was getting stronger by the day.

"And then there's the girl," Matthew added, locking eyes with him. "Seems you've had your own adventures since we last saw you. I think more than any of us put together."

JESS MICHAELS

Lucas shook his head slowly. "I know I can trust you," he said. "I know that even if I haven't shown it as of late."

Simon exchanged a brief glance with Matthew before he said, "You can. And judging from the fact that you reached out after so long, it makes me think you need to. You need *us*. Why?"

Lucas ran a hand through his hair. It felt oddly short, and he shook out his fingers before he said, "I...I'm a spy."

There was silence in the room for a beat, two, and then Matthew got up suddenly and laughed. "I said it, didn't I? And everyone said, 'Don't be foolish, Tyndale.' But here he's admitted to it. Damn, why didn't I make a wager?"

Lucas stared at him. "You guessed?"

Matthew shrugged. "It's something that's been bandied about over the years as a reason one would separate himself from people who care for him, yes. And since you had been in service, since you were very secretive about leaving it...everything added up."

Simon nodded his agreement. "Yes, but it is one thing to joke about spies and another to know one. You aren't in jest, are you?"

"No." Lucas sighed and was shocked at how heavy a weight had been lifted from his shoulders through his confession. "I was recruited by the War Department during my time as an officer. And I...I loved it. I loved the investigating, I loved feeling like I was truly helping my country. Like I was...worth something."

Simon jerked his face toward Lucas. "You were always worth something."

Lucas walked away. He wasn't going to get into all his secrets. Not today. Not ever if he had anything to say about it. "Either way, that is where I've been these past few years. I didn't want to endanger anyone else with my life. But half a year ago, I was injured by a traitor to our cause. A spy turned...I don't know what to call him. Double agent?"

Matthew's eyes widened. "My God."

"I nearly died," he admitted softly. He'd tried to avoid those words whenever possible, avoid the fear that thinking them engen-

158

dered, but there it was. He had never felt he had much to live for, he'd always guessed he might die in the service of his country...but to truly face death? That was something very different.

Simon sank into the settee. "That's why you have the limp."

Lucas nodded. "Yes. A few weeks ago, I was turned over to...to Diana. Her father was a War Department surgeon, and he died the day I was attacked. She has some of his skill and every other physician had done nothing but make it worse."

"So she isn't your mistress," Matthew said.

Simon's lips turned up in a half grin. "Oh, I think she is. The spark between you is far too obvious."

Lucas bent his head. "I should not pursue whatever is between us. But you saw her. She is stunning and that is the least of her qualities. She is so very clever and challenging and has a deep strength and goodness that I could not match if I put every effort into the attempt."

Simon drew back. "Are you in love with her?"

Lucas froze at the question. At the reaction to the question that made his heart throb and the voice in his mind scream *yes!*

He pushed that voice away. Pushed that physical sensation away. Loving her? That was impossible, no matter how true it felt. No matter how much it made him dream of a life he had turned away from long ago.

"She is helping me," he said softly. "To heal and to investigate what happened to me that day."

"You're still investigating?" Matthew asked. "Despite the injuries?"

"I am. And she's had some keen insights that have helped me. And troubled me." He thought of the doubts that had begun to enter his mind about her father and pushed those away with all the other emotions he'd stifled since his friends arrived.

Matthew gripped his hands before him, and his frustration was clear. "What if we could help?"

Lucas shook his head. "No. I cannot say much about it. It's secret and it's dangerous. I won't expose any of you to such a risk. Especially considering how much you all have to lose now."

Simon stiffened, and Lucas could see he was thinking of Meg and the child she carried. From the protective hardness that came over his friend's face, Lucas had no doubt he would die to keep her safe if need be. He would not risk her or himself if he didn't have to.

A fact that relieved him greatly, for he didn't want to have to argue the point.

"So we cannot all become spies, as we dreamed as boys," Simon said. "But that doesn't answer the question of how you want our help."

Lucas sighed. "My superiors and I have come to the conclusion that this man, this traitor in our ranks, might be flushed out if he saw me return to Society. His fears of what I might remember could drive him to make mistakes. And drive him to reveal himself without meaning to do so."

Matthew pushed to his feet. "You want to be bait."

Lucas almost laughed. "That seems to be the consensus of everyone who hears the plan. Yes, I will be the bait in a trap that could bring a murderer to justice. But I have not been in Society for years. I wondered if you might be persuaded to help...reintroduce me?"

Simon and Matthew exchanged a look, and then Matthew shrugged. "I'm certain that could be arranged under one condition."

"What is that?" Lucas asked.

Simon folded his arms. "Once you're back in the flock, you won't leave again. No more running. Not from your friends. Not from whatever pushed you away from your future in the first place."

Lucas sucked in a breath. There was no running from what had dragged him away from his future. He'd tried and never fully succeeded.

"Perhaps it's...time to face it all," he admitted slowly. "And I promise you, these invitations would not endanger anyone. Just put me in the public eye where I could be seen again."

"Well," Simon said, coming over to sling his arm around Lucas. "I have a few ideas about that."

CHAPTER 17

Diana cast her gaze toward the house above and tried not to let her thoughts wander too far. It was almost impossible when all she wanted to know was whether Lucas was well. Whether he was able to face the friends he so cared about despite whatever had inspired him to push them all away. She longed, in some foolish part of herself, to be with him. To support him.

"You and I are of a mind," the Duchess of Crestwood said as she sank down into the bench along the garden path and gently settled her hand on her belly. She looked up toward the house, as well, her concern plain.

The difference was, she had a right to feel that way. Diana's cheeks grew hot with a blush. What this woman must think of her, despite all her outward kindness and friendliness.

"I do not know Willowby's intentions," the duchess continued. "But I can assure you that Simon and Tyndale's are only the most loving. Their entire group of friends has missed him keenly, especially considering all the turmoil and joy that has come to our circle in the last year and a half."

Diana swallowed hard. "I am certain it is none of my business."

"Isn't it?" She glanced back up at the house. "It seems *he* feels differently."

Diana shifted at those words. At what they meant in this context. At the idea that this lady knew she and Lucas were lovers. That she labeled Diana a whore, however quietly.

"You know what I am," she said.

Meg's cheeks darkened and she darted her gaze from Diana's. "His friend," she said.

"Your Grace," Diana began.

The duchess smiled. "Oh, please don't do that. We are a very informal group, with too many dukes and duchesses to go around Your Gracing everyone. It gets too confusing. Please call me Meg, and I shall be very forward and call you Diana in return."

Diana blinked in confusion. "Meg?" she repeated.

"Excellent," Meg said. "You've made this very easy, with far less argument than I encountered with, say, Adelaide or Helena."

Diana shook her head. "I don't—"

"It seems very possible you might know them soon enough," Meg sighed. "Assuming all goes well with the gentlemen, as I'm sure it will."

Staring at the duchess, Diana tried to think of something to say. Here she'd thought Meg viewed her as Lucas's mistress, but she was speaking to her as if she were something more important. Someone that deserved a place at a table full of dukes and duchesses in the upper echelon of Society.

"I think you may be mistaken in your view of me, Your Grace."

"Meg."

She clenched her hands in front of her. "Meg. I-I am not going to be a part of your circle, no matter how this meeting of Lucas's goes today."

"Are you not?" Meg laughed, and it was a gentle, playful sound. "I know there are a great many unsavory tales of those with titles, but I assure you, we have not an ogre in the group. They're all good men with many fine qualities. And the wives, thus far, are a girl's dream when she thinks of the friends she would be lucky to have in her life."

"I'm certain you are right. It isn't a slur on any of you, I assure you. It's just that I am...I'm..."

Meg lifted her brows when Diana didn't finish and nodded. "You are...?"

Diana folded her arms and fought not to turn away. "You will make me say it out loud? I'm staying in his house, unchaperoned. I'm his..."

"His mistress," Meg finished. "Yes, that is how it appears. I admit that idea made me a bit uncomfortable at first, but having talked to you, I'm beginning to think my view of it isn't entirely true."

Diana drew back. "I assure you, it is. There is nothing between us outside of our—our arrangement."

She blushed even hotter at those words. Here she had been telling Lucas that she didn't want to be seen as a lightskirt by his friends and now she was defending her position as just that. All the while, the duchess gave her a knowing look.

"We are not a...a typical group of friends, my dear. Our ranks are filled with men who have suffered greatly and women who have had their own secrets. So if you were Willowby's mistress and nothing more, I assure you it would not make me like you less. But that isn't what you are."

"I would think I know what I am more than anyone. What do *you* think I am?" Diana asked.

Meg laughed again. "Someone who makes Lucas Vincent, Duke of Willowby, stop running. A woman who holds his arm with great protectiveness when he enters into a room where he is uncertain. A woman who seems to belong here in this place. *That* is who you are."

"He...he didn't stop running because of me," Diana whispered, for she had no answer for the rest of Meg's charges.

"If you insist," Meg said. "But I'd still like the rest of the duchesses to meet you."

Diana stared down at herself and blushed yet again. "Your Grace, this is the finest outfit I'm in possession of. Not fit for the company of duchesses, I think you would agree."

"The color is pretty on you," Meg said. She stood slowly, steadied herself and then approached Diana. She moved around her, examining her. "You and I are of a similar size, and since I am not currently wearing my usual wardrobe, I think I could solve your problem of dresses."

Diana's mouth dropped open. "You cannot be serious that you are offering to let me borrow your clothes?"

"No," Meg said. "I'd let you keep them. Simon will buy me new things after the baby, for I'm certain my body will change. You would look lovely in my green silk—it will bring out your eyes like jade." She clapped her hands together. "Oh, jade! I have the prettiest necklace and it—"

"Please, Meg," Diana interrupted. "You are too kind, but…"

"No buts," Meg said. "Really, let me do this. At least do not refuse me out of hand."

Diana sighed, for the offer was very tempting. She could tell from the gorgeous cut of Meg's current gown that whatever she offered would be beautiful beyond Diana's wildest dreams. That charity felt…wasted. She had no life or place amongst these people.

Yet she felt so comfortable.

"Ladies!"

Both of then turned, and Meg broke into a wide grin as the men strode down the garden path toward them. Diana pushed aside her feelings about Meg's offer and stared at Lucas. She could not fully read him, but she saw that he looked…relaxed. Happy. And she drew her first full breath since she'd left him nearly an hour before.

The Duke of Crestwood extended his hand and Meg took it, stepping into the circle of his arm with a smile that could have lit a thousand nights. Diana shifted in the face of such adoration between them. It felt almost accusatory as she glanced at Lucas and found him smiling at her.

"Miss Oakford, Willowby tells us you are quite the horticulturist," Tyndale said. "And that your garden far outstrips this one."

Diana shook her head. "I often wonder if Willowby had a head injury when he saw my little garden, that he was so enchanted by it when he had this to come home to."

"Home is where the tasty chicken is," Lucas murmured. "There were a great many things to recommend your garden, Diana."

She blushed and was pleased when the others moved to a different topic. Lucas complimenting her garden felt like...exposure somehow. This important thing, laid bare to those who were all but strangers.

"So we'll have a ball," Crestwood was saying with a smile for Meg.

She laughed. "In my condition? You might want to have someone else do it."

"Well, not Adelaide," Simon said. "For she is in a similar condition, though not as far along as you. What about Charlotte?"

"I would say Charlotte or Emma would be best." Meg said, clapping her hands. "Oh, a ball. How lovely to have everyone together."

Tyndale smiled, but Diana thought she saw a tension to his lips. She would have taken more time to wonder at it, but her heart had begun to race. "A ball?" she repeated.

Lucas turned to her. "Yes. Diana, I-I told my friends the truth. About me. About you."

Her lips parted. She had not been prepared for that statement. "I—oh."

"The truth?" Meg repeated, tilting her head. "Well, I look forward to wheedling it out of Simon."

"As do I," Crestwood muttered.

Meg's cheeks brightened and she laughed as she said, "But for now, I think we should go." She moved toward Diana, hands outstretched, and leaned in to buss her cheek gently. "You think about what I offered. You'll need it even more now if there's to be a ball and I would love to be of help."

"Thank you," Diana said, feeling Lucas's stare focused on her. "I appreciate the offer, I assure you."

Meg turned to Lucas and kissed his cheek, as well. "So lovely to have you home, my friend. I know James and the others are also dying to see you, so we must arrange that before any ball we host or else you will be surrounded and that would be quite awkward."

"Quite," he agreed with a smile.

Diana watched as he said his farewells to Tyndale and Crestwood. Both gentlemen acknowledged her, and then the small group headed back toward the house, leaving Diana alone with Lucas. When they were all out of earshot, she moved forward. She needed to touch him. To make sure he was whole after what was likely a taxing ordeal, no matter how well it had gone.

"You look happier," she said softly.

He looked down at her and nodded. "That was a reminder of the piece I've been missing in my life. And how foolish it was for me to throw it away when—"

He cut himself off and paced away from her. She pursed her lips. When he pulled back like this, when he cut her away from his past or his pain, it made her position very clear, no matter how strenuously he denied it.

"You told them you are a spy," she said in an effort to change the subject. For her own sake as much as his.

He nodded and faced her. "If I'm going to use their hospitality to reenter Society and goad our traitor, I felt it was only right. And I admit that when I saw them, I *wanted* to tell them. So that they'd understand why I disappeared. That it wasn't because of them."

She folded her arms. "Well, it is good you have *someone* to share your past with."

He arched a brow and she shifted, for she knew her tone had been petulant. Unfairly so, likely. He owed her nothing, after all. Still, she wanted more.

"You think I don't share my past with you?" he asked.

She shrugged. "You keep hinting about some horrible thing that happened to you and yet you do not reveal yourself in any meaningful way. I've confessed some of my darkest secrets and yet I know so little about you."

"Not all your secrets."

She drew back. "I beg your pardon?"

"Come, come, Diana. Don't play at something that neither of us will believe. You have told me a great deal and I am honored that you would trust me. But please don't pretend that you have emptied your soul to me. I can sense that there is much more you're holding back."

She took another long step away from him, shocked by his casual observation. Shattered by how right he was. The secret he wanted to know was looming over her at present, and to have him mention it, even without understanding it, cut her to her aching heart.

"Well, then I suppose we both have our secrets," she said. "And we shall both keep our own counsel on them."

He opened his mouth like he wanted to say more and she leaned forward, secretly hoping he would. But he didn't. Instead, he sighed. "Meg told you to think about an offer. What was it?"

It was like a wall of ice went up between them. The matter was closed, it seemed. "She has offered to share some of her gowns with me so that I might be more presentable as your companion."

His eyebrows lifted. "That was kind."

"Yes." She nodded. "Meg is very kind. Insistent, even, though I tried to explain to her that I wouldn't be accompanying you to any event, so it was unnecessary."

He stared at her. "What do you mean? Of course you'll attend any ball or event I go to."

She gasped. "Are you mad? You are trying to reintroduce yourself into good Society as a way to lure your traitor, and you want to take your mistress with you? Don't you think that will cause a stir?"

"I suppose it might," he said. "But a stir wouldn't be the worst outcome. Besides, I want you there with me. You are my partner in this, aren't you?"

She swallowed hard. His partner? That implied a certain connection, a certain intimacy. And yet it wasn't true, not really. As she'd already pointed out, there was such a wall between them on so many issues.

Perhaps it was time to stop pretending that wasn't true.

"We are not partners," she said softly, and watched how he recoiled at that quiet denial. "We are two people thrown into a terrible, common experience. And we became lovers. But we both made it clear from the beginning that it was nothing more than that, didn't we?"

"Diana," he said, lifting his hands as if to protest.

She shook her head. "Please don't. You are going to be able to investigate your case without any help from me the moment you step back into Society's gaze. Every time I check your shoulder, it's better and better. Your limp is barely noticeable. You don't even need my skills as a healer anymore."

He moved closer to her, pressing into her space. She fought to hold her ground rather than fall into his arms or run away. "What do you mean by that? What are you saying?"

She drew in a long breath. "Perhaps it's time that we stop pretending, Lucas. Perhaps it's time for us to...part ways."

He caught her elbow and shook his head. "No. You are saying that because you're afraid to attend a ball?"

"No!" she cried out, but she knew that was a lie immediately. From his expression, so did he. "There are many reasons for us to end this affair," she corrected herself. "Certainly one of them is that you are entering into the next arena of your case and of your life. One where I most definitely don't belong."

"Because I've taken you to my bed?" he asked.

She nodded. "That's part of it."

"Well, I hate to disabuse you of the notion that all ladies are pure, but I happen to know that all my recently married friends who are dukes bedded their ladies before they said their vows. We are human, my dear, no matter what titles are laid upon our heads at birth. A lady has desires as much as a woman whose father was not called 'my lord'."

"Yes, a lady. Meg is a *lady*. All of your friends' wives are ladies. I am not. My father was half a step above a merchant in their eyes. I am the kind of woman who would tie their ribbons or clean their chambers, Lucas. I do not belong in their world. In *your* world. You are a duke, for heaven's sake."

His breath was short and he stared at her. Just stared at her. Then he said, "No. I'm not."

She threw up her hands. "You can wish you weren't, you can run as far and as fast from it as you like, but you are who you are. You are the Duke of Willowby, Lucas. The most recent one in what I assume is a long line. To pretend otherwise is—"

He caught her arms again, and the sudden action stopped her talking, as did the forlorn, pained expression on his face.

"Listen to me, Diana. I'm not saying I'm not the duke because I don't want to be. I'm telling you...I'm telling you I'm not the duke because the last Willowby wasn't my father."

CHAPTER 18

The world swam around Lucas as he said the words out loud. He had never confessed this to another person, not even the friends he held so dear. The secret had rotted him out from the inside the moment he learned it.

The secret had made him into the man he was today.

Diana touched his cheek and he was grounded again. He looked into her eyes, those jade eyes that had captivated him from the first moment he saw her, and he was able to draw breath once more.

"Lucas," she whispered. "What are you talking about?"

He shook his head. "You wanted my secret, Diana. Well, that is it. He wasn't my father. I wasn't his son. What I have is not earned. It should not have been inherited. But here we are."

She looked at him a long moment, and then the calm expression that she always wore when doing her work as a healer crossed her face. She took his arm and guided him to a bench in the garden. He sank into it, grateful that his legs no longer had to hold him up.

"How did you find out?" she asked.

He rested his head back and stared up at the swirling clouds above for a moment. Memories flooded his mind, and he braced himself against the emotional impact of what he was about to say to her.

"He always *hated* me," he said, feeling the effect of those words. "I never didn't know it. *She* hated me, too, as you saw when we first arrived. They sent me to school as soon as they could, to get me out of their house and their sight. I suppose I thought it normal, just the way a family behaved. I thought I'd never belong anywhere until I was twelve and met the others, the dukes. When I was invited into their club I began to feel that I belonged."

She nodded. "That certainly explains your closeness to them."

"Yes, but our bond was built on one common ground. That we were all the sons of dukes, almost all of them undependable or cruel in one way or another. We turned to each other for support and information and brotherly love. And then I lost the one thing that bound me to them."

She shook her head. "What bound you was your love for each other. It was palpable in that room earlier."

"But they don't know," he said. "I've never told anyone what happened."

"What *did* happen?" she whispered.

He clenched his fists against his legs. "Our friend Robert, the Duke of Roseford...he's always been wild. He arranged for us to gain entry into a club. We were gaming and there were, we were..."

"There were women," she supplied gently.

"Yes," he said with an apologetic look for the uncouth topic of women he'd bedded in the lifetime before he knew her. "I was sixteen and it was my first time really seeing the world of men."

She smiled a little. "At that age, I imagine you must have been drunk on far more than just spirits."

"Yes. We were having a fine time until I turned and my father...*Willowby*...he was standing there three feet away, glaring at me. He was furious I was in this club carousing, as he put it."

She blinked. "But *he* was in the club."

"A fine argument, but not one I could make to him when he was half-drunk and filled with indignant rage. He dragged me out by my collar in front of my friends and threw me into his carriage. It was the longest ride home of my life with him screaming and yelling about all my failures."

"Oh, Lucas." Her voice cracked. "I'm so sorry."

"I had been resentful of him for years. Resentful of his coldness. I'd spent time with Tyndale's father by then, and our friend Kit, his father is Duke of Kingsacre and also so kind. I realized not all fathers treated their sons like mine did and had begun to hate Willowby with as much strength as he despised me. It was the perfect storm. A man and a boy nearly a man, both one drink too far into their cups, with so much between them that had been unsaid for over a decade."

"So you said it," she whispered, and reached out to thread her fingers through his.

He stared at their interlocked hands, surrendering to the peace her touch seemed to give every time she shared it. In this moment, when he was raw, it gave him the strength to say what happened next.

"Yes." His voice cracked. "I told him I was tired of his cruelty and his coldness. I told him I deserved his regard and his respect, if not his love."

She nodded slowly. "That was brave of you. What did he do?"

"Hit me so hard with the back of his hand that I tasted blood," he said. "And then he told me I deserved nothing because I wasn't even his true son."

Her expression gentled with deep empathy. "Oh, Lucas, he was intoxicated and cruel—it's very possible he was just lashing out at you."

"I thought the same in that moment. I was so stunned, I couldn't believe it was possible. If I wasn't his son, who was I? I couldn't think of an answer. But what he said to me in that heated moment turned out to be very true. My mother verified it."

She caught her breath and Lucas fought for his. There were so many memories coming back up to torment him. He recalled his mother's face when the two of them stumbled into the foyer. How disgusted she'd been as she glared at them from the hall.

"Why would she do so?" Diana asked.

"He gave her no choice. When we arrived here, at this very house, he dragged me inside. There she was, roused by the racket. He started bellowing at her to manage her bastard, as she should have done for all these years. She was *not* drunk, and there was a moment when all the color went out of her face. I knew then. In that moment, I knew."

"What did she say to you?" Diana asked, her hand tightening against his. "Did she explain?"

"In a way. She was enraged at first, not that he had struck me or railed at me, but that he would tell her secret. She kept asking him how could he, after all these years, how could he? It all came out then, as I watched them scream out their hate to each other like he'd screamed it out to me. It was like I wasn't even in the room and they hashed out the whole sordid thing as I'm sure they had many times before, only in private."

"She had strayed," Diana whispered.

"With a servant, of all things," Lucas said, almost laughing even though there was nothing funny about the most painful memory of his life. "My father's valet—well, his previous valet. And that affair happened during a time where my father knew full well the child could not be his. So I am not a duke, I simply wear the costume. I suppose living a life of lies helped me with my role as spy. I should be grateful, perhaps."

She turned farther into him and her warm hands lifted to his cheeks. She smoothed her thumbs against his skin and whispered, "That is not true. *They* lived a life of lies, not you. Whatever your mother did wasn't your fault. You couldn't change it."

"Neither could Willowby, though I know he wanted to," Lucas said. "I was born during their marriage—to protest my parentage would have been fruitless and caused a scandal that would have destroyed us all, not that my father cared about anyone but himself. He spent all those years looking at me and seeing the man whose tainted seed would be carried on in *his* line, and he was horrified. No wonder he despised me."

"He was a cruel person who could lay the sins of an adult onto an innocent child, no matter how he felt about his lines or his title or his fortune," Diana murmured. "Oh, Lucas, that is a burden to carry."

He shrugged. "But I didn't carry it. I ran from it, you see. I ran that very night, to our friend Hugh's house in London. He was the only one who had inherited by then. He let me in and asked me about what had happened, but I wouldn't tell him. I couldn't. I was too crushed."

"And even when that first horrible reaction faded," she asked. "Could you have confessed to any of them, if only to ease the burden?"

"I could have," he admitted. "Most of them have brutal pasts with their own fathers. I'm certain they would have been kind and supportive. But when they looked at me, they would have seen that I didn't belong. At least that's what I thought. So I never told a soul."

She dipped her head, and her voice was far away when she said, "It ate you alive, that pain that could not be spoken. That loss that couldn't be shared."

He stared at her, for there was an expression on her face that told him she understood those concepts on a far deeper level than he knew. He didn't understand what had broken her, but he was more comfortable knowing that he wasn't alone in the kind of pain that blossomed now in his chest.

"Yes," he admitted. "It damaged everything in my life. Like Hugh, all my other friends eventually sensed something had changed, but I pushed them back and pretended it didn't matter. When Willowby died two years later, I entered the military rather than face the past and the future. Perhaps I wanted to die, I don't know. I became a spy to forget what I am, but it slaps me in the face at all turns. If you think you don't belong here, well, neither do I, Diana. So *there* is my secret. There is the truth."

Diana was silent for a long moment. So long that he feared perhaps his secret had changed the way she viewed him, as he had once feared it would change his friends and their view. That no matter what she said, she knew what he was and that was all she could see now. Like his father had. Like his mother.

But then she took his hands and kissed first one palm, then the other. "That you shared this with me means so much to me, Lucas. And perhaps having said these things out loud will give them less power."

"I don't know about that," he said, and pushed to his feet. He walked to the edge of the fountain and watched the water endlessly fall. He understood that feeling. Forever falling, forever lost. He turned and found her watching him closely. "I think I owed you that secret. After all, you told me yours."

Something in her face shifted. That guilt and pain he often saw in her returned. It reminded him there *was* more to her past than what she'd shared.

"You were right when you said that I haven't been completely open with you," she said.

He caught his breath and hated himself for pressuring her. "But I was unfair to accuse you of that. In the heat of the moment I said it, but I don't think you owe me or anyone *anything*, Diana."

"Only I do," she said softly. "And of course it would be today of all days that I would see it."

"Today?" He tilted his head. "What is so special about today?"

"It is the day before tomorrow. And tomorrow means everything." She sighed. "You had a long day, Lucas—do you think you're up for a little trip?"

He blinked. "A trip?"

"Back to my cottage here in Town. I was going to make an excuse about needing herbs so I could return there tonight or tomorrow, but perhaps it is time for all the lies to be stripped away.

Perhaps it's time you really understand, as I now understand. If you want to, then I'll ask that you come with me."

He hesitated. From her expression, it was clear her secret was dire. Life altering. And if he knew it then they would both be laid bare. There would be nothing left as a wall between them.

And that was terrifying.

But the idea of knowing her, *truly* knowing her, was also tempting. Temptation won.

"Yes," he said softly. "I would be honored to return with you and to know whatever you *want* to share."

"Then let's go now," she said, and held out a trembling hand.

He took it, guiding her toward the house, guiding them both toward a future he feared and anticipated in equal measure.

L ucas had allowed there to be silence between them on the long ride across London back to her little cottage. Diana appreciated that deeply, for right now she could think of no words to say.

Enough had been said already.

She'd never intended to tell Lucas the full truth about her past. She'd never meant for anyone to know. But when he told her his secret, when he confessed it all out and asked for nothing in return, the last barrier she kept between them had melted. After all, this secret had brought her pain for so long. As she had suggested to him, perhaps speaking it out loud would take away the power of it.

The carriage stopped and Lucas helped her out. His hand was warm, comforting as he took her arm and guided her to the door. She opened it and they stepped inside.

Both of them drew a breath at once, and she glanced at him. He looked as pleased to be here as she felt. Back in this place where they had started. This place that was so separate from his world and whatever they would face there in the next few days and weeks.

"What can I do?" he asked. "Make a fire in the parlor? Help you get something from the study?"

She shook her head. "What I have to show you is not inside. We must go to the garden."

He released her arm and motioned for her to lead him. She did so on shaking legs, with a throbbing heart that felt like it was loud enough for the neighborhood to hear.

She walked through the cold, dark back parlor and through the doors that led outside. The sun was warm on her face, but that felt like a slap when she considered what she was about to do. Say. Feel.

Lucas followed her silently as she maneuvered her way through her herb plantings and the few flowers scattered through the small outdoor space. Finally she reached the big oak tree in the back corner of the space, and she stopped and stared at what she saw there.

Two little markers, memorials for the dead. One was for her father and her mother. The other was small—tiny, really—like the person it represented. The life lost before it had even begun.

"Diana," Lucas said softly.

She didn't look at him, but kept her eyes on that tiny marker. "My mother's name was Mira. I always loved the way my father said it. It could be a love poem or an admonishment or a prayer. When my baby was born so early, unable to take a breath, gone before I even got to hold her, I called her Mirabelle. At least in my head."

Lucas's fingers closed around her arm and she looked at him at last. He was pale and his lips trembled. "Your child."

She nodded. "That ill-fated affair with Boyd Caldwell brought me more than just a sad story about innocence lost, you see."

His jaw twitched. "Caldwell. *That* was the spy your father brought here? The one who seduced you?"

"I assume you know him," she whispered, her cheeks filling with heat.

His gaze darted away as he jerked out a nod. "I do. I...I know him, though not well."

She glanced back at the memorials. "When I realized I was breeding, I tried to hide it. Eventually, I was forced to tell my father what had happened between us and how Boyd had abandoned me after he got what he...wanted. I have never seen him so enraged. I don't know if he confronted Caldwell—we never spoke of him again. We came to London, where he could watch and help me while he worked. Until...until I started having pain. Too early, too soon. My father tried to help, but he couldn't save her. He barely saved me. She is buried here, which is why I put a memorial marker for them beside her. So I could visit them together."

She blinked and realized tears were streaming down her face. "Tomorrow will be one year since she died."

He swayed slightly, and then to her surprise, he drew her in and held her tightly against his warm, broad chest. His hand came up into her hair, gently smoothing her locks. "I'm so sorry, Diana."

She buckled then, the weight of the grief she had carried with her for a year hitting her all at once. He held her, keeping her upright and never speaking as she cried for the daughter she had never known, then for the mother who had also left far too soon and the father who had been snatched from her. She wept for them all until her chest stopped hurting and the tears faded to shudders and then stopped.

"Mirabelle is a beautiful name," he said, drawing back to wipe tears from her cheeks before he handed over a handkerchief he withdrew from his jacket pocket.

She wiped her eyes and nose and nodded. "I sometimes wonder what she would have been like. Looked like."

"Beautiful and accomplished like her mother," he said with a smile. "There is no way she could not have been with you as her influence. I'm glad you have this place to visit with her."

She shook her head. "I'm not sure Father wanted to have it, honestly. He seemed to do it out of guilt rather than a desire to remember. He was forever encouraging me to let her go, forget her."

Lucas flinched. "That isn't very kind."

"No, perhaps not. But he was a surgeon, of course. A doctor who saw death regularly. He could set it away. He expected me to do the same. He wasn't much comfort...after."

Lucas tucked her into his arms again and they looked at the markers together. "Then let *me* comfort you. We can stay here tonight. I'll have supper sent over—we can be here in this place where the case and the duties don't matter. And tomorrow we can see her again, visit her and set some flowers here for her birthday."

She glanced up at him, shocked by the kindness of his response to a child he didn't know, hadn't been his. But of course he would be. Despite his gruff beginnings with her, she had swiftly realized that while he might be complicated, he was not cruel. He was giving and caring, deeply passionate and highly attuned to those around him. Perhaps those things had been honed because he was a spy, but they hadn't been born from his profession.

They were just...him. And that was why she loved him.

She jolted at that realization, which hit her in the heart and almost made her buckle with shock and pain and terror. She couldn't deny it was true though. She did love him. She would always love him.

Even though there was so little time left for them now.

"I would like that," she said, wrapping her arm around his waist and leaning into him. "If you are willing."

He leaned down and pressed a kiss to her temple. "Whatever you need, Diana. Whatever you need and more."

She smiled, but she knew then and realized she'd never be able to forget, that what she needed was the heart he wouldn't give. And the future they couldn't have.

CHAPTER 19

It had been four days since Lucas and Diana had returned from her cottage, and he had noticed the changes in her. Although she still bustled and treated his wounds, she was quieter, reflective as she processed her grief. He was processing too. Both of them had confessed a great deal about themselves, so much so that he knew they were both feeling exposed.

In fact, she had exposed far more than perhaps she knew. When she'd told him that the name of her lover, the father of her child, was Boyd Caldwell, everything in him had frozen. One of the few things he recalled about the day he'd been attacked were his traitor's guards walking past the hiding place, saying part of a name.

Cal—

He and Stalwood had pored over the first and last names within their ranks that could match. He knew Stalwood had reviewed each one, more than half a dozen, including Caldwell, himself, but they'd never come up with a solid connection.

Only now there was one. Caldwell had been close enough to Diana's father that Oakford had let him into his home. Let him near his daughter. Diana thought they'd been investigating a case together.

Thoughts that had haunted Lucas ever since, thoughts that had begun to breed more and more suspicions about Caldwell. About Oakford, himself. He knew he would have to broach those thoughts with Stalwood sooner rather than later. But once he did...

Well, Diana might find out. If his suspicions proved true, they would very likely break her heart. He wasn't ready to do that, especially since she'd shared so much.

Especially since he was shockingly not uncomfortable, either in the sharing or the knowing. In fact, he felt...*closer* to her. He had that night after she confessed when he simply held her while she fitfully slept. He had the night they'd returned when he made love to her in the hopes that pleasure would ease some of the pain.

He did now as he sat across from her watching her pour tea and peruse the sideboard of breakfast pastries awaiting them this morning. "I received an invitation," he said, forcing away his more troubling thoughts about the case and about her, and breaking the quiet at last. "To a ball at the Duke and Duchess of Abernathe's."

She slowly turned, her hand shaking so much that the plate she held trembled. "I see."

"It is tonight," he said. "And there was also a message for you from Meg. My assumption is she might wish to meet with you this afternoon to share her gowns."

"The only reason I'd do so is if I would attend the ball as your companion," Diana said, setting her plate down and taking a seat beside him. "I don't think that is wise."

He frowned. She was so certain she didn't belong in his world. That she would be seen as less by his friends and peers. "I would like you to come," he said softly.

"And draw negative attention to yourself?" She shook her head. "It isn't just going to be your friends there, is it?"

He pursed his lips. "No, that would not serve the purpose of the ball, of course. There will be many of rank there."

"Then I don't belong," she said, and pushed the uneaten food away. "That's the end of the discussion."

He leaned over and caught her hands. Slowly, he drew them up to his lips and pressed a kiss against her knuckles. He felt her shudder, shift, soften. He smiled. "Please attend."

"You think you can seduce me into it?" she asked.

He arched a brow. "I know I can. But I don't want to. I want you to be there because you'll meet my friends as a group. Because I'd like to dance with you. Because I'd like to discuss any information that might be gleaned from our going. And because I'd like to see you as the shining, glorious star of the evening and know that I get to take you back to my bed at the end of the night."

She sighed, but it was obvious he'd won even before she said, "Very well, though I think you might be disappointed. Give me Meg's letter and I will write to tell her I'll come to her this afternoon to accept her offer."

"Good," he said, handing the letter over with a grin. "You'll be of great help to me, I'm certain."

She gave him a look and he saw her anxiety. "I'll remind you of that after, when you are sorry you took me."

She pushed to her feet and went to refresh his tea from the sideboard. When she turned her back, his smile fell. Once more he was plagued with troubling thoughts that had nothing to do with the ball. Thoughts of how hurt she might be by the investigation he was bound to do.

And how hurt *he* would be once he lost her.

A s Meg entered her parlor, Diana turned and was surprised to see a wide grin on her new friend's face.

"I'm so glad you came!" Meg said, and folded her into an embrace that was only made awkward by the pregnant belly that came between them. Diana found herself settling her hand on the swell and remembering her own months of confinement.

Meg tilted her head. "Are you well?"

"Yes," Diana said, jerking the hand away. "I'm sorry, just woolgathering. You were so kind to invite me and to renew your offer of loaning me some clothes for tonight. I admit I have no idea what to do or say or think when it comes to such an event. I fear I shall muck it up entirely."

"Well, we'll help you," Meg said as she took her arm. "Now come up to my chamber and we'll start. The others are very excited to meet you."

"The others?" Diana repeated as she followed the lead of the duchess.

"Yes. Emma is busy as a goose preparing for the ball, with Charlotte's help, but Adelaide is here and so is Helena."

Diana stopped in the middle of the hallway and forced Meg to do the same. "The other duchesses?" she asked.

Meg tilted her head. "You needn't look so frightened. Have I bitten you yet?"

Diana couldn't quite muster a laugh at the gentle teasing. "No, not yet. But it's just..."

She couldn't complete the sentence and Meg put her arm around her. "I recognize you're nervous. I even understand why. But I assure you, Adelaide and Helena are the sweetest and kindest women you could ever hope to encounter. You will feel nothing but welcome from them and friendship. They're incapable of anything else."

Diana nodded slowly. Meg was so earnest in her praise that it was hard not to find some faith that she might be right. They walked up the stairs together and Meg took her to an open door. She could hear female voices from inside, quiet laughter, and she drew a cleansing breath to ready herself. They entered and two ladies turned from an open wardrobe in the dressing room.

One was blonde, with loosely done locks that framed a very pretty face. She also had a pregnant belly of her own, though not as large as Meg's. The other was slender, willowy, with a shock of auburn locks done in a simple chignon. As Diana and Meg entered, both the ladies' faces lit up with happy, friendly smiles that could not help but put Diana at ease.

"Diana, ladies, is here at last!" Meg said, drawing her forward. "Diana, may I present Adelaide, Duchess of Northfield, and Helena, our newest duchess. She was just married to the Duke of Sheffield recently."

"Sixty-seven days to be precise," Helena said, and Diana was surprised to find the lady had a very American accent. Helena stepped forward to catch Diana's hands in greeting. "I'm still blissfully counting each and every one. Hello and welcome. We're so happy to meet you."

"We are," Adelaide agreed. "And I hope Meg has told you that there are too many of us to call by title, at least amongst friends. You will call us Helena and Adelaide."

Diana laughed as her nervousness continued to fade. "I admit, neither of you seems a woman who could be denied. So if you insist, I cannot see how I'd say no."

They talked for a while, of frivolous things. With each passing moment, Diana felt herself becoming more and more comfortable. She had been so far removed by this echelon of Society that she had pictured the women within it as cold, detached, unfeeling.

But that notion was being disproved at a rapid pace. All three ladies were amusing, welcoming, intelligent and clearly in love with their respective husbands. It was nearly impossible not to like them with all her heart and want to be part of their little circle.

Not that she could be, not truly. If their husbands had formed a club of dukes, *this* was a party of duchesses, and that was something Diana would not be a part of, despite the love she could now privately admit she felt for Lucas.

"Adelaide, your taste is impeccable," Meg said at last. "Will you come look through my things and help me decide what Diana should try on first?"

Adelaide smiled at Diana and the two ladies stepped away to the wardrobe to discuss, leaving Diana alone with Helena.

"You seem a very happy newlywed," she said.

Helena's face lit up. "Indeed, I am vastly content. You have not yet met Baldwin...er, Sheffield, but he is the greatest of men. Not that we did not have our struggles."

"Hearing you speak of him with such warmth and seeing your unmistakable joy, it's difficult to picture that."

"In a way, I'm much like yourself. I was not born of this world. Not that I am anything as interesting as a healer to a spy." Helena blushed.

Diana laughed, though it was a nervous sound. Lucas had told her it was likely all the duchesses would now know their secret, but that he trusted it would never leave their circle. It sounded better, she supposed, than a mistress. "You're American—I think that is very interesting."

Now it was Helena's turn to laugh. "I am that. From Boston, though it hadn't felt like home for a long time. I belong here now. But when I first arrived here, this—" She waved her hand around to indicate the fine chamber. "—wasn't my station, either. I was nothing more than my cousin's companion when I met Baldwin."

Diana blinked. Looking at the lovely woman before her, she could scarcely picture that she hadn't always belonged in the warm group of her friends. "A companion?" she repeated.

Helena nodded. "Due to many circumstances, things felt rather...*dire* for a long time. I could not believe that we could find happiness as we have. But I hope you'll see me as proof that obstacles of class can be overcome. For us. And for you and Lucas."

Diana caught her breath. "I-I am not...Lucas and I are not courting."

Helena arched a brow. "Are you not? Then perhaps I misunderstood the situation."

Diana ducked her head. Helena didn't sound like she thought she'd misunderstood anything at all. And yet Diana refused to be comforted by the words. The situation with Lucas was far more complicated than whatever had separated Helena from her duke.

Diana had to remember that for herself as much as for anyone else in her acquaintance.

She did not have to respond, however, for Meg and Adelaide returned to her with a lovely gown in each of their arms. Diana caught her breath at the bright jade of one choice and the dark, alluring blue of the other.

"You'll try on both," Meg insisted, "for a start. And I am going to send word to Willowby that he will not see you again until the ball. You'll stay here with me and I'll help you do your hair, as well. You'll accompany Simon and me in our carriage."

Diana shifted. "Oh, but—"

"Don't argue with her," Adelaide said with a theatrically put-upon sigh. "She wins."

"Every time," Helena said with a nod.

Meg seemed pleased by the teasing of her friends and said, "You see?"

"Very well." Diana threw up her hands in surrender, for there seemed no room to argue. Even if there was, she was not entirely put off by the idea of being pampered and prepared by her new friends. "I am, apparently, at your mercy."

"Isn't it so much easier just to admit it?" Meg said with a bright laugh. "Now which dress should we try first?"

Diana sank into the moment as she stared from one gorgeous gown to the next. "Could I—could I try on the green first? It's beautiful."

"Indeed," Meg said with a wide grin. "It matches your eyes to perfection and I cannot wait to see it on you."

Diana turned and let Helena begun to unfasten her current, plain gown. This was all a fantasy, a fairytale story where the common-place girl became a princess thanks to friends. And while she might enjoy indulging in the idea for a while, she reminded herself not to get too wrapped up in it.

It would end. And sooner rather than later.

CHAPTER 20

L ucas shifted and glanced at his pocket watch for what must have been the tenth time in as many minutes. The Abernathe ball was in full swing, but Diana had yet to arrive with Simon and Meg. He jolted when Graham Everly, Duke of Northfield, slung an arm around him and laughed.

"You're a bit obvious, mate, checking the door every thirty seconds. She'll get here when she gets here. And I hear she'll be worth the wait. When she arrived home, Adelaide could not stop waxing poetic about how lovely the mysterious Miss Oakford was in the dress the three of them picked out for her."

Lucas pursed his lips and refocused on the small group of his friends. He'd come early to James's house for the reunion and now was surrounded by Graham, Ewan, Baldwin, Matthew and Robert. Simon had not yet arrived, of course, and James was busy with Emma, welcoming their guests as each was announced. Only two of them were missing. Kit was in the countryside with his ailing father and young sister. Hugh had been invited, but then it had been determined that he was not in London, a fact that disturbed his friends, though they hadn't gotten into the specifics. They'd been too busy shaking hands, swapping stories and asking him questions about his life as a spy.

A grand homecoming, indeed, and one that had warmed his heart.

Now Lucas stood with the men, with them acting as if he'd never been gone from their circle. In a way, it felt like he hadn't. Like he'd come home after a long time away, but found his chair and his bed and his life just as comfortable as it had ever been.

"You're being preposterous," he said, forcing a benign look on his face. "You know my...*situation*...and why Diana is part of it. To pretend otherwise is..."

He trailed off in the sentence, because at that moment Simon and Meg were announced. They stepped into the room together, and behind them was Diana. She was wearing a beautiful green gown, one that matched her eyes to perfection. It was cut just a fraction too tight in the bosom, as it had not been made for Diana, but the smaller Meg. That only served to accentuate those beautiful curves of hers.

Her hair had been done by Meg's maid, it seemed, and the woman had done magic, winding and twisting and curling until all those luscious locks were like a crown fit for the most beautiful queen in all the country. All the world.

"You were about to tell us how you are unmoved by the entirely fetching Miss Oakford," Robert, Duke of Roseford, drawled with half a grin for him. "If that is true, perhaps *I'll* ask her to dance. She is stunning."

Lucas shot his friend—who also happened to be the most wild and inappropriate of the group—a glare. The very idea of the handsome, smirking, seductive duke putting his hands on Diana, even for just a dance, made Lucas's blood boil.

"I think he might have an apoplexy if you keep teasing him, Roseford," Matthew said with a laugh. "You are too cruel."

"Shut up," Lucas managed to mutter. "Diana is...well, she deserves better than any of us. Excuse me."

He felt his friends' eyes on his back as he departed their company and began what felt like an eternity of walking across the room toward her. She was talking to Meg and Emma now. Emma was clearly cooing over the gown that suited her so well. But Diana kept watching him from the corner of her eye, and when he reached them, she let out a breath like she'd been holding it.

"Good evening, ladies," he said, and reached for Diana's hand. It was shaking when she offered it, and he lifted it to his lips. "You look wonderful," he said quietly.

"I-it is all Meg's exquisite gown, I assure you," she said.

Emma snorted out a laugh. "It is not."

"Never deflect a compliment, my dear," Meg said, and her gaze held firm on Lucas. "Especially one that is so sincerely meant."

Simon and James stepped up then, taking their wives' arms. James grinned. "The arrivals have slowed now, so I think we can call this ball official."

"A great thanks to you, Your Grace, for making the arrangements so swiftly," Lucas said, forcing himself to look at Emma and away from Diana. She was a lovely woman, with kindness aplenty. It was obvious that James was devoted to her and their young daughter, heart and body and soul. Something he'd never imagined was possible for his friend when they were younger. To see James so at ease gave him nothing but pleasure.

"I'm happy to be of assistance," Emma said, reaching out to squeeze his arm. "Especially if it brings one of my husband's oldest and dearest friends back to our circle."

"They are beginning a waltz," James said, drawing Emma a bit closer. "We always dance the opening waltz, my dear. Do not deny me now."

Emma blushed and glanced up at him. "As if I could ever deny you. Enjoy yourselves tonight, you four. I hope we'll talk often later."

The two swept off then, and Lucas watched as James spun his wife into the dance, his hand just a bit too low in the small of her back, their eyes locked.

"They look very happy," Diana observed, her tone a bit far away as the foursome watched them dance. "And she is lovely."

"She is," Meg agreed. "I could not have picked a better bride for my brother. To see him so happy is…it's…"

She caught her breath and reached up to wipe a sudden tear. Simon tugged her closer. "Oh dear, this baby turns my wife into a water pot on more days than not. Happy tears, sad tears, tears over a torn hem…"

Meg swatted him playfully and was now chuckling through those very tears. "You are a cad, sir."

"And yet it is too late to escape me, for you are mine, or so the minister declared," Simon said with a laugh. "Come, I will dance you around the floor, and all will be well before the last strains of the music."

If Meg was going to argue, he did not allow it, but all but carried her off to the dancefloor, where they joined James, Emma and the rest of the revelers.

Lucas smiled at Diana. "You do look wonderful."

She blushed, and the act put him to mind of all the times they had made love. That flush of pleasure was something he very much enjoyed putting on her face, no matter how he found a way to do it.

"And you are handsome, not that you do not know it," she returned. He offered her an arm and she took it, allowing him to step her farther into the room. "How was your reunion?"

He glanced down at her, for he heard her concern in her voice. "Far better than I ever could have dreamed," he said, choosing pure honesty with her. He knew he could trust her with it. "All my concerns, gone in an instant. Though they certainly have a romantic notion of what it is to be a spy."

"Can one even be a spy if *nine* of his closest friends and all their wives know the truth?" she asked.

He smiled. "Well, my future with the department may yet be in question. I am better, yes, but my body is not the same. Perhaps it never will be. But if I were able to return to the work I love, I know for certain that I can trust those men and their wives with my life and the lives of those I work with. I believe that with all my heart."

She turned toward him with a half-smile. "Yet you feared what they would think of your secret."

He found his hand lifting, his body filled with a desire to touch her cheek. But he was well aware that the room was watching him, agog over the long-missing Duke of Willowby. To be too forward with Diana was not the best of ideas.

He clenched his fist at his side. "That's different," he said softly.

She nodded. "Of course it is." She might have said more, but in that moment, her eyes went a little wide as she looked at a point over his shoulder. "Is that Stalwood?"

He glanced back at him. "Yes. He's an earl, of course."

"Yes," she said with a shake of her head. "I know it, but sometimes I forget. To me, he'll always just be an old friend of my father."

Lucas winced at that reminder. He had some things to say to Stalwood tonight about the subject of Diana's father. Things that would hurt the man, would devastate her if she realized he suspected them.

He forced a smile. "He thinks very highly of you."

She blushed a little. "And will you discuss what we've gone over in your case? Would you like me to be a part of that?"

Before he could answer, he felt a tap on his shoulder.

"Are you going to introduce us?" Robert said when Lucas turned to see who had interrupted their conversation and saved him, albeit without meaning to, from a very uncomfortable lie he was about to tell.

He felt Diana shift at his side, and gently touched her arm before he smiled at the others and then made the introductions to the dukes and duchesses she had not yet met. After a moment of their welcome and kindness, he felt her relax a fraction and watched as she fell into conversation with the others.

Seeing her so relaxed should have made him happy. He liked that his friends liked her. And that she seemed to fit in with their tightknit little group. And yet, all he could think about was the subject they had been discussing when they were interrupted.

His case. Her father. And the secret that he was keeping from her about both.

D iana stood along the back wall of the ballroom, watching. It was a rather interesting exercise, for the room was a cacophony of sound, color and movement. Couples swirled around her, both in the flirtatious dance of courtship and the more regulated one of the dancefloor. Then there were the servants, moving through the crowd in every effort not to exist, even though they saw all. The men found each other in groups to talk politics, sometimes too loudly. And the women did the same, though their voices were raised in a wider variety of topics. Often their eyes fell on her, and there was no mistaking their interest and judgment.

Regardless of the attention, though, Diana felt like she was looking in through glass. She was still very much on the outside of this world. Lucas's world, for as she found him in the crowd, talking to James and Graham, it was clear he belonged. Whatever he felt about himself when it came to the truth about his parentage, he was a duke. And this was his universe.

"You're frowning," Helena said as she sidled up to Diana and slid a hand through her arm. "Are you well?"

Diana smiled at her friend. "Of course." They stood together for a moment, and then she sighed. "It is a very different world, isn't it?"

Helena laughed softly. "Oh, yes. Indeed it is. Are you feeling as if you don't belong?"

Diana nodded while she continued to look at Lucas. "I don't."

"As you know, I've felt the same. But I promise you, all in our circle like you enormously. We were just having a duchess meeting on the subject. So if you...*wanted* to be part of this world you would have all of us on your side. A formidable group, I assure you."

Diana faced her. "Of course Emma, Meg, Adelaide and Charlotte are wonderful. And it's clear they all are darlings of Society. All the women watch them, and I heard three ladies discussing the cut of Charlotte's gown a moment ago. She makes fashion. But…"

"But?" Helena encouraged her.

"Is it enough?"

"Why would it not be?" Helena asked, her tone very gentle.

Diana sighed. "Well, they've been watching me tonight, as well. Frowning. Talking behind their fans. Glaring at me. Would your circle be enough?"

Helena nodded slowly. "I understand those feelings. When Baldwin and I announced our engagement, there were women who gave me the cut direct. I won't say it wasn't hurtful or uncomfortable. But if you love him, I can also tell you that it is more than enough."

Diana froze. There were those words again, but this time they were spoken from another person's lips. They felt so much more alive. "I suppose the more important issue is if he loves…well, in theory it would be me."

"In theory?" Helena tilted her head.

Diana couldn't look at her. "We are speaking in hypotheticals, after all. We have to."

"Very well. In hypotheticals, I see the way he looks at you. It isn't just desire in his stare. It's caring. Concern. His face lights up when you're near. He's…alive. From an outsider's perspective, that is very much like love. But what about you?"

"If I were to feel such a thing for him," she said slowly. "It would feel like being woken up after a very long sleep. Like finding a half that I hadn't realized I was missing. But not a half that smothers or takes over the whole. Something that can allow itself to be separate, too."

Helena swallowed hard, her eyes now sparkling with tears despite her smile. "That is a very apt description. One that I think fits all in our circle. To find someone who both completes you and can allow you to be free, that is a rare thing. One that you should, *hypothetically*, not throw away out of fears that you won't fit into his world. If you fit into his life, that is all that matters. At least you should tell him your heart and give him a chance to refuse or accept it."

Diana's aforementioned heart leapt at that suggestion. To tell Lucas these feelings, that was courting disaster. And yet she knew Helena was correct. If she walked away without doing so, she feared she would live with that regret forever.

And she knew something hard and sharp and painful about living with regrets.

She looked across the room again. Lucas had left the side of his friends and now crossed the chamber to Stalwood. The two men shook hands and then talked with their heads close together for a moment. Lucas nodded, glanced over his shoulder, and then the two men exited the room together.

She refocused her attention on the case and smiled at Helena. "You've given me much food for thought. I think I'll take a moment and ponder it."

Helena leaned in and surprised Diana by pressing a quick kiss to her cheek. "In truth, I may be selfish. You and I could help each other, too, to find our way through this world. If I can do anything to help, please come to me."

"I will," Diana assured her before she slipped away to follow the men from the room.

She would have to face the truths that Helena had offered up to her. That was clear. But for now, she had to focus on the case that had brought Lucas to her. Perhaps once that was resolved, the future they could share...or not...would be clearer.

At least she hoped it would be. Because her heart was already deeply involved, and she didn't look forward to losing it if Lucas chose to walk away.

CHAPTER 21

"You have concerns," Stalwood said as he motioned Lucas into one of James's back parlors and shut the door firmly behind them. "I can see them all over your face. Has something happened?"

Lucas shifted. He'd been thinking about this moment for days and dreading it with every fiber of his being. What he was about to say was unthinkable, and a betrayal of the secrets Diana had shared.

And yet there was no way around it. Stalwood needed to know his thoughts. They could save a hundred men. A thousand.

"I do have concerns," he verified slowly as he moved to the sideboard and poured them each a drink of James's best scotch. "God, that isn't the right word for them. Worse than that."

Stalwood took the offering, but didn't drink as he continued to stare at Lucas with apprehension clear on his face. "This is about Diana, isn't it?"

"Diana?" he repeated in surprise.

Stalwood nodded. "You've already told me things that worry me. She is a beautiful woman, not to mention clever and kind. You have a charisma that is hard to deny. Perhaps I was a fool to place you two into the same environment and not think that nature would run its course."

He blinked. Stalwood was mentioning indelicacies, dancing around the subject of their affair because it was obvious. Too obvious to anyone who knew him, who knew her. And yet he didn't fear it. He didn't regret it, even if he should. And it wasn't the subject he wanted to discuss at present.

"No, it isn't Diana that brings me concern," he said. He shook his head. "That isn't entirely true. Let me explain."

Stalwood took a seat and glared up at him. "Please do."

Lucas sank into the chair across from his superior and said, "I have gone over every paper, compared every note and taken into account all the things I know, all the things I've learned from Diana, and I'm coming to one conclusion over and over."

"Which is?"

"George Oakford may have been involved in the acts of treason," Lucas said, though his voice felt slow and sounded far away as he forced himself to say those awful, terrible words. They rang in the air around him, and Stalwood jerked to his feet.

"George Oakford," he repeated, his lined face twisting with the same horror that burned in Lucas's chest. "No. That cannot be. What is your evidence?"

"He was there that day," Lucas began. "Unexpectedly, uninvited. He gave an explanation at the time and I cared so deeply about the man that I fear I might not have dug deeply enough. But how would he know my location? It was a secret that was jealously guarded, considering the nature of my investigation. I suppose it is possible he did overhear my plans from someone else. Or perhaps..."

Stalwood shook his head. "That is not enough to convince me."

"Nor me," Lucas reassured him. "So there is the rest. Diana told me that Oakford brought another spy into their home two years ago. That she believed that this man was working with her father on a case. But you told me that Oakford was not given cases. I know that idea troubled you."

Stalwood paced a moment and then nodded slowly. "Yes. I admit, that Oakford would work behind my back raised my suspicions. We were old friends and I was his superior. If there were an innocent explanation, then he could have and I think would have talked to me."

"I agree," Lucas choked out. The words came harder now. "Diana also mentioned a special knot her father used to close the bandages on wounds. Something complicated and not easily learned. Yet that was the knot on the bandage wrapped around my leg when I woke up after my injury."

Stalwood wrinkled his brow. "But you believed Oakford to be dead when you saw him lying on the ground. He could not have tied off your wound."

"I would think not. But perhaps his partner, the man who shot me, did. Although why he'd try to save me after shooting me twice and causing me to fall ten feet is beyond me. Or perhaps..."

"Perhaps?"

Lucas got up now. He hated to say the next. "What if...Oakford was pretending the initial injury?" he suggested. "He wasn't hurt at all, but he wanted me to think he was in the event that I survived. What if he came to my aid? We were...I thought we were close. Diana said he thought of me as a-a son. Even if he were a traitor, it doesn't follow that he truly wanted me to die. He might have even thought that my injuries would close the case."

"But Oakford did die. We had a body."

"Mutilated, which you didn't tell me," Lucas snapped.

Stalwood let his breath out in a long sigh. "I'm sorry you heard about that. I did not want you to carry even more guilt. His body was damaged, yes, but we identified him through his clothes and personal effects. We buried him."

"I have reason to believe Oakford might have come to despise his partner." He cleared his throat. "A personal reason. If that man turned on me, tried to kill me, and George intervened, they might have quarreled..."

"You think that was when he *truly* shot Oakford, along with all the other servants, in the scuffle," Stalwood finished. "But why would he hate the partner?"

"Diana," Lucas said softly.

Stalwood blinked a few times, his expression heavy with shock. "Diana," he repeated slowly and in a tone thick with understanding.

Lucas winced, for he hated to reveal even a sliver of the secrets she had whispered to him in confidence. But this was a traitor. A murderer. A man that had turned against his own and caused Diana's father's death. That had to justify what he was doing...somehow.

"I do not wish to get into the details," he said, and hoped Stalwood would respect that. "I will just say that Oakford believed that Diana had been...harmed by his partner. To know that would rot him out. Drive him to rage, even. They were in deep together, but if Oakford hated him..."

Stalwood nodded to show that he understood the path of Lucas's thoughts. His expression was grave. "Very well, let us say that is true. That still leaves us with an unidentified man in our ranks."

"Not unidentified," he said. "Diana named him. And the name matches even more of our evidence. Boyd Caldwell."

Stalwood swayed slightly at the invocation of that name. "You said the men guarding the estate that day said part of their employer's name that day. Cal—"

"You looked into Caldwell with all the rest, I know. Did you eliminate him?" Lucas asked.

Stalwood shook his head slowly. "He was one of the men we couldn't exclude by an alibi at the time of your attack. But we couldn't find anything especially suspicious about him, either. But if he is linked to Oakford...and Oakford was there the day you were shot..."

"It's a good lead, as much as I hate it," Lucas said, and rubbed a hand over his face. "I cannot tell you how much I hate it. To think that George Oakford could be a traitor, in league with a killer...it turns my stomach."

Stalwood was pale as paper. "Everything in me wants to shove this information away. Burn it from my mind if I could. But I know you're correct. There are pathways here that the evidence reveals. And until we prove them wrong or right, we cannot dismiss them. Even if it breaks my heart and yours."

"It does break my heart," Lucas croaked out. "Worse, it would break…"

"Diana's," Stalwood said, his tone pained. "Does she know your suspicions?"

Lucas flinched. "No. What she told me was not told as part of the investigation. I didn't reveal to her what I thought when she said that name…Caldwell. And I won't. I won't tell her."

"That's for the best," Stalwood agreed. "Until we know for certain, keep the communication open. We may need more details that she would be loath to share if she thought they would destroy her father's memory."

Lucas wrinkled his brow. *That* was not why he was keeping his thoughts secret from Diana. After everything she'd lost, he had no intention of stealing her love for her father, her belief and faith in his goodness. Not until they knew everything. Perhaps not even then.

If he could protect her, he would.

"Willowby?" Stalwood said, sharp.

He jolted. "Of course. Of course I will not tell her," he said.

"Good." Stalwood smoothed his hands over his waistcoat. "Bloody hell, I hate this. I'll return to my office and do some work on my end. I'll reach out to you as soon as I can to further this investigation."

The two men locked eyes, and then Lucas motioned to the door for his superior to leave first. He followed, his hands shaking as he tried to regain composure before he returned to the ballroom where he'd have to face the world, his friends and Diana.

. . .

D iana hid in the shadowy dark of an alcove in the hallway, watching as Stalwood and Lucas headed toward the ball-room. She leaned heavily against the wall, for her own legs would not hold her.

There had never been an intention in her mind to eavesdrop on the men. She'd had every plan to simply join them in their discussion and add whatever information she had to Lucas's. Because she'd been foolish enough to see herself as his partner in this investigation. To believe him when he said she was. To believe in him at all.

But when she'd begun to open the door, she'd heard her name. Her father's name, and the word *traitor*. It had shocked her so much that she'd stood there, silent and dumbfounded as the two men talked about the evidence Lucas saw against her father. About how he'd gleaned that information from *her*.

She'd listened as he'd danced around the edges of her secrets so that Stalwood couldn't possibly misunderstand them. Tears filled her eyes and she fisted her hand on the wall as she fought not to let them fall.

She'd trusted him. With her body. With her past. With her heart. And here he'd been using her in order to sully her father's name. Her heart ached and she wanted to scream in response.

She wanted to run away from this and him and never come back. And yet that wasn't possible.

"Diana, is that you?" She turned to find that Emma had come up the hallway while she'd been lost in her thoughts. The pretty duchess reached her, and her expression softened. "Oh, dearest, what is it?" Emma caught her hands and drew Diana closer. Her kindness was so honestly meant, and yet Diana wanted to run from it, too.

She forced herself to remain calm and said, "I-I was a bit over-whelmed and got lost on my way to the retiring room."

Emma wrapped an arm around her and guided her down the

hallway. "You know, I've lived in this house for over a year and a half and I am still getting lost from time to time. Let me take you there, for I could use a moment, as well."

Diana nodded and let herself be taken to the room where the ladies took their air and gathered themselves. Only she knew there would be no gathering herself. Not today. Perhaps not ever.

L ucas forced a smile as Diana and Emma entered the ballroom together. Once again, seeing her with the wives of his friends made him feel comfortable somehow. He didn't want to think about that overly much. Just as he didn't want to think about Stalwood, who had already left to follow up on Lucas's theories.

He would have to face that when the time came. Have to decide what to do and what to tell Diana if his ugly theories were correct. But for now, he intended to enjoy the time they had together.

He left the refreshment table and crossed to Emma and Diana, who lifted her gaze and watched him as he approached. With each step, his heart sank, for there was something...changed in her gaze. Empty. Pained.

He reached them and bowed slightly. "Ladies," he drawled as greeting. "Wherever did you two run off to?"

"The retiring room," Emma said with a concerned glance at Diana. "We were both a bit overcome by the warmth of the ballroom."

Diana shot her a brief, grateful look, and Lucas held back a curse. Something had obviously happened to her tonight, while he was distracted by his work. Perhaps someone had been unkind to her or she'd been reminded of something painful in the surroundings. Either way, he wanted to help.

"Perhaps you would grant me this dance, Miss Oakford," he said, holding out a hand. "A bit of movement might relieve some of your discomfort."

She stared at him a beat. Another. The coldness didn't leave her expression. "Of course, Your Grace. I see no way to refuse such an offer," she said at last.

He wrinkled his brow at her carefully chosen words, but smiled at Emma and guided Diana to the floor. The music began and they swayed into the steps. He was a bit slower than those around them, perhaps. After all, his arm and his leg were still pained, especially after getting so little rest for them today. But he was pleased that he was still capable of at least a modicum of grace.

"What is wrong?" he asked at last, when they had settled into the movements.

Her gaze left his and her lips pursed. "Nothing at all."

He pivoted them and shook his head. "I think I know you better than that, Diana. I can see something has happened—did someone say something to you to hurt your feelings? Or is it something else? I understand that you could have been reminded of your father or your...your daughter..."

She did not answer, though her green eyes, now dark with emotion, flashed over his face. But it was like she was seeing him for the first time. Like she didn't know him, despite all they'd shared.

That disconnected expression hit him in the gut like a knife blade and made him want to claw her close and fix whatever had changed her expression.

"I want to go home," she said softly.

He pressed his lips together. That was not an answer to his question. Nor did it explain why she seemed to hold him responsible. But it *was* a request he could honor. "I admit, I am not particularly comfortable either, and my body is punishing me for all this activity. We could depart early. I'm certain Abernathe won't mind, as I've completed the mission I came here to fulfill."

Her brow arched and she said, "I'm sure you have."

He turned her a few more times, concern growing in him with every moment. At last the song ended and he executed a bow. She curtseyed with the barest of politeness and then turned on her heel as if to abandon him on the dance floor entirely.

"Diana," he managed through gritted teeth as he caught her arm and guided her from the floor instead. "What is wrong?"

"Nothing," she said, perhaps a bit too loudly, for the eyes of some in the crowd shifted to them. She blushed in the moment she realized that, and tugged her arm from his. "Just a headache, Your Grace. Nothing for you to be concerned about."

He shook his head slowly. She was correct, of course. If she did not wish to include him in her troubles, he was owed no explanations. He was not her family, he was not her husband. And yet when she said it, he realized how untrue it was. Her wellbeing was his concern. Her happinesses and her heartbreaks, her laughter and her tears—in the weeks they had spent together, they had all become so very important to him.

In that moment, when she would barely look at him, when she had pulled away from him in body and soul, he recognized why. He recognized, suddenly and powerfully and deeply, that he loved her. He loved Diana Oakford with a power that nearly dropped him to the floor and made everything else around him fade.

"Is everything all right here?" Simon asked as he and Meg approached.

Diana's cheeks darkened with embarrassment. "Yes. I am just...weary."

"I have finished my business," Lucas said, somehow managing to find words when his mind was still reeling from the recognition of his heart. "I'll take Diana home."

She jerked, as if that wasn't what she wanted, but she didn't argue.

Simon wrinkled his brow. "I'll go have your carriage sent around so you can say your goodnights," he said softly, sending Meg a meaningful look.

Meg returned it, but her expression was bright and kind as she looped her arm through Diana's and said, "I know everyone will be very sad to see you go. But I will expect you to join the group of us for tea in a few days."

Diana cleared her throat and said, "Of course. I will want to return your gown."

Meg pursed her lips, but maneuvered Diana to the group of friends, who were standing together on the edge of the dancefloor. Lucas managed to say his goodnights, ignoring the questions in the eyes of his friends. He had no answers, so it was impossible to address what he didn't understand.

He was more focused on Diana, who was quiet and stiff as she said her farewells and embraced each duchess in turn. Meg was last, and Lucas heard her whisper, "Is there anything I can do?"

Diana looked at her evenly. "No. You've been lovely. Thank you for that." Then she turned and speared Lucas with a long look. "Your Grace."

He flinched. She had always switched back and forth between calling him by his given name and addressing him more formally. In fact, she was the only person he knew that could "Your Grace" him and not make his stomach turn.

But now when she said it, it was not a playful tease or a formal acknowledgment. It was a way to distance herself. Until he could talk to her, until he could be alone with her and really understand what had happened to change her feelings toward him, he wasn't going to be able to cross that distance.

He took her arm and led her from the ballroom and into the foyer. Simon stood at the door, and Lucas could see that his carriage was waiting outside.

"Good night," Diana said to his friend, then detached herself from Lucas's touch and slipped out to the carriage to be helped in by his footman.

Simon stared at him. "What changed?"

"I have no idea," Lucas said softly. "But I'm going to find out."

He moved to join her, but Simon caught his arm, holding him steady. Lucas looked into his friend's eyes. Normally Simon was playful, light, nothing but kindness, but now his expression was intense and focused.

"I almost lost Meg," he said quietly, "because I was not willing to speak my heart. I feared the consequences so much that I almost created far more dire ones. I make up for it every day, but I will never truly be able to erase those months and years that I was not brave. Don't do the same. If you love this woman, don't lose that chance at happiness out of fear for the consequences."

Lucas swallowed hard. He had not been around for Simon and Meg's desperate and difficult courtship. One that had broken up her prior engagement to Graham, one that had temporarily destroyed the friendship between the men. He'd heard about it, of course, in letters from a few of the others. Now he saw the truth of it in Simon's stare. The pain of it. And the desperation Simon felt that he not make the same mistakes.

"It's complicated," Lucas murmured.

Simon shook his head. "If you don't think it always is, then you should talk to each and every one of your friends who has been married recently. It's worth it. You're no coward, so fight."

Simon released him and stepped away. Lucas nodded slowly. "I'll think about it."

"See that you do. I'll come call in a few days. Let me know if you need anything in the interim."

Lucas turned away, back to his carriage, where he could see Diana sitting, waiting for him, though he did not think it was with happy anticipation. Simon's words rung in his ears. His admonishment to fight for her. For a future he had not dared to envision for over a decade.

He had no idea if there was anything to fight for, if Diana's changed behavior was any indication. But if there was, he had to decide if he could fight for it. Fight for her.

CHAPTER 22

Diana had expected Lucas to get into his carriage and immediately begin an expert interrogation of her. She had braced for it, for it seemed impossible to hide her feelings from him. They were too powerful. They boiled in her like witch's brew and burned her from the inside out.

And yet he had not done that. Not for the entire ride from the Abernathes' London home to his own. No, he'd only watched her. Silent yet focused, his dark gaze always following her every move, planning his reactions for the right moment.

She had been so foolish to let herself love a spy. She knew the very calculation and the manipulation that would follow were part of who this man was. She'd known it from the beginning, and yet she had believed in him. She'd slipped into a blissful confidence that it could be different. Tonight had slapped her in the face with the truth.

Everything between them had all been part of a deeper goal of his. She was a piece on his complicated chessboard. Perhaps that was all she'd ever been.

And yet she still loved him.

The carriage slowed as it entered his drive, and stopped. Still he said nothing as his footman helped her down. He didn't even try to take her arm as they walked up to the house and into the foyer, where Jones took their wraps.

"I'm going upstairs," she said, refusing to meet his eyes. Meet his eyes and the pain would follow. She knew that now.

He nodded. "I'll go with you."

"Why?" she asked before she could stop herself. Immediately she regretted it, for he leaned in and brushed his fingertips across her cheekbone. That gentle touch made her heart flutter, her body react, her anger dissipate for a brief moment.

"Do you really think I'm going to let you pretend that things didn't change?" he asked. "We are not finished, Diana. I want to talk to you."

She let out her breath in a burst and turned toward the stairs. She felt him watching her as he followed her up. But what could she do? Her emotions were so close to the surface, if she let them out she could lose control. This was not a man to lose control with.

He was always in control.

She opened her door and turned back to him. "Can't we leave it be?" she asked. Her voice trembled.

"Fight," he said softly.

She tilted her head, for the whispered word was no answer. "I beg your pardon?"

"Nothing," he said. "I can't leave it be."

She clenched her jaw in frustration and walked into her chamber. She threw herself into the chair at her dressing table and began to tug the pins from her hair. She had been so happy to have it put up—she'd felt like a princess when she looked at herself in Meg's mirror all those hours ago. Now she recognized it for what it was. A mask. A costume.

As fabricated and false as any moment between her and Lucas, now poisoned by his conversation with Stalwood.

He shut her door and leaned against it, but made no move to come to her side or touch her. At least he gave her that. "Tell me."

"Am I your foot soldier now, Your Grace?" she asked, tossing a pin on the table and watching it bounce off the surface and clatter to the floor below.

He recoiled. "What?"

She pivoted in her chair and looked at him. "That was an order, was it not? To report?"

"Diana," he said, pushing off the door. His face was twisted with pain, with confusion, with desperation. All of it seemed so real. Like her anger and her heartbreak actually moved him. She had to force herself to remember that what she'd heard earlier proved his expression wrong.

"I thought you were going to tell me when you were meeting with Stalwood," she snapped.

His eyes widened. "Is *that* what this fit of pique is about? That I didn't tell you that Stalwood and I were meeting? Diana, you have been a great help to me, I appreciate that more than you could ever understand, but let me be clear: this is my case. *I* decide what I should share and not."

She glared at him. "Yes, that is patently obvious. As is the fact that I am an *idiot* for thinking we shared anything more than a few nights in a bed."

He recoiled. "You cannot be this upset about a meeting, Diana. To think that nothing else mattered because I went into a parlor without you. That's madness."

"George Oakford is the traitor," she said softly. "That is what you told the earl, isn't it?"

He froze, his expression going blank because he'd spent years learning how to do that. How to turn emotion off and on. How to lie without blinking.

"Tell me to my face that it wasn't," she continued, rising to her feet and stepping toward him. "Lie to me, Lucas, as you have been for weeks."

He lifted his chin. "You eavesdropped on my meeting."

She folded her arms. "Do not turn this on me. I followed you because I was stupid enough to believe I was a *part* of your investigation. A partner, you said. I would have come into the room and never hidden, except I heard my name. And then his. And all those ugly words you said about him."

He shut his eyes briefly and all the air exited his lungs in a long exhalation. For a flash of a moment, he looked exhausted. Overwhelmed. Devastated in a way she never would have expected.

Then he opened those same dark eyes and held her steady with them. "I would not have had you hear those things," he whispered.

She barked out a humorless laugh. "I assume not, Your Grace. After all, they revealed me to be a fool for believing in you, in us. I'm certain you would not want me to know that you seduced all my secrets from me, things I would never have told another person, and then cavalierly handed them over to Stalwood. Will they be included in the report, as well? Passed around to the other agents?"

He moved to her now in three long steps and caught her arms, drawing her up against his chest. She caught her breath at being so close to him, at the passion that flashed in his eyes.

"That is not what this is about!" he all but shouted. "I struggled with giving Stalwood even the skeletal information I did."

"It didn't seem like a struggle," she whispered as she carefully extracted herself from his arms and backed away once more. "You seemed to hand him my life on a platter like it was nothing more than another piece in a puzzle. Like my heart didn't matter."

"Of course it matters," he said softly. "Diana, when I began to suspect your father, I didn't tell you because I knew it would break your heart."

"You knew I wouldn't believe it," she corrected, anger bubbling up in her chest and making her clench her fists at her sides. "And I don't."

"You don't have to," he said quickly. "He's your father, and if you can hold him innocent, keep your memories as only positive, I would want nothing less for you."

She stared at him. "But you will continue to investigate him."

He hesitated, and she knew the answer even before he slowly nodded. "Yes."

She spun away. "I heard what you told Stalwood." She thought of each piece of evidence he'd laid out. And she violently pushed away the sliver of doubt that entered her mind when she considered them all put together.

"I'm sorry," he said. "I would not have wanted you to find out that way."

"No." She didn't look at him still. "You wouldn't have had me find out at all. When I heard you accuse my father, that was shocking. When I heard you hand over the most painful moments of my past to someone else when they were told to you in confidence, that was chilling. But when you told Stalwood that you would lie to me, keep me in the dark so you could continue to use me...*that* was devastating."

She faced him at last and found him standing, his head bent and his shoulders slumped. "Would it make any difference if I told you I said it that way so Stalwood would not suspect my deeper feelings?" he asked. "That I was planning to keep the truth from you, for now, because I didn't want to hurt you as you are hurt now?"

She clenched her teeth. How she wanted to believe that. To think that his lies were told to protect her. But she didn't. She didn't have any faith left. It had been whittled away, sliver by sliver, by Caldwell and his empty seduction, by the loss of her child, by the death of her father and now...this.

This final heartbreak that stole her breath and made her want to run. Made her need to run. That was the only way now.

She moved past him, careful not to touch him, and went over to her wardrobe. She opened it and began to remove her clothing.

"What are you doing?" he asked.

She glanced at him. "Now that I know the true purpose of your investigation, I cannot take part in it anymore. My father is dead and I won't be a part of sullying his name. As for your injuries, we both know you are more than capable of healing on your own. You probably have been for days. Staying was…a mistake. And it's one I can no longer afford to make."

He opened and shut his mouth and she waited for him to argue. To demand. To refuse. But at last he simply nodded slowly. "I understand, Diana. I understand why you can no longer bear to be in the same space as me. I won't stop you. It would be unfair to do so. But won't you wait until tomorrow to go?"

She stared at him. If she waited for tomorrow, she might wait another day, and another. She might let herself be swept up by this man and all the things she'd secretly come to hope for. If she'd learned anything from her father's pragmatic view of grief and loss, it was to ride away from both as swiftly as she could.

"No," she said. "That would not be wise."

He seemed to buckle and caught the back of the closest chair to maintain his stance. Then he nodded. "Very well. I'll have one of my footmen accompany you back to your home. He will help you light your fires and see that you are safe."

"You needn't—"

He moved forward. "Please let me have that, Diana. Please."

She caught her breath at the desperation in his tone. Pained and so very real. It felt so real. She wanted to trust it. She couldn't.

"Fine." She turned her back to him. "Let me gather my things, will you?"

"Yes," he said softly. "Of course. I'll make the other arrangements."

She knew he hesitated, standing at her door for too long before he left her alone. When he did, she collapsed to her knees, covered her face and cried. For what she'd believed and hoped for. For what she'd lost. And for what she'd never had at all.

Lucas's hands shook as he watched his servants place Diana's very few things up into the carriage that would take her home. Far away from him. The "footman" he was sending to help her was actually one of Stalwood's guards. He'd given the man strict instructions to stay and watch the house, watch over her.

It was the only way he could give her what she needed. The only way to let her go because she couldn't stand to look at him anymore. No one's fault but his own, and yet it felt like his entire being was under attack.

When he turned, he found her standing behind him. She had changed from her pretty gown, back into her plainer clothing, and yet she looked more beautiful to him than she ever had.

"That's all of it?" she said, her voice barely carrying.

He thought she was asking him, but it was Jones who answered as he entered the foyer from behind Lucas. "Yes, Miss Oakford," he said coolly. "That is all. May I do anything else for you?"

"Leave us," Lucas whispered, for he could not dare speak harshly or he would scream.

The butler frowned and did as he was told. Slowly, Lucas shut the door and faced her. This was their last moment alone. Perhaps their last moment ever, and he could think of nothing to say. Not when she stared at him like she didn't know him at all.

"I never meant to hurt you," he said, and the words felt false. Like they were an excuse, when he had none.

She nodded slowly and let out a small sigh. "I suppose you didn't. You are who you are, Lucas. And your duty is important to you. I know that."

He wanted to tell her that he loved her. He wanted to shout it from the top of his lungs until she believed him. And yet he saw how self-serving that would be. It was a way to manipulate her. To try to erase the damage he had done with his lies.

And she deserved better.

She moved forward, and he stiffened as she reached out to him. But she didn't slap him, though perhaps he deserved it. She didn't demand she be set free, back to a life that could not include him.

She reached up and cupped his cheek. She stared into his face,

JESS MICHAELS

and for a moment all the harm he'd done was gone. She was Diana again. His savior, his light, his life.

"Lucas, don't—don't let any of this push you from your future," she whispered.

He wrinkled his brow. "You are determined to save me still?"

"I suppose I'm a fool, but yes." Her fingers traced his cheek gently. "You've run from your life for a long time, because of mistakes that were not your own. But you've been brought back here, to your friends and your home and a future that you once let be stolen. I would hope that perhaps this will keep you from running again."

He let out his breath. "If you would want me to try to make this life, then there is no way I couldn't grant you that boon, Diana. I owe you that. I owe you much more."

She leaned up then, her lips coming to his. Everything in him wanted to drag her close, to claim her with the kiss she granted, to force her to feel what he had stolen from her heart. But he didn't. Somehow he just let her brush her lips to his, feather-light, like a butterfly's wings. And then she was gone.

"Goodbye," she said, reaching past him for the door.

"Goodbye," he whispered in return, that one word like a sword being stabbed through his heart. He watched her leave his home. Watched her leave his life.

And knew that nothing could ever be the same.

CHAPTER 23

It had been two days since Diana left. Well, thirty-seven hours and twenty-three minutes. He could have probably guessed to the second, but there seemed little meaning in that exercise. She was gone and everything in his body and soul hurt.

Now he stood in the hallway, staring at his parlor door, and he struggled to find the strength to open it. Not because of his injuries. The time with Diana had eased those so much that he could function. No, he hesitated because facing what was inside without her felt…impossible.

Slowly, he pushed the door open and drew a breath as his mother pivoted from the portrait of his father hung above the fireplace. Her dark gaze snagged his and then darted away as her lips pursed.

"You have summoned me," she said, and folded her arms. "And I have come. What is it you want?"

He flinched at her coldness but entered the room regardless. Diana had made him promise not to run from his life. To do that, he had to face the past.

"Good afternoon, Mother," he said. "May I get you tea?"

She shook her head. "No."

He sighed. "Can we not be civil?"

Her nostrils flared and then she shrugged before she settled herself into a chair before the fire. "I suppose we could try. Though I see little benefit from the exercise."

"There has been little in the past, hasn't there?" He took the seat across from hers. "There is so much between us."

She drew back a fraction, surprise washing over her expression. "You cannot have brought me here to talk about *that*."

He leaned forward, draping his elbows over his knees. "And yet I have."

She recoiled, her hands gripping the arms of her chair until her knuckles became white. "I will not."

"I understand why," he said slowly. "The topic is difficult for you. But you must know that it is difficult for me, as well. We have avoided it for years. Avoided each other. To the point where I did not even have you sent for when I was shot, almost killed."

Her lips parted. "Shot?"

"Yes." He drew in a breath. "In protection of my country, my king, I was shot six months ago. You did not ask me about my limp when you last saw me, but that is how I got it. I nearly died and I did not call for you. Would you have wanted me to?"

She was silent a long time, but her expression had become less confrontational, less cold. "I-I don't know," she admitted. "As you say, our relationship has never been a happy one. Perhaps it would have been hypocritical to come only because you were...did you really almost die?"

He nodded slowly. "I did. And someone who helped me recover pointed out that I'd been running from my life. We both know why. Perhaps it's time I stop."

She stiffened. When Willowby had died, she had wanted Lucas to take his place, to accept the role he hadn't earned. They'd had a terrible row about his decision to abandon that post. Even now he could see she was still interested in him doing his duty. To save face, perhaps. To make up for something. Whatever the reason, it made her lean forward in interest.

"You wish to take your father's place?" she asked.

He flinched. "Willowby's place, yes. But if I want to stop running, I need your help."

She swallowed hard. "How?"

"Was it an affair?" he asked.

She turned her face, her cheeks growing pink. "You cannot ask me such impertinent things."

Her harsh tone was back and he recoiled from it. It reminded him of too many times he'd heard it. Too many times he'd felt it cut him like a knife. Even now, it still stung.

"You act as though I had some part in your decisions," he said. "I only suffered from them. Are you really so cold as to say that I don't deserve to understand why you did what you did when it changed everything about my life?"

She glared at him and folded her arms. He drew in a long breath. Part of him wanted to keep pushing, but that was the emotional part. Perhaps it was time to treat this like an interrogation with a reluctant suspect. And the best way to do that was often to do…nothing.

He settled back in his chair, holding her stare evenly and said nothing. Time ticked by between them and he saw her grow uncomfortable. Saw her shift. Saw her blush.

Finally, she let out her breath in a huff. "It was an act of war!"

"That was why you chose my father's servant," he said.

Her shoulders sagged and he could see he had her surrender now. "He never wanted me. Your father, he made that clear. He wanted my father's money, he wanted…propriety in public. But me? He could barely look at me. I grew to hate him for it. Like a poison that crept into every corner of our life together."

Lucas stared at her. All these years, how he had resented her for what she'd done. For the parentage she had stolen from him, for the way she'd pushed him away. And yet now he saw her pain. She hid it well. Perhaps he'd inherited his own ability to do the same from her. But beneath that cold mask she wore, that lady-of-the-manor chilliness that kept a wall between her and everyone else, there was the pain. The regret. The loss.

"I made a mistake. Once." She shook her head. "And then there was you and there was no denying it. Especially when that cad of a valet decided to blackmail me for it."

Lucas lurched. "He did?"

"Yes." Her voice was thick with disgust. "He threatened to bring my world down around me."

"You must have been terrified."

"Indeed. I even tried to..." She blushed deeper. "Well, I tried to soften your father to me. To make it not so obvious that you weren't his. It did not work."

Lucas shut his eyes, pained by the idea of his mother, so alone as she tried to seduce a man who didn't want her to cover up being seduced by one who had used her. That rejection from the duke had sealed her fate, sealed his own.

"When you came, it ended it all," she said, lifting her chin. "And yes, I grew to resent you for it. Despise you for it. For your chin, which was like that other man's. For your laugh that was like his."

"So did Willowby. Even before I was told the truth, I knew the emotion," Lucas said softly. "It was no life for a child, to feel that hatred and not understand it."

She nodded slowly. "I know that. I knew it then, but I was incapable of anything else. In a way, it was a relief when you knew. When you left. When he died."

"I imagine so. He no longer controlled your purse. He no longer withheld your future. And I no longer reminded you of what you had longed for and lost." Lucas met her gaze. "And now, looking at me, with the years that have separated us, do you still despise me?"

She examined his face carefully. "When you said you almost died, I admit there was something in my stomach that...lurched. A great desire not to lose what I never wanted or cherished."

218

Her words were frank and they still hurt. But he'd asked her for her honesty and there it was. He found, in this moment of calm that had been made possible by Diana's pushing, that he could understand her. And see the hope that those words created for them.

"I was not his son," Lucas said. "But I am yours."

"So you want…what? Some kind of close bond?" She said the words like they were foreign. With a faint lilt of disgust.

"No, I don't think that's possible. We're not built for it, are we, after so much between us?" He sighed. "But that doesn't mean we must be completely estranged. There is something in the middle, isn't there?"

He shifted as he said those words. As he felt them in his heart. No matter what else had happened, there *was* a place for his mother in his life. Small, perhaps. Distant. But not broken. Not entirely.

Diana had given him the strength to see that. To be able to take the leap to say it to his mother. It was Diana's gift to him. Her last gift, perhaps, and that turned his stomach far more than the wait for his mother's response.

"I don't want to be estranged." Her words came deliberately. "But how do we move forward?"

"Carefully," he suggested. "Slowly and with a bit of understanding for each other. Something I don't think either of us has ever given to the other."

She nodded. "Very well. I think I can do that."

He reached out and took her hand. She let him, and he realized it was the first time he had touched her in years—decades, perhaps. After a few seconds, she released him and got to her feet. He followed. The discomfort still hung between them now, but it felt less awful. Less permanent.

It was a start.

There was a knock at the parlor door, and they both turned as Jones entered the room.

"You have an urgent message, Your Grace," he said as he handed over a folded sheet of paper. "I would not have normally intruded, but the man said it was most important and could not wait."

The duchess smiled. "It is likely for the best. I'll leave you to your urgent business. Perhaps you'll come and call on me for tea in a few weeks. We'll start with that."

Lucas nodded and watched as she left the room, Jones on her heels. He turned the note over and blanched. It was Stalwood's seal that closed the page. The man had a different one for different kinds of messages. This one indicated that the spy should come right away for a meeting. When Lucas opened the page, he was not surprised to find it blank. The seal was the message, nothing more.

He strode from the parlor and into the foyer, just in time to see Jones shutting the door and his mother's carriage pulling away. The butler seemed surprised to see him so soon and said, "Is there something you need?"

"My horse," Lucas said cautiously, for he had not ridden since the attack. "And quickly."

Jones stepped out to call on the footmen with the message, and Lucas shook his head to clear it. This meeting with Stalwood had to be about Oakford and Caldwell. And he could only hope it would help him clear his mind to work on that case.

Because right now he needed the distraction.

Diana stood at her kitchen table, chopping dried herbs before she slid them into marked vials for future medicines and tinctures. Normally the work was pleasant, for it helped her clear her mind.

Today...well, today was different. In truth, she feared every day would be different for the rest of her life, because of Lucas. It had been nearly two days since she slipped from his home, away from his life and returned to her own. Only the London cottage was now haunted by thoughts and memories of the man. Here he had touched her, here they had kissed, here he had held her, comforted her.

She shivered and some of the dried herbs scattered across the table. She swore and swept them off the edge and into her palm to try to fill the vial again.

She had every intention of going back to the countryside, but hadn't made the arrangements yet. "Not that it will be any better, I fear," she said, jolting at the sound of her own voice. Her house felt so quiet now without Lucas in it.

"Still talk to yourself, do you?"

She pivoted at the voice in her door. It was one she recognized, as was the gentleman who owned it. The one standing there, staring at her.

Boyd Caldwell.

Out of instinct, she scurried away from him a few steps until she flattened herself against the opposite wall. She had not seen this man for almost two years. Not since he seduced and then left her. He looked the same. Tall, broad-shouldered, with dark hair and green eyes. He was older than Lucas. Older and far less alluring.

She thought for a moment of the accusations that had been made about him being the traitor. She'd been so focused on her father, she hadn't let herself consider the other man.

Now she couldn't stop thinking of it.

"You look like you've seen a ghost," Boyd said, ducking into the kitchen and shutting the door behind him, though he had not been invited to do either.

She wiped her shaking hands along the front of her apron and tried to gather her composure. "You almost are. I have not seen you in two years, Boyd. What are you doing here?"

He smiled. Once, what seemed like a lifetime ago, she recalled being taken with that smile. Now she felt uncomfortable with it turned on her.

"I cannot come to call on an old friend?" he asked.

She swallowed past the lump in her throat. "We were never friends, Boyd."

That smile broadened, became a little lewd as his gaze flicked over her. "No. I suppose we weren't. We were much, much more."

"If you have come here for that, you will be sadly disappointed," she snapped as she folded her arms across her chest like a shield. "I know the truth about you now, Boyd."

He arched a brow. "Do you now?"

She realized in that moment that there was a double meaning to that statement. She'd meant it as a reminder that she now knew he had a family, a wife, that his advances were self-serving and had no future.

But she also knew about the suspicions that surrounded him. If true, she knew he was a traitor. A murderer. A person who had stolen her father and nearly killed the man she loved.

She lifted her chin. "I know about your family," she said. "Do you have other secrets?"

"As if you don't." The smile turned to a smirk, and he looked around her kitchen. "You are just like your father with all your weeds and potions."

She stiffened. "Yes, you knew my father well," she said, carefully testing the waters further. "If anyone was a friend to you in this house, it was him."

"Once," he said, the tone curt and short.

She tilted her head. "It is harder to be friends with a dead man, I suppose. And one whose daughter you seduced."

"Is that the story you tell yourself?" Boyd asked, facing her again. "That you were the sweet innocent who was taken in by a dark and evil man? You batted your eyelashes at me aplenty, my dear. Don't mistake the messages you sent."

"Why are you here?" she pushed out past clenched teeth. "I don't think we have anything to say to each other."

He didn't move, just remained in the middle of the kitchen, positioned between herself and both the door to the outside and the one to the rest of her house. Positioned between her and safety, she realized now with a creeping sense of discomfort and dread.

"You've taken up with the Duke of Willowby, I hear," he drawled. "Become his whore, but a whore he takes to proper parties, so *that* is something."

She froze and met his eyes carefully. There was something so feral in them. So dangerous, and in that awful moment she knew that all of Lucas's hunches about this man were correct. That he was the person who had nearly killed him. That he'd been a traitor and a vile betrayer to everyone who trusted him.

And she also knew, in a flash of heartbreak, that her father was likely also guilty. There was no mistaking their connection, especially since Boyd was here. Menacing and cold and dangerous.

"He was injured," she said, treading lightly. "I was asked to help and did so."

"There's a bit more to it than that," he said, that wicked smile returning to his lips. "And who can blame him? I know the charms you possess. I was the first one to sample them. Do you think I should tell him about that when he comes to rescue you? Or did you already confess it all when you gave yourself to him?"

She caught her breath. His words were coarse and crude, but they were also terrifying. Rescue her. That meant she was under threat. And so was Lucas.

She shook her head. "You can tell him anything you like, I suppose," she said softly, trying desperately to measure her tone. "I mean nothing to him. As you said, I was just his whore."

"So you think he wouldn't come for you if you were in danger?" he asked with a laugh. He reached into his pocket and slowly withdrew a small pistol. He pointed it squarely at her. "As you are in danger now."

She sucked for air, but couldn't seem to draw in enough as she stared at the weapon pointed at her. This man had killed before, in cold blood, and there was no reason to believe that he wouldn't do the same to her. One twitch of his finger and she would never again smell the flowers in her garden or walk in the hills around her home. She would never see Lucas again or feel his touch or be able to tell him that she loved him.

Grief welled up in her for all she would lose alongside her life.

"Steady now," he said. "No need to get ahead of yourself, my dear. You are a means to an end. A lovely piece of cheese for a rat or two."

She shook her head. At the very least she could try to save Lucas in this. "I'm telling you, he won't come for me. I don't mean enough."

"Is that why he put a guard on your house? Because you're meaningless?"

She blinked. "A-a guard?" she repeated.

"You didn't know?" he asked. "Well, it doesn't matter. I took care of the lad myself. What's one more dead spy now?"

Her stomach turned, but she forced herself to remain calm. "You are just trying to frighten me," she whispered.

"I hope it's working, for you should be frightened. For yourself. And for him. Because you're wrong about his feelings, I think," he said with a chuckle. "My people tell me that he cares for you. And even if he doesn't, the man wouldn't let a lover die. He lets his heart get ahead of his head that way. Besides, if he doesn't come, the other one will. And that would be as good a catch for this cat as Willowby."

"The other?" Diana repeated in confusion. "What other? Are you talking about Stalwood?"

His smile widened, impossibly cruel and callous. "No. I'm talking about your father, Diana."

Her lips parted. This man was mad. "My father is dead," she breathed.

He shook his head slowly. "No, no, my dear. Dead is what he wanted you to believe. I assure you, George Oakford is very much alive and well. At least he will be until I lure him to me with your life as bait and then put a bullet through his lying brain."

Diana stared at him, unable to think or speak or breathe. The world began to spin. Her father, alive? After all these months of mourning and pain, was it possible? Her breath came short as she was overwhelmed by emotion, and then she did something she'd never done before in all her years.

She fainted.

CHAPTER 24

Lucas carefully slung himself down from the horse, ignoring the massive pain that shot through his leg and shoulder as he did so. He handed over the reins to one of Stalwood's men and glanced up at the stylish townhouse before him. Inside he would have to face his superior and find out the truth about a man he'd considered a father.

He was not looking forward to what he would hear. His instincts already knew what it would be.

He climbed the long stairs and was greeted by Stalwood's butler. By the serious expression on the man's face and the way he took Lucas immediately down the hall, it was clear he was expected.

The man opened the door. "The Duke of Willowby, sir," he said into the room, then stepped aside for Lucas to enter. Stalwood was standing to the left at the window, looking out, his expression pensive.

"I got your message," Lucas said, "and came right away. I shudder to think of what you've found."

Stalwood turned and glanced at Lucas, then looked past him to the right side of the room with a pointed expression. Lucas followed his gaze and his heart lurched into his throat.

A ghost stood at the sideboard, drink in hand. It had to be a ghost—there was no other explanation, for it was George Oakford. The doctor was looking at Lucas, his expression hooded and unclear.

"What the bloody hell?" Lucas gasped.

Stalwood nodded to his servant. "That will be all, Jessup. No interruptions, no exceptions."

The door closed behind Lucas, but he continued to gape at Oakford. "Explain this," he hissed, his mind turning to Diana. Her heart had been broken by the death of her father. And here he was, in the flesh, as if the past six months hadn't happened.

"He showed up here an hour ago," Stalwood croaked. There was no doubt from his shaking voice that he was as shocked by this development as anyone. "It's why I called you here."

Oakford set his drink down on the sideboard and stepped forward. "Willowby."

Lucas didn't think, he didn't plan, he just swung on the man. His fist connected with Oakford's cheek and the doctor staggered back, catching himself on the sideboard edge.

"How could you?" Lucas breathed as Stalwood rushed forward to catch his arm and stay his attack. Pain throbbed through his shoulder but he ignored it. "Do you know what Diana has gone through since you 'died'?"

Oakford straightened, his hand straying to the cheek that was already swelling. "That was the worst part of all this, I assure you," he said.

"You want an explanation," Stalwood growled in Lucas's ear. "For yourself, for her. Well, he says he has one, and I have not yet heard it. Let him speak."

"You'll want to hear it," Oakford said softly. "But you must let me say it all because I need your help. *Diana* needs your help."

At that, Lucas went still, all his anger fading to fear. "Diana? Why?"

Oakford let out a sigh. "Let me begin at the beginning. I was always a pragmatic man, not prone to emotional displays."

"How is Diana in danger?" Lucas shouted.

"Because I brought a demon into our home," Oakford snapped back at last. "I exposed her to Boyd Caldwell, not thinking he would —would—"

"I know what he did to her," Lucas hissed in disgust. "And the consequences she had to face after, alone."

Oakford turned his head, and a flash of emotion crossed his face. "I failed her," he admitted. "So many times. But the reason I did this was for her."

"You became a traitor to the crown for Diana?" Stalwood asked, his tone as cold as ice. "Oh, I have a hard time believing that, *old friend.*"

"It's true. When my wife died, I realized how little I knew to help her. She had a future, but I could provide nothing but an education. What would I leave her when I was dead? A tiny cottage here, another in the country? A garden full of worthless herbs? What kind of life was that for her? My worries grew deeper as she grew up, became a woman."

"Is that when Caldwell approached you?" Lucas asked, trying to focus on the details, even as fears for Diana plagued him.

Oakford nodded. "He was injured during a case—that was how we crossed paths."

Lucas shivered. That explained the pattern he'd noticed in the attacks. Each man who had been replaced on his case had been injured. Oakford was the common element.

"Caldwell felt...angry that it had happened, and convinced that the War Department had seen him as expendable. I'd never seen such rage in another person." Oakford shuddered. "But when he said we could make money together, I listened. For her."

"Stop saying *for her*," Lucas growled. "Your daughter would never want you to trade your country and your friends for her comfort. To pretend that you did this in her name is to sully all that she is."

Oakford bent his head, and for a moment all the energy seemed to drain from him. "You're right, of course. I know it is my failing and no one else's. Caldwell assured me we could trade on smaller secrets, that no one would have to get hurt. Once people started dying, once he hurt my daughter, I *tried* to get out, but he wouldn't let me."

"He wouldn't let you," Stalwood repeated in disgust.

"It's true!" Oakford's tone was harsh with desperation. "He came to visit me in the country, threatening and demanding. He said if I didn't help him, he'd expose me. I'd have lost everything and Diana would have been swept up in it. He told me there would be but one last betrayal. He knew there were arms being moved, he also had contacts that could sell them to France for Napoleon's army. He told me that no one had to die for this act."

"Except all the men who would be shot thanks to the weapons!" Stalwood cried. "My God, George. For what? *Money*? If you'd been truly worried about Diana, you know I would have provided for her comfort and her future. You did this for your own selfishness."

Oakford flinched. "But then you showed up, Willowby," he said after a moment where he seemed to be gathering himself. "You were seen, and Caldwell was enraged. He despised you already and he wanted you dead. I crept out, hoping to intercept you. When you climbed the wall, I-I shot you."

Lucas stepped backward and felt the reaction in the very leg this man had shot. "*You* shot me?" he whispered in disbelief.

Oakford nodded. "I hoped that if I injured you, it would be enough for Caldwell. I fired the first shot so I could pretend I'd been injured, and then hit you. I assumed once you fell and saw me lying there, you would be distracted. I planned to bravely rouse myself, rush to your aid and get you out, and Caldwell would buy himself time and money by finishing the job."

"You nearly killed me," Lucas said.

"No, *Caldwell* nearly killed you," Oakford corrected. "He guessed that there was something afoot and came down after me. He shot you in the shoulder. I knew that was a far more serious wound. I convinced him that I would finish you and that he should go back to his dealings. But he was scared then, paranoid, certain that anyone could be against him."

"He shot the others at the house," Lucas whispered.

"Yes," Oakford said, and swallowed. "He killed them all. When I heard him start firing, I tried to get you up, get you moving. But I'd hit you wrong and you were unconscious from the fall. Your leg was bleeding profusely. I tied off the wound and was about to go when Caldwell returned. He wanted you dead, Willowby, so I fought him."

Lucas folded his arms. "Excuse me if I do not thank you for that."

"You shouldn't," Oakford said. "Caldwell ran after we fought, and I gathered up all the information about his contacts and...and the money he had hidden for the exchange for the weapons."

Lucas drew back. "So it was still all about the bloody money."

Oakford shrugged. "Easy for you to say, one who has always had it. I *needed* it. And I knew that if Caldwell didn't have it, he could do far less damage in the interim."

"Brave," Stalwood said, his tone dripping with sarcasm.

Oakford's nostrils flared slightly, but he continued, "Caldwell ran when he saw riders coming. Only I wasn't certain that he wouldn't turn back, turn on me. It was a split-second decision as the rest of the agents flooded in. I grabbed one of the servants, switched out clothes and personal items so that the body would look like mine."

"You mutilated that man's body," Stalwood said in horror. "And slithered off like a snake."

"You *coward*," Lucas snapped. "You could have stopped this that very day if you'd only turned yourself in and told everyone the truth."

Oakford clenched his jaw. "I suppose I am a coward. I didn't want to be swept up by this. To be transported or hanged. To have Diana sullied by what I'd done."

"So instead you devastated her?" Stalwood shook his head, and his expression was twisted with rage and disbelief. "You bastard."

"Why come back now?" Lucas asked. "You must know you won't be set free just for turning yourself in or turning on Caldwell."

"Because of Diana," Oakford said, stepping forward. "Caldwell knew I was alive—he's been trying to find me for months. He wants the information and the money I stole. He's desperate for it. I've been in hiding, but watching his every move. Only a few days ago, his eye turned elsewhere. Toward you, Willowby."

Lucas froze. That was exactly why he'd returned to Society, to draw the attention of the man who had nearly killed him. "He heard I was back in the ducal home," he said. "Did he think I could identify him?"

"He knew you were clever enough to put it all together," Oakford said. "And because of the fact that Diana was with you, he may even believe I was helping you."

Lucas lunged forward. "You think he believes Diana is in on your scheme. That *she* is the key to finding you."

He nodded. "Yes. He might not think she knows I'm alive, but he must assume that she could be key in drawing me out. And if it is true that the two of you are...close...perhaps bringing you to him in the bargain." Oakford moved to Lucas and caught his arm with both hands. "Please tell me that my daughter is safe in your home. Watched by Stalwood's men when you are not with her."

Lucas glanced at Stalwood. "N-no," he stammered as fear gripped him. "She was...she overheard us talking about our suspicions about you at the Abernathe party a few days ago. She left. Went back to your home here in London."

Stalwood sucked in a breath. "Did you not think that dangerous?"

"I sent a guard to watch over her, but I had no idea it was as bad as this. I had no idea her father was alive. If the bastard wanted to get to me, he could come for me at any time. I was the bait, not her. Christ, we have to get to her, to move her someplace safer. Now!"

All three men moved for the door together, and as they burst into the foyer, Stalwood's butler stepped into their path. "Your Grace, you had a message forwarded from your home a quarter hour ago."

He held out the paper, and Lucas grabbed for it in frustration. His mind swirled on Diana now and her safety. He couldn't think of anything else.

"We need horses, Jessup, immediately," Stalwood snapped.

The butler's mood changed in an instant. His posture changed into a military one and he scurried off to call for the mounts. As he did, Stalwood turned to Lucas. "What is the letter?"

Lucas jolted and stared down at the folded page. "I don't know." He drew a breath before he flipped the letter over and gasped.

"That seal," he said, touching the red wax. It had been stamped with the image of a reaper. The mark of death.

"Caldwell," Oakford breathed. "He used that seal for correspondence about our plans."

Lucas's stomach turned as he opened the letter and read it out loud. *"You are in my way and I grow tired of it. Come to where it began, where it ended for dear George Oakford. If you do not, his daughter may end there too."* He paused as a lock of hair fell from the page.

Oakford caught it. "Diana's hair," he whispered.

Lucas nodded. *"Come alone,"* he finished.

Stalwood shook his head. "Obviously that isn't going to happen," he said.

Lucas jerked his gaze over. "No, but it must look like I'm alone."

"It must look like you're with me," Oakford said, his eyes growing wide. "It's you and me he wants, not her. Perhaps if he can have us both, he'll trade her freedom and then..."

"You think I would allow you to involve yourself in this when you have already proven yourself to be a traitor?" Stalwood cried out, catching Oakford by the collar and shaking him. "How do I know you haven't orchestrated this whole thing as a way to get to Willowby?"

Lucas stared at Oakford, trying to read him. Trying to decipher if this were, indeed, a trap and a trick. "You hated Caldwell after what he did to Diana," he said softly. "You wanted out."

He nodded. "I told you I did."

"And you tried to save me," he said. "By bandaging my leg that day." Oakford bent his head in silence. Lucas glanced at Stalwood. "I'm willing to take the chance."

"Are you mad? You are one of my best agents, there is no way in hell that I would—"

"Diana is an innocent in this," Lucas interrupted. "I will not let the woman I love be murdered while we argue. Oakford is going with me, and that is the end of it. You will follow with as many agents as you can move in secret."

"I'll begin gathering them. It's a five-hour ride to that estate. We can leave within two. Excuse me," Stalwood said, and rushed from the foyer.

Lucas watched him go, then grabbed Oakford's arm and dragged him from the house.

"Where are we going?" Oakford asked as Lucas shoved him toward one of the horses Stalwood had called earlier.

He swung up onto his own mount and turned him toward the street. "To that estate. There's no way I'm waiting two hours to go after Diana. When Stalwood realizes we've snuck off, he'll rush his duties and can follow right behind."

Oakford smiled as the two men urged their horses into a run and entered the street together. "I want to ask you something," he said as they raced through the busy lanes toward the eastern edge of Town.

Lucas pressed his lips together. He didn't want to have a long conversation with this man, this traitor. He didn't want to think about anything but Diana and how he could save her. From Caldwell, but also from the pain that she would experience when she saw her beloved father was alive and had conspired against her and everyone he supposedly loved.

"You said you loved my daughter," Oakford said when Lucas was silent. "Is that true?"

Lucas glanced from the corner of his eye at this man he'd once called friend. "Did I say it out loud?" he asked. "Yes, it's true. I am in love with Diana."

Oakford nodded, and then he sighed. "Good. Because the likelihood I'll come out of this without my neck stretched is almost zero. I would be happy to know that she was loved and taken care of by a man I have long considered a son."

Lucas jerked his face toward Oakford. Not so long ago, those words would have meant a great deal. Now... "If I was your son, how could you do this? To me, but also to her? How could you do it to her?"

Oakford sighed. "I was weak, Willowby. I was up to my neck in problems and terrified for her future, so I was weak. I hope you'll be stronger. She deserves that."

"She deserves more," Lucas agreed, and then they rode in silence, both lost in thoughts of the woman they'd loved.

The woman they'd put in danger.

CHAPTER 25

D iana sat in a fine parlor in a comfortable chair. At the sideboard, Caldwell prepared a cup of tea for her. It all would have been very civilized if her hands weren't tied. If the other furnishings in this house weren't covered in cloths, because the place they'd broken into was unoccupied.

If she weren't in pure terror not just for her life, but for Lucas. And if she weren't still processing what Caldwell had told her hours ago in London: that her father was alive. A lie, of course. It had to be a lie. Why Caldwell would tell it, aside from causing her pain, was another question entirely.

"You like two sugars, do you not?" he asked.

She glared at him. "Why pretend you care? I'm not your guest."

He smiled over his shoulder. "One of the things that attracted me to you those two years ago was your fire," he said. "That must be what Willowby likes, as well."

"Do not compare yourself to him," she hissed, turning her face when he brought the cup to her and lifted it to her lips. "You are not half the man he is."

Caldwell's smug smile faltered a fraction. "Yes, so I've heard more than once. Do you really think he's worth more because of his title? His fortune?"

"No," she said softly, and thought of Lucas. Thoughts of him were all that kept her focused and centered in this terrifying ordeal. The only thing that kept her from succumbing to the swell of anxiety that kept rising in her chest. "He is worth more because of his goodness, his decency. His bravery and his heart. That is what makes him fifty times the man you are, you craven, bloodthirsty coward."

He set the teacup aside, and then he gripped her face in his hand, smashing her cheeks as pain shot through her.

"That's enough now," he said, quiet even as he hurt her. Controlled. "I've spent quite enough time hearing about the virtues of the Undercover Duke from my superiors and your father and everyone else. If only he'd died when he was supposed to, but that was Oakford's fault. He's the one who bandaged Willowby's leg so he wouldn't bleed out on the lawn right outside this very window."

Diana froze, thinking of what Lucas had told her about the knot in the bandage that had been around his leg when he woke up after the attack. That knot she'd recognized and tried so hard to explain. And yet here was the best explanation.

One that said this bastard wasn't actually lying to her. That her father was alive.

She turned her face and wrenched her cheeks from his grip. "What makes a man like you?"

He smiled. "A lifetime of scrambling for every little thing I earned. Of watching men like Willowby be given what they did not deserve. Of being injured in the field and realizing I was risking my life for nothing."

"What about your family?" she asked. "What about your wife and your children? Are they not worth being decent for?"

He turned his head. "My wife and children mean nothing to me. I married because it was expected and her father's name helped me in my position. She is but a burden, as are they."

There was something in his tone when he said "they" that belied those cold words. She thought he didn't care about his wife—that was true. But the children...that might be a different story.

He walked away, back to the sideboard. As he did, she looked out the large window and saw a puff of dust coming up from the direction of the road. Her heart leapt. Rescuers. Lucas. Only she didn't want Caldwell to notice that.

She had to distract him and give whoever had come for her their best opportunity. She knew only one way to do that.

"Did you know about our daughter?" she asked, every word like a stab to her broken heart.

He spun around and faced her, his face bloodless and shocked. "What?"

"I became pregnant after our ill-thought tryst," she whispered. "Did you not know?"

"Liar," he spat.

She bent her head and the tears came easily. "I wish I were. But it's true."

He was silent for a long time, what felt like an eternity. Then he said, "Oakford never told me. Even when he tried to break our partnership, he never said a thing."

She flinched, for that statement was, once again, proving that her father had been a traitor. She shoved her heartbreak aside and focused.

"I named her Mirabelle," she whispered. "She did not draw a breath."

His cheek twitched and he gripped his hands at his sides. Then he erased the emotion, using those same spy skills she'd seen her father and Lucas employ so many times. Push the pain away, erase the anger, leave behind...nothing.

"That is probably for the best," he croaked.

She struggled against her bindings. "For the best?" she screamed. "You heartless, empty bastard!"

He stepped toward her, but before he could respond, he glanced at the window. "Riders," he grunted. "Close, too."

She couldn't help but smile, and he looked down at her with a glare. "You knew, did you? Saw them coming?"

She shrugged her shoulders as best she could while tied. His anger returned, and he backhanded her. Her lip smashed against her teeth and she tasted blood. Some trickled from the small cut there.

"Good," he said. "A little blood will help. Now, let's get ready for our visitors, shall we?"

He left the room, tugging a pistol from his waistband as he walked, and she pulled against the bindings. "Boyd!" she called out.

He ignored her, of course. She drew a few long breaths. She could not focus on what was happening with Lucas right now. What she had to do was get herself free. Pain shot through her wrists as she twisted her hands, trying to get a sense of the knot he'd tied at her wrists. She could feel the loops of it against her flesh, and closed her eyes as she pictured the image of it.

When she had it in her mind, she slid her fingers along, trying to find the end of the knot. There it was, against her left palm. She began to push, twisting the rope, attempting to trace it backward through its path. Slowly, she felt it working, loosening by tiny fractions toward her freedom.

She heard voices outside, male sounds, shouting. Too far away to identify them. She had to hurry. She pushed more, pulled more, closer and closer but not quite free.

The door to the parlor opened, and she stopped fiddling with the rope as she looked up. Lucas entered first, his face drawn with anger and emotion. When he saw her, his expression lit with relief.

"Diana," he breathed.

Tears prickled and she blinked at them, not wanting to show weakness. "I'm fine," she whispered. "I'm fine—oh, you shouldn't have come."

"As if I wouldn't come for you," he said.

She glanced toward the door, expecting Boyd to walk through

next, but instead it was someone else. And as she stared, her heart nearly exploded from her chest. There was her father, in the flesh. A bit thinner, perhaps. His cheeks covered in scruffy facial hair. But here, alive.

And everything Caldwell had said was true.

"No," she moaned, her eyes coming closed as the world began to swim before her eyes. "No, no, no!"

In his years on this earth, Lucas had heard many a terrible sound. Death was common in his line of work and he'd listened to many a deathbed confession, many a pained moan.

But he'd never heard anything worse than the sound coming from Diana's mouth as she stared at her father and her world came crashing down around her. And even worse than that, he could do nothing in that moment to comfort her. He couldn't even touch her.

Even if he could, what would he say or do? Her father was alive and she had to accept that everything she'd ever believed about his heroism and goodness was a lie. He understood it, for he had endured the same set of emotions when he saw the man.

For her it had to be multiplied a hundredfold.

Caldwell entered the room, gun pointed at Oakford's back, a wide grin on his face. "Look at our little family reunion," he said, that cruel lilt to his voice like a file against Lucas's spine. "Say hello to Papa, Diana."

She had not stopped looking at her father since he entered the room, and Oakford had not looked away from her. She shook her head. "Why?" she whispered. "Why would you do this?"

"I'm sorry," he said softly. "The situation spiraled out of control and I should have protected you better. But I shall now."

With that, he turned to Lucas and pulled a pistol from his boot. Lucas staggered and Diana screamed as they both realized what was happening.

"You bastard," he growled. "You ever-loving bastard."

Oakford bent his head slightly. "I have to do what's best for Diana, and this is the only way."

D iana stared as her father backed up and glanced at Caldwell. His partner looked as shocked by this turn of events as he did. "You had a gun?" Caldwell murmured.

"Yes. We can talk about this, Caldwell," Oakford said.

Caldwell half pivoted toward him. "Talk about what? You betrayed me and you stole my money and my information. Do you know how much trouble that's caused for me since you pretended to be dead? I had a price on my head for a while, Oakford, and it's your fault."

"I have what you want," Oakford soothed, that same tone Diana had heard him use with injured men a dozen times, a hundred. "And I have Willowby here to boot. We can mend our relationship, can't we? Go back to our partnership."

"Father!" Diana screeched, struggling against her bindings. "Please don't do this. Please!"

Her father ignored her, but she saw Lucas watching her. His expression was twisted in pain as tears streamed down her face. "I'm sorry," she whispered and wanted to say so much more. "I'm so sorry."

"I know," he murmured back.

"How can I trust you after what you did?" Caldwell hissed, seemingly oblivious to the world of unspoken communication flooding between his two captives. "After the chaos you caused these past six months? For all I know, you're working alongside Stalwood and he has a dozen men coming here to destroy us all."

"He doesn't know," Oakford said.

Lucas set his jaw and his outrage was plain in every fiber of his being. "So *this* is why you showed up to my home today, told me these stories that Diana was in danger. Were you two in league, using her to get to me?"

Caldwell shifted. "You knew I had her?"

"I knew you've been looking for me," her father said with a shake of his head. "You must know I have done the same for you. I realized you took her and why—I owed you a boon for you to think of granting me one. Your letter to bring Willowby to you was well timed, it convinced him of my truthfulness. We were always a good partnership, Caldwell, even if this time it wasn't planned."

"You convinced me to come with you alone," Lucas breathed.

Her father nodded. "I thought a threat against Diana's safety might cause you to be undisciplined." He held Lucas's stare for a long moment and then looked at Caldwell. "So he's here. If you let Diana go, we can get rid of him together."

Diana struggled in her chair anew. Her hands were almost free. "No, no, please. Don't hurt him, Father. You love him—like a son, you used to tell me."

"I love you more," he said, glancing at her. "No matter what you think."

"Then don't take him from me." She stopped struggling. "Please, please don't take him away from me. I love him. I need him."

Lucas froze at those words. His eyes came to her and she held them for what felt like forever before he whispered, "Diana, let him do this. Your life is worth far more to me than my own. Look at me."

She turned her face and met his eyes. "Lucas…"

"I love you," he said, and it was so beautiful and clear, so true. She believed it even though this was a moment of panic. "I promise you, this is for the best."

"Well, this is all very romantic," Caldwell snapped, dragging her back to the moment and the dangers within it. "But there is no letting Diana go and killing him as an escape. Stalwood already knows—he must, if Willowby suspected you."

"Stalwood knows nothing," Oakford said softly. "When he delivered the case file to my old home here in London, where Willowby was staying upon his return, I snuck into the house and stole the incriminating facts. If Willowby suspected, it was not with evidence to back up his claims. It will take Stalwood months to sort through this new mess. Enough time for you to complete whatever plans you have and go wherever you desire. All you have to do is let Diana go."

Caldwell shifted, and it was clear his mind was reeling with all these possibilities. "No. I'm not letting her go. She's close to Stalwood. She wept on his shoulder at your false grave. If she loves Willowby, she would tell." He lifted his hand and pointed his gun at Lucas. "It would be better to kill this one now. Then if you return what you stole, you and I can negotiate about Diana. That's the best way."

He began to press the trigger, and Diana watched as Lucas braced for it. In that moment, her hands came free at last and she hurtled herself toward him, to block the bullet, to save his life.

The gun made an awful sound and Lucas watched in horror as Diana lunged from her chair, suddenly free of the bonds that had held her there, and threw herself in front of him.

Lucas cried out, and in that same instant, Oakford jumped in front of Caldwell. The bullet hit him instead of Lucas or Diana, and he staggered back as a circle of red spread across the shoulder of his white shirt. He dropped his gun as he fell, and it skittered toward Lucas.

He shoved Diana aside, swept it up and fired as Caldwell struggled to reload his pistol. His shot was true, hitting Caldwell between the eyes. He stood for a moment, a blank expression on his face, and then collapsed in a heap on the floor beside Oakford.

Diana screamed and Lucas turned toward her. He expected her to move to her injured father, but it was his arms she bounded into, her hands smoothing over him as she whispered endless, empty words about his health and his safety.

He pulled her close and kissed her, brief but powerful. Then he turned her toward her father. "He lied, Diana. He lied to protect you. Stalwood was coming all along, he knew it and so did I."

She gasped and turned to her father, who was lying on the floor, pressing a hand into the hole in his shoulder as he watched them. He saw her expression soften, a bit of her faith in this man returned with the truth the two of them had hidden in order to save her life.

"He needs your help."

She nodded and dropped to her knees beside him. He was already pressing a hand to his shoulder, and she tore a piece of fabric from his shirt to begin binding the wound as Lucas moved to ensure that Caldwell was indeed dead and unable to harm anyone further.

It was over. One traitor was dead. The other was now in the custody of the War Department, for Lucas had no intention of letting Oakford walk away when his actions had done so much damage.

Now there was just the fallout to handle, and the heartbreak that would flood Diana and put her in grief all over again.

CHAPTER 26

Three Days Later

Diana paced the parlor, certain she would wear a hole in Lucas's parlor carpet before this terrible day was through. She glanced at the clock on the mantel and sighed. He'd been gone far too long. It could not be good news that would come home with him.

The door opened in that moment, and she pivoted to watch as Lucas entered the room. His face was very serious and his eyes were locked on hers. Worried. Soothing. The same expression he'd had in the three days since her entire world had fallen down around her, everything she believed destroyed the moment her father had reappeared, alive and well.

"What was the decision?" she asked, her voice trembling.

Lucas came to her then, taking her hands in his as he searched her face like he could find peace there. She had no idea how that was possible, considering she felt none within herself.

"It was a long argument," he said. "Stalwood and I took up in your father's defense and presented the evidence that he had actually turned against Caldwell in the end. That he took that bullet in order to protect me. We left you out of it, of course, as we agreed upon."

She pursed her lips. "Yes, *you* agreed upon that, you and Stalwood and my father. I still think I should have been there." She turned away and paced to the window.

"You should have been," he said softly. "This decision will affect no one more than you. But it is the only way we can protect you in some way from the truth of what your father did and why."

Her hands shook as she faced him. "What was the panel's decision in the end?"

"They considered his injury and his actions as a whole." Lucas let out a long sigh. "And determined that he should not be hanged for treason."

Diana's legs nearly went out from under her. She leaned heavily on the window ledge as she stared at him in disbelief. "Truly? They won't put him to death?"

"No," he said. "They won't. But he...he will be transported, Diana. As soon as his injury allows for travel, a week or two at most, he will be sent away. The panel felt he would at least be able to do some good amongst the prison population."

She stared at him as numbness overcame her. Transported. Although it was better than death, the end result would be the same. She would never see her father again. Perhaps he would be allowed a letter to her from time to time, but the distance between them would be insurmountable.

"I see," she said at last, the only thing she could think to say. "It is fair, I know."

"Fair to him," he corrected. "None of this is fair to you, Diana. You will be able to see him as much as you like in the time you have left. Stalwood and I demanded that be true. Stalwood will actually be monitoring him in his own home until the time is right."

She nodded slowly. "Stalwood was a friend, for his part of the bargain. Were there any other censures?"

He shifted, and she knew there had been. "His lands have been seized. His property and funds now belong to the crown."

She bent her head. "So I have nothing."

"Yes." He cleared his throat. "I did not tell them about your daughter's grave, but I did argue that you ought to be able to live in the home if you'd like. They agreed to lease the property to me, though it will still belong to the crown. You won't lose the ability to visit Mirabelle there for as long as I'm alive."

Her heart stuttered as she looked at him. "You did that for me?"

He nodded. "I would do anything to lessen the pain of this. Anything in my power."

"Thank you," she whispered, her love for him bubbling up in her. But she didn't speak it. She had done so in the height of their terror a few days before, he had said the same. In the time since, she had stayed at his home, and the topic had not come up again.

She had to assume he had only said those words out of terror in that moment. Facing death, they had seemed to have less meaning to him. Now he had forgotten them.

And she could live with that. There was so much else she'd have to face now. Losing Lucas was just the worst of it.

"We can go there whenever you'd like," he continued. "Just say the word."

"You would take me home to the country?" she asked. "No, that would be too much. I ought not even stay with you anymore. I think my family has trespassed on your good graces long enough."

He wrinkled his brow. "Take you home? *This* is your home, Diana."

She stared at him in blank surprise. "Lucas."

"It has been madness since you were taken. Madness for longer than that," he said, and ran a hand through his hair. "I should have been clearer, but I didn't want to overwhelm you when there was so much for you to handle already."

She swallowed, but she could think of nothing to say but his name. "Lucas…"

He shook his head. "I love you, Diana."

Those words hit her harder than a runaway phaeton, and everything in her wanted to lean into them and him and stay in his arms forever.

A more rational part tried to keep joy at bay. "You said that in a moment of great peril," she began. "I would not be so cruel as to hold you to it."

"I meant it, peril or not, Diana. I knew it before I said it that day. I knew it and I knew what I wanted." He moved forward, and she found no strength to step away. He cupped her cheek and she shivered, for the feel of his skin on hers was heaven. "I love you and I want to marry you."

If she hadn't already been leaning against the window, she would have fallen over. "What?"

"You are everything I have ever wanted, everything I shall ever want." He held her gaze steadily. "I have not ever felt for anyone even a shadow of what I feel when I touch you or see you or even merely hear your name. I could not live my life without you."

"That would make me a duchess," she said, dumbfounded.

He nodded. "Yes, it would. And a duchess with duties, for I have realized, thanks to you, that I cannot turn away from this life anymore. I have given up my position at the War Department, effective immediately. Though Stalwood did ask that I make myself available to review case files from time to time. Something I would only do if you would be agreeable to such that."

"Stop," she breathed, her head spinning as she steadied herself on the back of the closest chair. "You are ahead of yourself with all these plans and questions. The fact of the matter is that I don't belong here. Not in this world, in your life."

He smiled, a crooked little expression that was wry and warm. "Oh, my darling, neither of us belong here, do we? But we belong together. I need you. I need you at my side. And I want to be there for you, as well."

What he was offering was everything she'd ever wanted or

desired. Everything she'd never dared to hope for. But there was still fear there. Fear and uncertainty.

"It wouldn't be easy," she whispered.

"Sometimes it wouldn't be," he conceded with a tilt of his head. "But I think we've both learned through bitter experience that is true of life in general. I bore a great weight on my shoulders, until you took some of it for me. I hope I did the same for you."

She nodded. "You did. I never knew how much my secrets ate at me until I was able to speak them."

"Then be my wife," he whispered again. "Spend a lifetime with me where we'll share not only our joys, but our pains. Where neither one of us will bear the full weight of either. We'll do it together. Be my partner in the truest sense. Be my heart and my love until there are no more sunrises for us. Please. *Please* don't turn away from the happiness we could have. Love me and marry me."

His face was close to hers now, his breath gentle on her lips. He slid his arms around her, and suddenly she was home. The most perfect home she had ever known or would ever know again. It was everything, and in that moment she knew she could not walk away from it. There had been too much loss in both their lives to accept another.

"I do love you, Lucas," she said as she leaned up to brush her lips to his. "I do love you, and I will marry you."

He said nothing, only pulled her closer and deepened the kiss. But she needed no words. She felt his joy and his relief in the way his mouth moved against hers. She felt the future laid out before them, far happier than the past.

Because they would be together, and that would always be enough.

EXCERPT FROM THE DUKE OF HEARTS

THE 1797 CLUB BOOK 7

Order the next book in the series - Available now!

Spring 1812

It could have been called a 1797 Club party, thanks to the number of friends Matthew Cornwallis, Duke of Tyndale, had in attendance. Dukes abounded, in seemingly every corner. Once upon a time, he would have enjoyed this moment when they were all together. It had become so rare over the years as his friends grew into their titles, their marriages, their responsibilities. But at present, it was not joy in Matthew's heart as he watched them from a distance.

It was something far darker, far uglier. Something he did not wish to name. More than half of his friends were here with their wives. They spun around the dancefloor in pairs, eyes locked, hands inappropriately low, laughter echoing, cheeks filling with color thanks to whispered words.

They were all happy. He should have been happy for them. He was. And he wasn't. Because he was standing on the outside now, looking in on a world he should have joined years ago. Except Angelica had died.

All he was left with were regrets.

Suddenly Robert Smithton, Duke of Roseford, slid up beside him. Wordlessly he handed Matthew a scotch and then lifted his own glass to clink it against Matthew's.

"To the bachelors," he said, staring out at the dance floor and their friends. "Those of us left, that is."

Matthew shut his eyes. There were days when his grief still felt so raw, no matter how many years had passed since the death of his fiancée. Today was one of them, and Robert's words were like a knife in his heart.

"Sorry," Robert said softly.

Matthew's eyes flew open and he stared at his friend. Robert was almost his polar opposite, a man driven by pleasure and nothing more. He didn't allow deeper emotions, so he never experienced the pain that went with them.

But he was also a brilliant mind, a loyal friend and someone Matthew cared deeply for, regardless of his judgment of Robert's decisions.

"I must look like hell if you're apologizing to me," Matthew croaked out before he took a sip of his drink.

The tension on Robert's face bled away and he grinned, the rogue in full force at that moment. "I'm apologizing because I'm an ass," he said. "But you know that. You're always telling me much the same."

Matthew drew in a deep breath as the pain faded a fraction. Leave it to Robert to do that. He did appreciate it.

"Well, you're no more an ass than usual," he said softly. "So I forgive you this once."

Robert tipped his head. "Much obliged, Your Grace."

Matthew sighed as his attention returned to the others. The music had faded now and they were joining up in little clusters, the women comparing gowns and smiling at their husbands. Every once in a while Ewan, Duke of Donburrow, brushed his hand over his wife Charlotte's swollen pregnant belly, and a shadow of a smile crossed his normally serious face.

"It's the end of an era," Robert mused.

Matthew jolted from his own thoughts and nodded. "I suppose it is. They have all found their matches, leaving only a handful of us without such happiness. But it was bound to happen, wasn't it? We're of an age to do such things. Someone will be next."

Robert snorted out a laugh of derision. "It won't bloody well be me," he said, and downed his entire drink in one slug.

Matthew laughed with him. "No, my assumption is that you will be last—you enjoy your life too much to surrender it willingly."

For a brief moment, a shadow crossed Robert's face. Matthew tilted his head at the sight of it, for it was an expression he'd never seen before on his old friend. Before he could press, Hugh Margolis, Duke of Brighthollow and another of their bachelor friends, approached.

Matthew's concern shifted. In the past six months, he'd seen a change in Hugh. His hair had grown out, his cheeks were slashed with stubble more often than not. More than that, there was something deeply troubled in his dark gaze. Whenever he was asked about it, he waved the question off.

But tonight some of that trouble seemed faded. He grinned at his friends, back to the light and lively companion he'd always been. He even slung an arm around Robert. "And what are you two talking about so seriously, eh?"

Robert rolled his eyes. "How very romantic our friends have all become. And we were debating who would enter the snare of marriage next." He winked at Matthew. "And we were discussing how miserable Tyndale is."

Hugh's smile fell and his expression gentled. "Are you very miserable, Tyndale?"

Matthew shook his head. It was a funny thing. Once you lost someone, it was like you turned to glass. Everyone else tiptoed around, trying not to upset or break anything. He was growing tired of it, in truth.

"It's been three years," he said softly. "I suppose Robert is right that I ought to be over the loss by now and not roaming around like the maudlin hero of a romantic novel."

Robert shrugged. "In my experience, ladies trip over themselves for a maudlin hero. You must start using it to your advantage."

Matthew couldn't picture doing anything of the kind, but he played along for Robert's sake. "And how do you suggest I do that?"

It was like he'd offered his friend a thousand pounds, Roseford's eyes lit up so bright. He was practically bouncing as he said, "Let's get out of this stuffy party and go somewhere fun."

Hugh shook his head. "I shudder to think what you define as fun, my friend. Where exactly do you mean?"

Robert grinned wider. "The Donville Masquerade."

Matthew stared at him, his mouth slightly agape. "The sex club," he said with a shake of his head. God's teeth, everyone knew about the Donville Masquerade.

Robert drew back. "You limit yourself, my dear old friend. Not just a sex club. There's drink, gaming and dancing, and yes, I think a night with a comely lady would do each of us good."

"Christ," Hugh said with a slight laugh. "You and your appetites."

Robert wrinkled his brow. "And since when is indulging in pleasure such a terrible appetite? It can't have been so long since you did the same."

Hugh shifted. "Well...nine months," he admitted.

Robert's eyes went impossibly wide and his mouth twisted in horror. "No. That...can't be true. Is that even possible? Matthew, tell him that he will turn into a monk if he doesn't change his ways."

The two men faced Matthew and now it was his cheeks that filled with color. "I doubt I'm the one to tell him such, considering how long it's been for me."

Robert drew back. "Longer than nine months?"

Matthew cleared his throat. "I'm not sure this is a proper topic—"

"Ten months?" Robert pressed. "A year?"

"Honestly, Roseford, you are—"

"More than a year?" Robert nearly recoiled into the crowd.

Matthew let out a long sigh. He knew his bulldog of a friend, and there was no way he'd let this go until he had uncovered the number. "Fine. Three and a half years."

Robert stared, unspeaking. Even Hugh jerked his face toward Matthew like he'd declared he had decided to take over Spain. Matthew pursed his lips and forced himself to remain impassive beneath their horrified expressions.

"How are you both not...dead?" Robert said. "You are dead, for that sounds like living in a grave."

"Roseford," Hugh said, voice heavy with warning.

Robert waved him off. "It's settled, we're going to the Donville Masquerade tonight. I have a membership and you two will come as my guests. I shall brook no refusals."

With that, he turned on his heel and strode from the ballroom, likely to call for his carriage.

Matthew stared at Hugh and found him looking back. Brighthollow shrugged. "He isn't entirely wrong, you know."

"Of course he isn't," Matthew said. "He never is. Not entirely."

"We probably both could use a break from our troubles. Nothing says you have to spend an evening with a lightskirt, after all."

Matthew shifted. He rarely thought about sinful things anymore. Those thoughts had seemed so wrong after Angelica's death. Eventually he'd just purged them from his mind and become the monk Robert had first accused Hugh of being.

"You're right," he said with a sigh. "And I'll go, if only to keep him from having an apoplexy in the middle of James and Emma's ballroom."

They moved to say their goodbyes to their friends, but Hugh

caught his arm before they could reach anyone. He tugged Matthew to face him and his expression was serious.

"You aren't betraying her," he said softly.

Matthew's lips parted and he nodded. "I know."

Except that wasn't true. What Robert wanted from him felt exactly like a betrayal of the woman he had once loved, the one he'd lost. And that's why he had no intention of doing it. Not even when surrounded by "temptation" at the wicked Donville Masquerade.

Order the next book in the series - Available now!

The Undercover Duke

The Duke of Hearts

The Duke Who Lied

The Duke of Desire

The Last Duke

Seasons

An Affair in Winter

A Spring Deception

One Summer of Surrender

Adored in Autumn

The Wicked Woodleys

Forbidden

Deceived

Tempted

Ruined

Seduced

Fascinated

The Notorious Flynns

The Other Duke

The Scoundrel's Lover

The Widow Wager

No Gentleman for Georgina

A Marquis for Mary

To see a complete listing of Jess Michaels' titles, please visit:

http://www.authorjessmichaels.com/books

ABOUT THE AUTHOR

USA Today Bestselling author Jess Michaels likes geeky stuff, Vanilla Coke Zero, anything coconut, cheese, fluffy cats, smooth cats, any cats, many dogs and people who care about the welfare of their fellow humans. She is lucky enough to be married to her favorite person in the world and lives in the heart of Dallas, TX where she's trying to eat all the amazing food in the city.

When she's not obsessively checking her steps on Fitbit or trying out new flavors of Greek yogurt, she writes historical romances with smoking hot alpha males and sassy ladies who do anything but wait to get what they want. She has written for numerous publishers and is now fully indie and loving every moment of it (well, almost every moment).

Jess loves to hear from fans! So please feel free to contact her in any of the following ways (or carrier pigeon):

www.AuthorJessMichaels.com
Email: Jess@AuthorJessMichaels.com

Jess Michaels raffles a gift certificate EVERY month to members of her newsletter, so sign up on her website:
http://www.AuthorJessMichaels.com/

facebook.com/JessMichaelsBks
twitter.com/JessMichaelsBks
instagram.com/JessMichaelsBks
bookbub.com/authors/jess-michaels

Made in the USA
Monee, IL
02 October 2023

43857460R00152